'Why did you offer to make me your mistress if you did not mean it?'

His husky laughter made her frown as he said, 'Are you disappointed now that I've changed my mind? Maybe I shall take you, after all . . . Be warned, Louise, I am only a man, and I can be noble for only so long.'

She felt a frisson of unease at the veiled threat in his voice. Somehow she knew that her will was not strong enough to resist him if he really wanted her.

'Oh, I think I have nothing to fear, my lord,' she said, turning away from him. 'You have made yourself my protector, and I think your sense of honour will keep me safe.'

A shudder shook her as she felt the touch of his hands on her shoulders. 'You are safe enough as long as you do not provoke me too far, Louise—but be careful. My patience is wearing thin!'

Anne Herries was born in Wiltshire but spent much of her early life at Hastings, to which she attributes her love of the sea. She now lives in Cambridge and often writes in her garden surrounded by glorious trees and birds which are so tame they come to the kitchen door to be fed. She is happily married and credits much of her success to her husband, who has constantly encouraged her to continue with her earliest dream—writing.

Anne Herries has written four other Masquerade Historical Romances—*Devil's Kin*, *The Wolf of Alvar*, *Beware the Conqueror* and *Demon's Woman*.

RAPHAEL

ANNE HERRIES

MILLS & BOON LIMITED
15–16 BROOK'S MEWS
LONDON W1A 1DR

*First published in Great Britain 1986
by Mills & Boon Limited*

*Australian copyright 1986
Philippine copyright 1986*

ISBN 0 263 75543 6

*Set in 10 on 10½ pt Linotron Times
04–1086–78,600*

*Photoset by Rowland Phototypesetting Ltd
Bury St Edmunds, Suffolk
Made and printed in Great Britain by
Cox & Wyman Ltd, Reading*

CHAPTER ONE

JEWELS GLITTERED and flashed in the light of a thousand candles as the richly-gowned courtiers moved restlessly through the long gallery, the sound of their voices reminiscent of the incessant buzzing of flies about a dung-heap. It was a warm summer night, and the air was heavy with the musk of expensive perfumes, which veiled a less pleasant odour. To a casual observer it might have seemed merely another tedious court function: a prelude to the more important events which were to take place within the week. Yet the stranger was instantly aware of the underlying tensions that flowed beneath the surface, tugging this way and that as they swirled insidiously through the various factions present. Behind the smiling, painted faces were seething hatreds, jealousy, greed; the lust for power and revenge on old enemies concealed by polite laughter and outward protestations of friendship. It was an uneasy gathering this night in the palace of the Valois kings.

The stranger's presence was noted as he paused for a moment on the threshold of the gallery, surveying the brilliant scene from eyes that were surprisingly keen beneath the lazy lids, which gave his patrician features a habitual air of boredom. Only the slight flaring of his nostrils and the sneer on his full, sensuous mouth betrayed a hint of the contempt he felt for the people he watched with seeming detachment.

Further down the gallery, two young women were among those who had noticed the tall stranger. One was pretty, with fair, curling hair peeping from beneath her lace cap; she had a pert nose, brilliant turquoise eyes, and was inclined to plumpness, though as yet only sufficiently to enhance her seductive charms. Her

companion was slender and slightly taller. Dressed in a
modest gown of pearl-grey satin, her quiet beauty
seemed at first glance unremarkable beside the first girl's
obvious appeal. Her hair was the colour of Burgundy
wine and swept up in a thick coil beneath the stiff silver
head-dress. Her eyes were grey, and strangely serious
for one so young; but when she laughed, the change in
her was breathtaking, as if the sun had suddenly broken
through a bank of cloud.

'Who do you think he is?' Marie de Galliard's turquoise eyes gleamed with excitement as she touched her
companion's arm, her fan fluttering flirtatiously as
she knew herself observed by the stranger's coal-dark
gaze.

Louise de Granvelle glanced at her, a hint of amusement in her face. Marie was a distant cousin and some
five years her senior. As children they had been close
friends, but it seemed to Louise that the older girl had
somehow changed since she came to live at Court. At
times there was a sly look in Marie's eyes, and they were
too knowing for a woman of but three and twenty. Yet
perhaps it was that she herself was a country girl, un-
used to the ways of the most sophisticated court in the
world. Perhaps it was naïve of her to judge her cousin
by the rigid standards she herself had been taught to
respect.

'Of whom do you speak, Marie?' Louise asked,
though she too had noticed the handsome newcomer.

It would have been difficult to remain in ignorance of
his arrival when so many eyes were turned in his direction. There was something different about him; and it
was not just the colour of his hair, which had the
blue-black sheen of a raven's wing, or the tiny, barely-
healed scar at his right temple, that made him stand out
from others as richly garbed. It was the sheer arrogance
of the man as his gaze travelled slowly round the room;
and his almost belligerent stance as he stood with feet
apart, his sword hand resting lightly on his hip. Although

he was not wearing his sword, the gesture was instinctive, giving a clue to the nature of the man.

'The tall, handsome man in black and silver, of course,' Marie replied, a note of impatience in her voice. 'Can you not see him there by the entrance? By his complexion I would judge him an Englishman. Do you think they are truly a cold race? What fun it would be to seduce such a one! I am sure he is interested in me—see, he comes this way.'

Louise laughed, her eyes lighting from within. Sometimes her cousin's remarks were rather shocking, but of course, Marie must be jesting. She could not mean that she would deliberately set out to seduce a stranger merely for the sake of amusement?

The younger girl was aware that Marie had a lover, but could not in her heart condemn her cousin for seeking solace in the arms of another man. Marie had been wed at fifteen to a man almost old enough to be her grandfather. Having borne her husband a son in the first year of her marriage, who could blame the pretty young woman for considering her duty done?

No, Louise would not condemn Marie for her infidelity, though such behaviour would be frowned upon by her own family. All her relations were strict Huguenots, and her father was distantly connected by marriage to Gaspard de Coligny, the Admiral of France. It was at the Admiral's bidding that they had come to Paris, to attend the wedding of Princess Margot of the House of Valois to Henri, King of Navarre.

Monsieur de Granvelle had at first resisted the urging of his kinsman; and Louise knew that despite the apparent friendship between the Admiral and King Charles IX, her father was not the only member of the Huguenot nobility to distrust the ruling House of Valois. They were suspicious of the Queen Mother, Catherine de' Medici, and they despised the young king, who was said to have fits of madness, when he ran wild through the palace, terrorising his servants.

'The Italian Woman is still the true ruler of France,' the Seigneur de Granvelle had grumbled, striding restlessly about the great chamber of his château in La Rochelle. 'The Admiral is unwise to trust her—look what happened to the Queen of Navarre. I vow it was Madame Catherine who sent her to her grave!'

'Hush, Father,' André de Granvelle warned. 'Such talk is treason, and dangerous if it should reach the wrong ears.'

'And who will betray me in my own house?' The dark brows drew together in a scowl.

'In times like these, we can be sure of no one. It would not be wise to make an enemy of Madame Catherine if we are to visit the Court.'

Louise had heard their conversation as she sat stitching quietly by the window; it was clear her family distrusted the Queen Mother, but she herself was not sure what to believe. It was whispered that Jeanne d'Albert had visited the little shop on the quay opposite the Louvre, purchasing some wedding finery from Monsieur René. Monsieur René was the Queen Mother's glovemaker, and so the rumours began. Still, it seemed unlikely that the Italian Woman should want to poison her latest ally. Why should she, since the Queen of Navarre had signed the marriage contract, thereby granting her dearest wish?

The musicians had begun to play, and Louise forgot the whispers and disturbing rumours as she watched the dancing, secretly longing to take her place among that merry throng. Politics meant little to her, and she intended to enjoy her first visit to Court—if only someone would ask her to dance!

'He is coming towards us. I'm sure he means to ask me to dance!'

Louise heard the excitement in her cousin's voice. For a moment she had forgotten the stranger in her pleasure at watching the dancing; the courtiers' gowns were so lavish that they looked like a sea of brightly-coloured flowers waving in the breeze. Taking her eyes from the scene that fascinated her, the girl saw that Marie was correct. The man with the scar at his temple was indeed making his way slowly but surely towards them, and it was now possible to see that the deep cut had been recently inflicted on him. The skin had healed, but was still a livid purple. Realising suddenly that she had been staring at him rudely, she felt the colour come and go in her cheeks as he stopped before her.

'Mademoiselle, will you honour me with this dance?' he asked, and though his French was perfect, the accent was distinctly English. It sounded strange to her ears, and her lips quivered.

Marie had guessed right, she thought, he was from that island across the Channel. A cold, damp place, she had been told, where the sun hardly ever shone. It was not surprising then that his skin should be so pale; but perhaps it was the blackness of his hair that made the contrast so startling.

Her confusion at being addressed by the stranger was such that she could not speak for a moment. Marie, however, had no hesitation. She gave him a brilliant smile and laid her hand on his arm.

'I should be delighted, m'sieur,' she said, fluttering her fan like an accomplished coquette.

Louise blushed, looking down at the tip of her satin slipper in embarrassment. The invitation had clearly been for her, but Marie had placed the stranger in an impossible position. No gentleman could be so impolite as to point out her cousin's mistake.

'Your pardon, madame,' the Englishman said coldly. 'I was inviting your companion to dance with me.'

Louise gasped, and Marie turned a most unbecoming shade of pink. Wishing the ground would open and swallow her up, Louise was about to refuse his request when he grasped her arm and began to steer her forcefully towards the space occupied by those already twirling gracefully to the music.

'M'sieur,' Louise said agitatedly, fanning her heated cheeks. 'Would it not have been more polite to dance first with my cousin and then with me?'

The fine, dark brows rose in lazy amusement. 'It might have proved less pleasurable, however, since I have no wish to dance with the lady.'

A tiny shiver went through Louise as he placed one hand at her waist, directing her in the stately dance. There was something distinctly unnerving about this man, something that she found fascinating, while it frightened her.

'I think you have not long been at Court, mademoiselle?'

'Two days.' Louise dared to glance up at him then, averting her eyes as she saw the gleam of laughter in his. 'Since my cousin believes you a stranger here, m'sieur, how can you know that?'

'There is still the bloom of the country air upon your cheeks, and that innocence in your eyes is as yet untainted by the corruption of the Medici Court.'

'M'sieur, have a care, I beg you! Such words are treason, and there are spies everywhere.'

His mouth twisted in a wry smile. 'Are you one of Madame Catherine's spies, my little one? No, I think not. You have come simply to witness this great and glorious wedding, have you not?'

The mockery in his voice made Louise stare at him curiously, wondering at the scorn she glimpsed in the half-closed eyes. If he felt such contempt for the French Court and all its people, what was he doing here?

'My father, André and I came at the Admiral's bidding, though my father felt it unwise. Yet we could not show disrespect to the King of Navarre.'

'André?' The black eyes seemed to pierce her with their sudden sharpness. 'Your brother or your betrothed?'

'I have no betrothed as yet.' Louise flicked down her lashes, wondering why she should feel compelled to answer him with truth when the question was impertinent. She owed this stranger nothing, and yet she found herself unburdening her mind. 'The man to whom I was promised died fighting for his religion in the last civil war. My father has not yet arranged another match for me, but—but he intends to do so while we are in Paris, I believe.'

'And will you marry the man your father chooses?'

There was surprise in her face as she looked up at him. 'It will be my duty to do so. Besides, my father is a good man; he will choose wisely.'

'No doubt your obedience pleases him.' The Englishman's scorn flicked her on the raw. 'I had thought you a girl of spirit—seemingly I was wrong.'

'If you thought me a coquette, you were mistaken, m'sieur!' Anger brought her face glowingly alive, and she had never looked so lovely as in her righteous indignation. 'If you seek a mistress to amuse you during your stay in Paris, you had done better to invite my cousin to partner you. Perhaps she might have been fool enough to risk her reputation for your pleasure.'

'If she still has a reputation to risk?'

His arrogance was unbearable. Louise lifted her head with dignity. 'You will be good enough to conduct me to my father, m'sieur. He is talking with Admiral de Coligny by the window.'

The Englishman glanced round the gallery, which was hung with brilliant banners emblazoned with the twin arms of Navarre and Valois. Everywhere were silk hangings with the initials of M and H entwined with gold-embroidered fleurs de lys.

'You forget I am a stranger here. I cannot recognise the Admiral by sight, nor would I take you to him if I could. Pray forgive my wicked tongue, mademoiselle. I fear it has oft led me astray. I meant no insult to your cousin—or to you.'

Louise considered him from serious, grey eyes. 'I am not sure that I should forgive you.'

'Then walk away and leave me, for I shall not deliver you up to your friends just yet.'

The challenge in his eyes made Louise bite her lower lip. To leave him standing alone in the middle of the floor would excite comment and speculation. It would be the height of rudeness, and Louise had been strictly reared. The Englishman had gambled that she was incapable of behaving so badly, and she saw the triumph stamped all over his face. He was enjoying himself at her expense, and she knew a fierce desire to slap him.

'You think yourself clever, m'sieur,' she said between clenched teeth. 'But the dance is almost ended—I shall not have long to endure your impudence.'

'I see I owe you yet another apology. I doubted your spirit, and I was wrong to do so. I like you better when you spit defiance at me. I hope your father chooses a man for you, mademoiselle. You would terrify a boy —and you deserve better than some old goat with one foot in his grave.'

'I pray my father will choose a gentleman, m'sieur.' She gave him her sweetest smile. 'But perhaps you are not aware of the distinction?'

'*Touché*!' His laughter was unexpectedly soft, and it sent tiny shivers down her spine. 'I fear our time together is almost done. Will you introduce me to Gaspard de Coligny, if I humbly beg forgiveness and promise to strive to behave in the fashion of a gentleman?'

He was still mocking her, but strangely now she felt more amusement than anger. 'You have not introduced yourself to me yet,' Louise reminded him with a lift of her brows. 'You do not deserve that I should grant your request, m'sieur—yet I shall do so if you will be good enough to furnish me with your name.'

He swept her an elegant bow as the music ended. 'I am Raphael Carleton, mademoiselle. It was remiss of me not to mention it before—but I thought you and I had no need of names.'

What could he mean by that? Only that he had thought never to see her again once their dance was ended. She was not sure why his assumption should make her angry, but the urge* to strike him surged through her once more. She stared at him coldly, lifting her chin with haughty pride.

'I am Louise de Granvelle. I tell you for politeness' sake, though it interests you so little. Please come with me, Monsieur Carleton. Since you are an Englishman, it might be that my kinsman would wish to meet you.'

Her tone implied that it was highly unlikely, and Raphael smiled. He was not sure what devil had prompted him to plague her so. Perhaps it was something in her manner that reminded him of another. The smile left his lips, and ice crept into the slitted eyes. One finger stroked the scar at his temple, his mouth thinning with contempt; but this time the contempt was for himself alone. Only a fool would allow the memory of Helen's lovely treacherous smile to haunt him still; and whatever else he might be, Lord Raphael Carleton was no fool.

Louise was aware of a change in the man at her side, sensing his anger. It surprised her—if her earlier insults had not annoyed him, why should he suddenly be angry with her now? For there was a deep, cold fury in him.

She approached the Admiral hesitantly. Although he had always been kind to her, Louise was a little in awe of the great man. Normally, she would not have dreamt of interrupting his conversation with her father, but somehow she sensed a purpose behind the Englishman's request. It might be that he carried a message for the Admiral from Elizabeth of England.

From the expectant look on their faces, Louise knew that her father and his companions had been waiting for her to join them. She curtsied graciously to the Admiral, lifting her face to smile shyly at him.

'M'sieur, this gentleman wishes to be made known to you.'

A little to her surprise, Coligny smiled warmly at her

companion. 'You are welcome, my lord. I had news of
your coming, and am pleased to see you safely arrived in
these dangerous times.'

Louise frowned. The stranger was of some import-
ance, it seemed: a gentleman by birth if not by nature.
She wondered why he had not given her his full title, and
realised it must be that he hoped to embarrass her in
front of her kinsman. It was to be his revenge for her
scorn.

Raphael noted her look of accusation, but if he recognised the reason behind it, he ignored it. All at once he
was the perfect aristocrat. The exchange of compliments
between the two men was courteous, but not falsely
extravagant. They seemed to be measuring each other,
and the meeting was more than the casual affair Louise
had imagined.

'I believe you are visiting your cousins the
Montpelliers?' the Admiral said. 'While you are in
Paris, it would please me if we could perhaps dine
together one evening? There are things I should like to
discuss with you.'

Was Louise imagining things, or was there some
hidden meaning in the simple exchange? For a moment
the Englishman's eyes had the brightness of a hawk's,
but then the lazy lids came down and his lean face
resumed its habitual sneer.

'It would indeed be a pleasure, m'sieur,' he drawled.
'It might prove diverting—should I find the time. There
is, after all, so much to interest one at this delightful
Court, is there not?'

Louise saw her father's quick frown at what seemed to
be a deliberate snub to their kinsman. Lord Carleton's
voice had risen slightly, as though he wished to be
overheard. The girl was puzzled by this show of rudeness. The Englishman was not like any other she had
ever met, and she decided she disliked him. How dared
he ask to be introduced to her family, and then insult one
of the greatest men in France?'

'M'sieur?'

Lord Carleton appeared to start as the small, dark-skinned man touched him on the arm. The Italian—for his appearance proclaimed him to be one of the Medici retinue—had approached so softly that the girl had not noticed him until the last moment. Yet she sensed the stranger had been aware of him long before the rest of them. Louise wondered if the rebuff to her kinsman had been for the eavesdropper's benefit.

'Yes?' The English lord did not smile as he looked down at the newcomer, his fine brows arching in haughty enquiry. 'Did you wish to speak with me?'

'A lady wishes to speak with you, m'sieur.' The Italian seemed nervous, a thin beading of sweat along the line of his neat beard.

'A lady?' The Englishman's expression remained unchanged, though if he were in doubt of the lady's identity, he was the only one present who had not immediately guessed it.

It was clear that the servant did not wish to answer. His eyes swivelled nervously from side to side, and his manner became almost pleading. 'A very important lady, who prefers to speak with you in private.' He leant a little closer to Lord Carleton, his voice dropping to a whisper. 'One might say the most important lady in France.'

The summons was not unexpected. Madame Catherine would not long have remained in ignorance of the stranger's arrival; her spies would have reported the presence of an Englishman at court. Since he had not presented himself to her at once as the English Queen's ambassador, the Medici would be curious, and perhaps suspicious, that he should choose to arrive at such a time.

Raphael was aware of the speculation in the faces around him. An odd expression flickered briefly in the black eyes: an expression that was half mockery, half excitement. He had sensed danger lurking in the dark passages of the Louvre from the moment he arrived; treachery was in the air, and he would need to keep all his wits about him if he were to accomplish the mission which had brought him here. It was what he needed to clear his head of the bitter thoughts that lived with him day and night. He had heard much of the Italian Woman, and he thought she might prove to be a worthy opponent. Catherine de' Medici delighted in discovering other people's secrets; he wondered how long it would be before she knew exactly why he had come to Paris, and smiled inwardly. To pit his skill against a woman he suspected of being as devious as she was clever would be to taste the very nectar of the gods. Yet life was but a game, and to win, one must hazard all.

He swept the company an arrogant bow, amused by the confusion and suspicion he saw in their faces— especially one. If his own suspicions were correct, there would be a reckoning here before the game was played to its end. Meanwhile, it pleased him to keep them all guessing. Turning to the servant, he gestured imperiously.

'Pray lead on, sirrah. I am anxious to learn in what way I may serve your mistress.'

As he walked away, Louise saw an anxious look pass between her father and the Admiral. She knew little of politics, but she had heard enough of their private talk to realise that Gaspard de Coligny feared Madame Catherine more than any other of the Court. Unlike the Guisards, who had made no secret of their hatred ever since the Admiral had been accused of complicity in the murder of François, Duc de Guise, the Queen Mother seemed to vacillate between her Catholic allies and the Huguenots. At one moment she declared herself desirous only of bringing about a true peace in which the Protestants were to be free to worship in their own way; the next she was plotting secretly with the Cardinal de Lorraine and the Spanish ambassador.

For the present, de Coligny had the friendship of the

King, but it was well known that the young man was weak and lived in fear of his mother. And then there were always the Guisards waiting in the wings, eagerly anticipating their chance to seize power. Henri, the young Duc de Guise, had sworn vengeance on the man he considered responsible for his father's death. Only the King's promise of protection had brought about this uneasy truce—and for how long would it last?

There had been talk of another war. The Admiral was hot for a strike against Spain as a way of bringing peace and security to the Netherlands, but such a move would not be popular with the Catholics. Louise had heard it whispered that it might be wise to cultivate the friendship of Elizabeth of England, though secretly, of course. She guessed that was why her kinsman had been pleased to welcome the English lord, hoping perhaps for a message from across the Channel. Yet now that he had gone willingly to meet Madame Catherine, it seemed he might not be what they had expected: he might in fact be carrying a message of hope for the Italian Woman. The Queen Mother was trying to arrange a marriage between the English Queen and the Duc d'Alençon, despite the great disparity in their ages. If such an alliance were formed, it would give her far greater power, and the Huguenots could look for no help from Elizabeth.

Louise sighed deeply. The intrigues of politics were not for her. She did not wish to be caught up in the dangerous games these men played. She wished only to dance and enjoy herself. It was with a sense of relief that she saw her cousin signalling to her from across the room. Whispering an excuse to her father, which was scarcely noticed, the girl made her way across the floor.

Raphael frowned as he followed the small Italian from the gallery. It was a dangerous masquerade he had begun this evening, and one that could easily cost his life if he were careless. Already one man was dead—would he be the next? His frown was replaced by a mocking smile. At the moment he had the upper hand, and he believed he had confused his enemy. It would be interesting to see what happened next.

Pushing his private concerns to the back of his mind, he followed the servant into a small antechamber, looking round the tiny dark room with surprise.

'The lady will be here soon, m'sieur.' The servant bowed respectfully and departed, leaving Raphael alone.

He was alone, and yet he had the feeling he was being watched. The dark eyes narrowed in suspicion, his iron-hard muscles tensing beneath the velvet doublet. For a moment he thought he might have walked into a trap; then a heavy tapestry was drawn aside and a woman entered through the door it had concealed.

His first impression was that she could not possibly be the Queen Mother. Plump, short compared with his height, and plain-faced, she seemed too insignificant to be the power behind the throne of France. Then he gazed into her eyes and what he saw there startled him; she had the strange, fixed stare of a serpent coiled to strike. Yet, when she spoke, her voice was soft and almost conciliatory in tone.

'Thank you for coming to see me, Lord Carleton.'

So she knew his name. What more did she know? Raphael wondered as he bent his knee and kissed the hand she offered him.

'Your servant said that you wished to see me, Madame? Is there something I can do to help you?'

A secret smile lurked in her cold eyes. 'And would you serve me, m'sieur, if I asked you?'

'Perhaps—if by doing so I could also serve England.'

'Ah, I see you are a man who speaks his mind. Alas, I have not your freedom, m'sieur. I have always been a stranger at this court—like you.'

'Surely not, Madame? You are the mother of a king.'

'And the widow of another.'

Her eyes gleamed oddly, and Raphael wondered if

she were remembering the slights and insults she had
endured as a young bride from her husband's mistress. It
was said that she had had holes drilled in the ceiling of
her husband's bedchamber so that she could watch him
making love to her rival. Looking at her now, the
Englishman could well believe it.

He met her gaze steadily. 'So, Madame, what is it you
wish of me?'

She laughed suddenly, a high, mirthless sound that
sent a chill through him. 'You interest me, m'sieur.
Perhaps you should ask what I can do to help you . . .'
Her eyes darkened with triumph. 'You see, I know why
you came to Paris.'

Louise glanced anxiously at Marie's face, fearing that
her cousin might be angry because the stranger had
asked her to dance, but she seemed to have forgotten the
incident.

'Surely you do not wish to spend your time with old
men?' Marie teased. 'There is a young man who is dying
to meet you. He swears he will go into a decline if you
will not dance with him.'

Louise giggled, forgetting her earlier doubts about her
cousin. Marie was full of life and fun to be with; and she
was so tired of always being sensible. Just for tonight she
would be as reckless as her cousin.

'And where is this young man?' she asked provocatively. 'Why does he not approach me himself?'

'He fears you would not receive him.' Marie flicked
her fan open, directing her cousin's gaze with a flutter of
her lashes. 'See that divine creature, there by the Duc de
Guise, the one with the golden hair and blue eyes? It is
he who has fallen beneath your spell, you lucky girl.
Pierre de Guise is not a cold fish like that Englishman.
Indeed, I vow I am half crazed with jealousy.'

'A member of the de Guise family!' Louise blanched
with shock. 'I could not dance with him, Marie. My
father would be furious!'

'Oh, do not be such a little prude,' Marie pouted her rouged lips. 'Poor Monsieur de Guise wishes only to dance with you, and perhaps compose a sonnet to your beauty. I am not suggesting that you marry him—but where is the harm in one dance? Surely it is permissible tonight: are we not gathered here to celebrate the coming marriage of a Catholic princess to a Protestant king?'

Marie's arguments were convincing, and perhaps Louise wished to be persuaded. The life she led in La Rochelle was so quiet and so predictable. Inwardly, she was longing to be swept up by the gaiety of the Court, to dance and laugh—and yes, even to flirt a little. After all, what harm could it do to dance with this man?

There was a strange restlessness in her tonight. By some sixth sense, she knew it to be connected with Lord Carleton. His mockery had touched an exposed nerve, making her fully aware of feelings she had scarcely recognised before this evening; though they had always been there, buried in her subconscious. Feelings of rebellion and resentment against the strict régime of her days.

Her mother having died when she was born, Louise had been reared by her grandmother. Madame de Granvelle was one of those good, stern women who believed it right for children to learn the sorrows of life from an early age. She had beaten Louise with tears in her eyes; but they had not prevented her from making the punishment every bit as severe as she considered necessary.

'It is for the good of your soul, my child,' she would say when confronted by a white-faced but defiant Louise. 'So that you may learn to be a true Christian and a dutiful daughter to your father.'

Louise had learned to take her punishment without tears, crying only when she was alone in her chamber. She had learned to be a dutiful daughter; and if there was sometimes rebellion in her heart, she had learned to hide that, too—perhaps so well that she herself was hardly aware of it. Yet tonight it flared in her as never before, and she was swept away on a tide of recklessness. For once, she would do as she pleased!

A shy smile at the young man in question was enough to bring him hurrying to her side. He was indeed a beautiful youth, she thought, like one of the pretty statues with which the palace abounded, almost too perfect to be human; but the look of adoration he gave her was highly flattering. When he bowed and formally asked her to dance, she offered him her hand with a flutter of excitement. For the first time in her life, Louise experienced the sweetness of a young man's undivided attention. His compliments were like heady wine, warming her blood and bringing a flush of pleasure to her cheeks.

He moved with all the elegance of a natural courtier, and she felt as if she were floating on air. Her laughter rang out merrily in response to his teasing. The music was light and intoxicating as they swirled and dipped in that liveliest of dances, the gaillarde.

Louise was enjoying herself so much that she was unconscious of the eyes turned in her direction. Suddenly many in the room were aware of the beautiful young woman whose presence had at first gone almost unnoticed. When the music ended, the girl found herself besieged by eager partners. She was sorry to part from her charming gallant, but to have refused all others for his sake would have caused gossip; and even in her reckless mood, she was sensible enough to have a care for her reputation.

She did, however, grant him two more dances during the evening. Of all her new admirers, he was the one who pleased her most. Pierre could not have been more than a few months her senior; and she found his youthful adoration far sweeter than the practised flirting of the more sophisticated courtiers. Some of the men who begged for the favour of a dance alarmed her; their manner was often predatory, and the hard gleam in their eyes was somehow chilling to a girl who had hitherto led a sheltered life.

Therefore Louise kept her warmest smile for the young de Guise. It was perhaps even warmer than it might have been had her eye not chanced upon the tall Englishman. He had returned to the ballroom at last; but after a brief glance round the gallery, he turned away. So he had not returned in order to dance with her again! The girl was aware of a sense of pique that he had not bothered to seek her out this time.

'Mademoiselle—I have not displeased you?'

Louise realised she had been frowning. She looked up, smiling into her companion's adoring gaze. 'No, not at all, m'sieur. I was merely feeling a little warm.'

'Ah yes, the air is stuffy in here.' He hesitated, seeming almost diffident. 'Would you care to take a stroll outside for a moment, mademoiselle?'

Louise was tempted. It would be pleasant to walk in the cool of the gardens with her handsome gallant. She was nearly sure he wished to kiss her, and the idea brought a sparkle to her eyes. She had never been kissed by a man, except once or twice on the cheek by her father. Indeed, she had never in her life been allowed to be completely alone with a man who was not a close member of her family, not even Étienne, her betrothed. Madame de Granvelle had always accompanied them on their walks, keeping a discreet step behind, but near enough to see that nothing happened to besmirch the girl's honour.

It was more than she dared to leave the gallery with a stranger. Regretfully, she shook her head. 'I cannot, m'sieur. My father would never allow it.'

Did she imagine the quick frown of annoyance on his face? It was gone so swiftly that she could not be certain. He took her hand in his, his eyes filled with unmistakable longing.

'I would not ask you to do anything that might bring

harm to you, mademoiselle. Yet I cannot bear to think that we may never meet again.'

'My family is staying in Paris until after the wedding celebrations are over,' Louise said, gently removing her hand from his. 'I am sure that we shall meet again.'

'Promise me it will be soon,' he begged earnestly. 'Could we not arrange a meeting? Surely it would be quite proper for us to walk together in the morning when all may see us? Perhaps Madame de Galliard would consent to be your chaperon?'

'Perhaps.'

For the first time, Louise was a little doubtful. It was one thing to dance with this charming young man, another to make a secret tryst with him. She was not sure that she wanted to be drawn into an intrigue with him, despite his pleasant manners. Her mood of abandon had passed, leaving her curiously empty; it was with some relief that she saw her brother advancing purposefully towards her.

'Will you not introduce me to your companion?' André asked, and the girl shivered as she heard the harshness in his voice. Her conduct had been noticed, and André was displeased—which meant that her father would also be angry with her.

'Monsieur de Guise—my brother, André de Granvelle.'

Louise gave no sign of the anxiety she felt inside. She had long ago learned that it was useless to weep or beg for mercy. Her father was not by nature a particularly cruel man, but he expected a certain standard of behaviour from his only daughter; any lapse would be swiftly dealt with.

'Monsieur de Guise.' André bowed stiffly. 'It is an honour to have met you. You will excuse my sister now; it is time we were leaving.'

Pierre de Guise returned the bow, but elegantly and with a charming smile. 'The honour was mine, m'sieur, I assure you. May I congratulate you on the beauty of

your sister, whose grace and manners are a credit to the
House of Granvelle.'

The exchange of compliments was meaningless: a
polite ritual that barely hid the animosity felt equally by
each man. If Louise had been able to forget politics and
the hatred between the Guisards and the followers of
Gaspard de Coligny, these two could not. It was in both
men's faces as they bared their teeth in yet more tight-
lipped smiles that did not reach their eyes, and Louise
felt a hollowness in her stomach as André gripped her
arm, propelling her forward.

Glancing at her brother's profile as they walked in
silence from the gallery, Louise saw a muscle tighten in
his cheek. He was very angry, and she knew he was not
above taking a whip to her himself, since their grandmother had been unable to make the journey to Paris.

It was not until they were in the privacy of their coach
that André spoke.

'You have disgraced our family,' he said coldly.
'Father is displeased with you. You may consider yourself fortunate to escape a beating.'

'I am sorry I annoyed you, André,' Louise replied,
hanging on to the side of the unwieldy coach as it rattled
and lurched dangerously over the cobblestones. 'I
merely danced with Monsieur de Guise.'

'You were flirting with him like a wanton! Fortunately
the Chevalier de Leconte was not present to witness
your disgraceful behaviour this evening.'

'The Chevalier de Leconte?' Louise asked, wrinkling
her brow as she tried to fit a face to the name, and failed.
'Why should a stranger be interested whether or not I
danced with Monsieur de Guise?'

'You danced with that popinjay three times,' André
reminded her grimly. 'It is not for me to acquaint you
with our father's plans. However, you will learn soon
enough. I hope a night's reflection will be sufficient to
bring you to your senses. You will not dance with that
man again. If he speaks to you, you must make it clear

that you wish for no further acquaintance with him. Do you understand me, Louise?'

She understood well enough. It seemed that she was not to be punished this time, but a second lapse would be treated with severity. Since she did not really wish to become too involved with the young man in question, the threat was less distressing than it might have been. Yet she felt a sharp surge of rebellion, and her thoughts were not those of an obedient sister as she faced her brother in the darkness of the coach.

Why must she always obey? Why must her life be planned for her with no reference to her wishes? She had been taught that it was a daughter's duty to obey her father always and without question, but suddenly her mind was seething with doubts.

The moon had moved out from behind the clouds, and Louise stared out of the window at the dark shapes of the night-bound city. She did not know why this change had come about in her so suddenly, though she had been aware of it from the moment she heard the mockery in the Englishman's voice. It was the memory of that brief glimpse of scorn in his dark eyes that had brought on her mood of devilment.

Lord Carleton was different from any man she had ever met. He had spoken to her as though she were his equal, and not merely a woman. Even though he had mocked her, there had been no condescension in his manner; he had seemed to enjoy crossing swords with her, and was amused rather than angered by her defiance.

She sensed that there was some mystery about him —something that made him a possible danger to her family and friends. Perhaps he was a spy? There were many at Court; and he must have had a purpose in asking her to dance, since he had not cared to repeat the experience. For some reason, that still rankled in her mind. It was clear he had used her merely as a way of meeting the Admiral—but why?

It was impossible to understand the way his mind worked, and she abandoned the attempt. Yet she found her thoughts dwelling on the brief time she had spent with the English lord, going over every word he had spoken. Remembering something she had said to him, a chill ran down Louise's spine. Of course! What a fool she was not to have realised the significance of André's forbearance at once.

If she was not to be beaten for her behaviour, it was because her father did not wish her to be confined to her bed as a result of it. She had told Lord Carleton that her father was thinking of arranging a marriage for her —obviously he had made his choice.

A cold knot formed in her stomach and she felt quite sick. Who was this man? To her certain knowledge, she had never met the Chevalier de Leconte. Her restless fingers played with the jewelled handle of her fan, and she felt an intense desire to run far away from Paris and the unknown man who was to be her husband.

Yet where could she go but to her home in La Rochelle? She had no money of her own, and no one she could turn to for help. She had no choice but to obey her father.

CHAPTER TWO

LOUISE BREATHED deeply in the fresh, sweet air of early morning; there was nothing quite like the smell of a forest after a shower of rain, she thought. Her delight was intense as she gazed round the large clearing at the mass of jostling horses and their riders. Half the Court had gathered for the chase, which was to form the day's main entertainment. Later, there would be an informal picnic, and in the evening a masked ball was to take place at the Louvre.

For two days Louise's father had refused to allow her to leave the house at the Rue Saint-Denis, where they were staying. Missing the celebrations was a punishment, he said, for her disgraceful behaviour at Court; but he had been unable to refuse his permission when the Queen Mother sent a special invitation for Louise to join her ladies in the hunt. The select band of ladies who rode with Madame Catherine was called the Escadron Volant, and Louise was thrilled to have been asked to join them, although it was for just one day.

The huntsmen's horns sounded and the first of the riders began to move off. Marie edged her horse nearer to Louise, signalling to her that it was time.

'Stay close to me,' she said. 'Madame Catherine is always at the forefront, and she expects us to keep up with her.'

'I shall do my best,' Louise replied, her eyes sparkling. 'Thank you for lending me your horse, Marie. She is such a beautiful creature I am surprised you could bear to part with her even for one day.'

The chestnut mare Louise was riding was indeed a fine, high-spirited animal. While they were waiting for the chase to begin, it had constantly pounded the ground

with its front hooves, and it had taken all Louise's skill as
a horsewoman to hold her mount. Like her, the mare
was impatient to be off.

Marie smiled but made no reply, merely beckoning to
Louise as she spurred her own mount forward. The
horse she had provided for her cousin's use was not her
own, but she had no intention of telling her exactly
where it had come from. If all went as planned, she had
been promised both the horse and a purse of gold.

Following her cousin's lead, Louise gave the mare its
head and felt a thrill of pleasure at the sudden surge of
speed. She knew without a doubt that she had never
before been mounted on a horse of this mettle. It should
not be difficult to keep up with the leaders, even though
they rode at a terrific pace. It was no wonder that
the Queen Mother's ladies were named the Flying
Squadron!

The hounds had managed to put up a stag, and were
now in full cry as the royal party set out in pursuit.
Horses and riders plunged on in the shadowed coolness
of the forest, led on by the magnificent beast which
gallantly avoided the pursuing dogs until, at last, it was
driven into a dense thicket where neither the huntsmen
nor the courtiers cared to follow. An attempt to flush it
out by blowing the horns at full blast met with no
success, and eventually the hounds were recalled.

Louise was secretly glad that their prey had evaded
them at the end. It had been an exciting chase, but she
would not have enjoyed seeing such a beautiful creature
killed.

The dogs had startled a hare, however, and some of
the courtiers were in pursuit; it seemed poor sport after
the earlier chase, and Louise felt disinclined to join in.
When Marie rode up to her, she was pleased to hear that
the Escadron Volant was returning to the clearing,
where a picnic should now be awaiting the royal party.

'You and I are to go on ahead,' Marie said, 'to make
sure that everything is in readiness.'

'I'm not certain which way we came. Are you?'

'Just follow me,' her cousin replied confidently. 'I have ridden in this forest many times. We have only to follow this track to find our way back.'

It seemed a little strange to Louise that they should be sent on ahead to warn the servants that the hunt was returning, but she did not question her cousin. The order would have come from Madame Catherine, and must obviously be obeyed.

Trotting gently a short distance behind Marie's horse, Louise allowed her thoughts to wander. It was so peaceful and quiet now that the noise of the dogs and the horns had been left behind. All she could hear was the sound of birds singing, and a breeze sighing in the treetops. Sunlight filtered through the leaves, dappling the undergrowth with patches of gold and warming her face. It was not until they had been riding for some time that Louise realised the trees seemed to be getting thicker; now it was darker, and the sun could not penetrate so easily.

'Are you sure we are going the right way?' she called to her cousin. 'I do not remember the forest being this dense—and look, you can see that no one has ridden this way recently.'

Marie reined in, glancing back at her with a worried frown. 'I think you may be right,' she said. 'We must have taken the wrong turning a few minutes ago. You remember there were two tracks?'

'Yes. We have come the wrong way, Marie. We should go back and try again.'

'Perhaps we should split up?'

'No, we must stay together. If we are lost, it will be easier for a search party to find two of us.'

'As you wish.' Marie shrugged carelessly. 'We cannot be far from the clearing; the forest is not very large. You lead on, and I shall follow you.'

Louise turned her horse, looking anxiously now for signs of trampling in the undergrowth. She pointed a little to her left. 'See, this is the way we came.'

She gave the mare's reins a gentle flick, urging her
mount forward at a steady pace. It was not easy to find
the path they had taken, for it was not like following a
well-used track, and they seemed to zig-zag through the
trees. Louise had to be alert for every broken twig or the
imprint of a horse's hoof in the earth. Since the ground
was slightly damp, she was able to retrace their passage,
but it was difficult and needed all her concentration. It
was only when she saw the tiny clearing ahead where the
path had forked that she glanced back over her shoulder,
calling to Marie.

'It's here we went wrong . . .' she began, the words
trailing away as she looked in vain for her cousin.
'Marie? Marie—where are you?'

There was no answer, and her voice seemed to echo
eerily in the stillness. She called again urgently, straining
for a sound that would give a clue to Marie's whereabouts; but there was nothing. Nothing but silence. A
shiver went down Louise's spine. What could have
happened to her? Until this moment she had not been
particularly worried; for as her cousin had said, the
forest could not be all that big and they must eventually
find their way. Now, quite suddenly, she was frightened.
Something must have happened to her. She would have
to go back and look in case she had fallen from her horse
and lay injured. Yet even as she prepared to return to
where she had last seen Marie, there was a rustling in the
undergrowth and she cried out gladly,

'Marie, where have . . .'

The question died abruptly. She was staring not at her
cousin but at three rough-looking men who had come
seemingly out of nowhere. Her breath caught in her
throat as she gazed down at the men, who must by their
appearance be beggars or vagrants. Their faces were
gaunt and streaked with dirt; and they looked at her
strangely from sunken, haunted eyes.

'Who are you?' she whispered, gentling the mare as it
shied nervously.

The men surrounded her. She saw the leering expression in their eyes and stifled the scream that rose to her lips. She must not show fear. After all, she was mounted and they were on foot.

'I have missed my way,' she said, succeeding in keeping her voice level and calm. 'Have you seen a large party of huntsmen?'

'What will you pay to find your friends, lady?' one of them grunted, coming to take hold of the mare's bridle.

'I have no money,' Louise replied, lifting her chin proudly. 'But if you can help me, I shall see you are well paid for your trouble.'

The spokesman grinned at his companions. 'A fine lady like you must have gold—or some trinket—to make it worth our while to let you pass.'

Louise saw the menace in his face, and shivered. The others had closed in about her now, forming a semicircle about her horse's head. She realised they had no intention of allowing her to go on without payment—but if she gave them the small brooch she was wearing, it would not satisfy them.

'I have no money with me,' she repeated, fighting for control. 'Nor will I give you anything until you lead me to my friends.'

'Then we will take what we can,' the spokesman said. 'Your horse is worth a fair price—and your clothes would fetch enough to feed us for a month, I'll swear.' He grew bolder as he spoke, touching the heavy silk of her gown with his filthy hands.

'Keep away from me!' Louise shouted, striking at his fingers with her whip. 'Don't you dare to touch me.'

She struggled desperately to hide her fear, but their hands were clawing at her now from both sides. Lashing out angrily in all directions, she tried to force the mare's passage through them, but they held its head and would not let her pass. Now their leader had hold of her ankle; he was trying to unseat her even as she rained blows on his head and arms. She could feel herself slipping, and screamed aloud in despair.

A sudden cry caused her attackers to glance round in alarm. As a horse came crashing through the trees on the other side of the clearing, they ceased to pull at her clothes and fled back the way they had come.

Louise's mount reared in fright, almost accomplishing what the vagrants had tried and failed. She held on, wrestling valiantly with the reins as she brought the mare under control once more. It was a moment or two before she was able to recognise her rescuer.

'Monsieur de Guise!' she cried in relief. 'How glad I am to see you.'

'Mademoiselle de Granvelle!' he said, dismounting and coming towards her swiftly. 'I pray I was in time to prevent those ruffians harming you?'

He held out his arms and Louise slid down into them, allowing him to hold her for a moment. She was trembling, and did not at first resist when he pressed her close to his chest. When she drew away, he let her go reluctantly.

'I—I am better now,' she said, smiling shakily. 'In a little while we must return the way I came a few minutes ago. I fear something must have happened to my cousin. She was behind me, and then she disappeared. I am afraid those men may have harmed her.'

Pierre's face took on an odd expression. 'You need not fear for Madame de Galliard; I passed her just a moment ago. She said she had somehow lost sight of you and asked me to look for you while she went for help. I am sure she will be with the other ladies by now.'

Louise frowned. How could he have passed Marie coming from the other direction? It was impossible —unless she had been going round and round in circles!

'Do you know where the others are?' she asked doubtfully. 'I seem to have lost all sense of direction.'

'You may rely on me, mademoiselle.' He smiled, taking her hand in his own to kiss it. 'In a moment, when you feel well enough to ride, I shall help you to mount.'

'I have stopped shaking now. It was fortunate for me that you came this way . . .'

Louise saw the tiny flicker of satisfaction in his eyes and wrinkled her brow, feeling suspicious. It was indeed lucky that he had chosen to take this route—and it was more than a little strange that he had just happened to see Marie. Now that she thought about it, the vagrants had run away very quickly. A little too quickly! Marie had deliberately led her in the wrong direction, knowing this would happen. She had waited her chance and then slipped quietly away. It had all been planned so that Pierre de Guise could rescue her.

'You planned this with my cousin!' she accused furiously, and saw the truth in his guilty flush. 'How could you be so cruel? I was really frightened for a while.'

'Oh no,' he said, catching her wrist as she tried to pull away. 'I swear that was not part of the plan. You must believe me, mademoiselle. I wanted only to find a way of being alone with you for a little time. I swear on my honour that you were not meant to be attacked.'

He reached out for her, trying to pull her to him once more, but she avoided her grasp, her eyes glinting angrily.

'I think you forget yourself, m'sieur!'

'Forgive me, I beg you. I was mad to plan such a trick—but I did it for love of you. Since we first met, I have not slept for thinking of you. Will you not grant me one kiss?'

'Since you arranged this little masquerade with my cousin, I can see no reason for a reward, m'sieur.'

'Please do not be angry with me. I wanted only to be with you—to hold you in my arms. I knew your brother would never allow us to meet.' He caught her hand again, looking at her wretchedly. 'I would do anything if you will only forgive me, Louise. I adore you—I worship you! My life is nothing to me without you.'

Louise could not remain unmoved by his protestations. She looked at him uncertainly. 'It was a
foolish jest none the less. Do you swear before God that
those vagrants were not part of your plan?'

'I will swear it on the holy relics if you will forgive me.'

'Well, I suppose you meant no harm.' Louise sighed
deeply. 'You could not have known what would happen.
Now, take me back to my cousin and the other ladies.'

He held her hand still. 'Will you dance with me
tonight?'

'My father has forbidden it. You know our families
hate each other.'

'I could never hate you.'

'Nor do I hate you, m'sieur.' Louise smiled sadly, her
anger fading. 'But we must return to the others. I shall
be missed. If my father hears of this accident, he will not
let me attend the ball tonight. It was fortunate he and
André were too busy to come today.'

'Then we must go.' He kissed her hand lingeringly
once more before helping her to mount. Then, as he
stood looking up at her, 'I shall see you tonight?'

Louise remembered her brother's warning, but she
was moved by the pleading in the young man's eyes. She
realised he must have been desperate to conceive this
foolish plot with Marie's help—she must not forget
Marie's part in it!—but she was sure he had meant no
harm. The courtiers often played tricks on one another,
sometimes from spite or malice, but more commonly as
a source of amusement. To make a fuss over the incident
would only cause the other ladies to laugh behind her
back.

'I have been forbidden to dance with you, m'sieur, but
I cannot help answering if you speak to me. Besides, we
shall be masked. How can I be blamed for dancing with
you if I did not recognise it was you who asked?'

Pierre's eyes gleamed with laughter. Her answer
pleased him. He had begun to believe there was no way
to breach her defences, but now she had given him hope.

As they rode back to the clearing—which Pierre found with ease!—he regaled her with gossip about the courtiers, telling her all the most amusing stories. His wit was slightly malicious, but Louise could not help laughing at his tales. So she was relaxed and smiling when they reached the clearing, where long tables had been set with a delicious buffet of cold meats, bread, wine and sugared fruits.

Everyone was either sitting on silken cushions or strolling from one group to another as they sipped their wine from silver cups and nibbled at morsels of venison. Louise knew their late arrival had been noticed, and she could hear the whispers begin to circulate. Her cheeks were flushed as Pierre helped her to dismount, and she hurried to join Madame Catherine's ladies.

For a moment the Queen Mother's dark eyes were turned on her; Louise shivered as she saw the cold calculation in that ominous gaze. Finding her courage, she curtsied to her hostess, apologising for her lateness.

'I lost my way, Madame,' she said, loudly enough to be heard by others. 'Fortunately, Monsieur de Guise chanced on me as I was being attacked by some beggars. Was that not lucky?'

There was a tiny ripple of laughter, and Louise realised that the jest was already being whispered of. She saw a gleam of amusement in Madame Catherine's eyes, and was glad she had decided not to make a fuss. It was obvious that they all knew what had happened—and from the sly look on Marie's face, there was no doubt that she had enjoyed spreading the tale.

'You are forgiven, Mademoiselle de Granvelle. Please try not to get lost on your way to the Louvre this evening.'

The titters behind her increased as Madame Catherine turned away. Louise bit her lip, holding her head high as she saw the sly looks directed at her. Most of them probably thought she had been a party to the plot as a way of meeting a lover in secret. It was unkind of

Marie to spread the story, and she felt hurt by her cousin's behaviour. Her reputation must suffer for it, and her father would be furious when he heard the story—and now he must do so in time!

'Would you care for some venison, mademoiselle? Or perhaps a glass of wine?'

Louise turned sharply as she heard the unmistakable accent. Looking up into Lord Carleton's face, she saw that he, at least, was not laughing at her. Indeed, there was the hard gleam of anger in his slitted eyes.

'Thank you, my lord,' she replied with a little toss of her head. 'Getting lost has given me an appetite, I fear.'

She saw a flicker of appreciation in his face as he offered her his arm. 'I, too, was a latecomer to the feast. Shall we see what we can find to tempt us?'

Louise took his arm gratefully. She was still aware of the whispers and sly glances, but they had lost their sting. She ignored everyone but her companion, allowing him to pour her a cup of sweet red wine, and laughing as he piled her platter with the choicest cuts of meat and the finest fruits.

'Have a care, or you will make me grow fat and ugly!' she cried. 'Then my poor father will never find a husband for me.'

'You have ridden hard, and need some sustenance to carry you through all these festivities,' he replied with a wry smile. 'Besides, you must know there are a dozen men here who would marry you, given the chance.'

Louise arched her brow. 'Because I am the daughter of a wealthy man?'

'Do you wish me to say it is because you are the loveliest woman at Court?'

'No.' She shook her head positively. 'That would be merely flattery, my lord. I know I am not the most beautiful woman at Court, nor do I expect to find a perfect man—it is simply that I should be happier if I thought my husband truly cared for me, and was not interested only in my inheritance.'

His lips twitched. 'Are you a believer in love, mademoiselle de Granvelle? I had thought you far too sensible—and only too willing to marry the man of your father's choosing.'

The smile died from her face, and she shivered, despite the warm sun. 'I must when the time comes. I have no choice. Please do not tease me about it, my lord.'

'No . . .' His look was serious, for once. 'I suppose you are bound to obey your father. Yet others in your situation have learned to take their pleasure where they can—as you will do in time.'

They found a space under the shade of a tree, and sat down to eat. Louise knew that he had been hinting that she would take a lover, as many women did once they had given their husband a son—as Marie had. Letting her eyes travel round the clearing, she wondered about the private thoughts behind the smiling faces. The Court was always buzzing with some new scandal; men and women took new lovers and discarded old ones almost as easily as new gloves. Would she become like them one day?

As though he were aware of her thoughts, Lord Carleton set out to amuse her and bring the laughter back to her eyes. Since he was skilled in the art of conversation, she was soon laughing at his jests, forgetting everything in the pleasure of the moment. It was not long before some of the courtiers drifted over to join them. Raphael was telling a long, involved story about the English Court. His audience drew closer, fascinated by the titbits of scandal he dropped temptingly every so often.

Louise listened to the slow drawl of his words, realising how cleverly he drew his listeners into the conversation, so that they, too, were soon recounting stories of their own. The group gathered about them grew larger as they were joined by the brightest and wittiest of the company.

Glancing casually across the clearing, Louise found
herself looking directly at her cousin, and shivered as she
saw the cold gleam of hatred in Marie's turquoise eyes.
The shock ran through her, making her feel slightly sick.
Why was she looking at her like that? What had she done
to deserve Marie's hatred? She had believed that today's
little escapade had been merely a thoughtless jest on
Marie's part, but now she wondered if her cousin had
meant her harm. Yet why should she? Perhaps that look
was not for her. It might be only that she had a
headache . . .

Louise's reverie was interrupted as one of the
courtiers spoke to her. 'And what is your opinion,
Mademoiselle de Granvelle?'

'I beg your pardon, m'sieur, I was not attending. Pray
repeat your question.'

'Lord Carleton was saying that French women
are exciting lovers but seldom faithful to their
husbands . . .'

'You misquote me, m'sieur.' Raphael's mouth twisted
wryly. 'I said I would always choose a French woman for
my mistress, but think twice about marrying her if she
happened to be beautiful. Lovely women are as in
inconstant as the moon—no matter whether they be
French, English, or any other nationality.'

There were cries of 'shame' and pouts from the
women, but the men laughed and echoed his sentiments.
Louise wrinkled her brow, staring at him thoughtfully.

'Then, in your opinion, a woman cannot be both pure
of heart and beautiful? You are very hard on us, my lord,
for if we have virtue we must make ourselves ugly—and
if we are ugly, no one will care if we are virtuous.'

'Well said, mademoiselle!' one of the ladies cried. 'I
can vouch for several ladies I know who have both
qualities.'

'Show me such a paragon, and I will marry her,'
Raphael quipped.

'You are unkind to doubt us all,' a pretty girl said,

smirking at him. 'Perhaps you would prefer an ugly
wife?'

'At least I would be sure her brats were my own. And
if she possessed a fortune, her kisses would taste sweet
enough.'

Laughter and a murmur of agreement from the gentlemen greeted this statement. Louise was quiet for a
moment. Conversation such as this was the lifeblood of
the Court, and no one took it seriously for most of the
time. Yet there was just a trace of bitterness in Lord
Carleton's voice, and she thought she caught the glint of
ice in his black eyes.

'You would be faithful to your plain wife, I suppose?'
she asked, lifting her gaze to meet his challengingly. 'Or
perhaps you consider fidelity a virtue in a woman, but
unnecessary in a man?'

'Now that is another matter entirely.' There was more
laughter and cries of 'shame', but he refused to give his
ground. 'As yet, I have not found a woman I would care
to marry, but if I did . . .'

'You would be as unfaithful as the next man!' one of
the ladies cried.

'Perhaps.' Raphael shrugged his shoulders, seeming
to lose interest in the conversation. He turned his dark
gaze on Louise, and she saw that he was angry, though
few would guess it. 'I believe Madame Catherine is
leaving with her ladies. Perhaps you should join them,
mademoiselle?'

He stood up, offering his hand to help her to rise.
Louise accepted his assistance, avoiding his eyes as she
thanked him. She heard the courtiers' laughter as she
walked away, and wondered at the disappointment she
was feeling inside. The other night she had thought Lord
Carleton somehow different from the others, but today
he had proved himself as insincere as all the rest. He
had been drinking steadily for the past hour or more,
and seemed quite happy to carry on as he was all day.
She was grateful to him for helping her through an

embarrassing situation, but sad to find he was not the
man she had first thought him.

Louise was not sure why the discovery was so disappointing. After all, she would be going home
soon, and her father had told her he had already begun
negotiations for a marriage between her and the
Chevalier de Leconte.

It could make no difference to her what kind of a man
Lord Carleton was!

Marie came to meet her as she joined the group of ladies
preparing to return to the Louvre.

Seeing Louise's angry look, the older girl had the
grace to blush. 'Are you very cross with me?' she asked
in a hushed whisper. 'Pierre told me you were attacked
by some beggars. You must know I would not have
wanted harm to come of our little masquerade? I am
truly sorry for it, Louise.'

'I know you were not to blame for what happened
—but you need not have told everyone it was a plot so
that Monsieur de Guise could find me.'

'It was far better than I should. No one thinks
the worse of you for it. Indeed, you took the jest so
well that I have heard only praise. Besides, Madame
Catherine asked where you were, so I had to tell her
the truth.'

Was there just a hint of jealousy in Marie's eyes?
Louise could not be sure. Perhaps she was making too
much of the incident. It had been meant as a harmless
prank, after all. Marie could not know how angry it
would make the Seigneur de Granvelle. Louise sighed
deeply. When her father heard the story he would blame
her, and this time she could not expect leniency! Fortunately, he would not be present at this evening's entertainment, as he had left Paris on some business. So she
would have to make the most of tonight and face her
father's rage when he returned.

Shrugging her shoulders, Louise smiled a little tightly.

'I know you meant it only as a jest, Marie. Shall we forget it and be friends again?'

'I have always been your friend,' Marie replied, her eyes lighting with mischief now. 'Most ladies I know would thank me for the chance to be alone with such a handsome and ardent lover!'

Louise shook her head, but made no reply. She knew her protests would not be believed. Nor would Marie be the only one to think the worst of her. The fact that her and Pierre's families were enemies would make it seem all the more likely that she was involved in a secret love-affair with the young man. It would be an amusing story for the courtiers to laugh about behind their hands.

Not that it was a secret any more, Louise thought ruefully. Riding back to the city with the other ladies, she was teased unmercifully about her handsome admirer. It was clear that several of her companions would not be averse to meeting the young de Guise in a secret rendezvous. She would have to be careful what she did in future, she realised. It was all too easy for an unmarried woman to lose her reputation at Court. It might be wiser not to dance with Pierre tonight.

It was easier to make the decision than to keep it, Louise discovered when she and Marie joined the merry throng already gathered in the brightly-lit gallery that evening. The Court was in the mood for celebration now that the eve of the royal wedding had arrived. Tomorrow, 18th August 1572, the ceremony would take place in front of the great cathedral of Notre Dame, where all the people of Paris could witness this wondrous event.

These past few days had seen a few setbacks, not least of which was the Princess Margot's reluctance to take the King of Navarre for her husband. It was common knowledge that the wayward girl's heart was given to the handsome Henri, Duc de Guise, and that she would have married him long ago had her mother allowed it. Her passion for the young man, who was the uncrowned

king of Paris and beloved of its citizens, had brought the
pair of them close to ruin; only Henri's hurried marriage
to Catherine, Princess of Clèves, and a prolonged
absence from Court, had averted disaster.

However, the Queen Mother's will had prevailed.
The princess was outwardly obedient, even if her dark
eyes did stray too often to those of the man she loved;
and though the long-awaited dispensation from the
Pope, allowing the union between a Catholic and a
Protestant, had not yet arrived, the French King had
convinced Navarre's uncle, the Cardinal of Bourbon,
that it was on its way.

So the marriage could take place at last, and the
celebrations would continue for days afterwards. The
excitement was infectious, and it was difficult for Louise
to remain untouched by it all. She had never seen so
many beautiful gowns or such wonderful jewels as the
courtiers wore; the men as splendidly dressed as their
ladies on this momentous night.

The girl could not but be glad that neither her father
nor André was present. Marie was considered a sufficient chaperon because of her status as a matron.
Privately, Louise thought it fortunate that both her
father and brother had been too concerned with politics
to take much notice of what went on at Court. Had
either of them realised that Marie's husband allowed her
to do exactly as she pleased, they would have considered
she was too free in her manners and likely to be a bad
influence on her cousin. If that had happened, Louise
would even now be sitting alone in her room at the house
in the Rue Saint-Denis.

Realising that she would probably be excluded from
many of the celebrations once her father heard the
stories about her and Pierre de Guise now circulating at
Court, Louise let herself be swept up in the gaiety of the
occasion. She found herself dancing continuously with a
succession of masked partners, many of whom it was
impossible to recognise.

The masks were often very elaborate, sometimes representing horned beasts or demons. Everyone was trying to guess the name of their partner, and there was a great deal of laughter as mistakes were made.

Louise was wearing a white mask trimmed with silver to match her gown. She had chosen to hide only the top half of her face, which was perhaps not such a complete disguise as that of many others. Most of her partners seemed to know her name, even though she could not always guess theirs. Lord Carleton's accent gave him away instantly, however.

'Will you honour me with this dance, mademoiselle?' he asked in a husky voice that was a vain attempt to hide his identity.

'Willingly, my lord,' Louise replied, taking his hand with a smile.

'Ah, you know me. I wonder why?' The sensuous mouth twisted a little wryly.

Her laughter rang out gaily as they began to dance. 'Your accent betrays you, m'sieur.'

'I am glad it amuses you,' he said, his eyes mocking behind the black velvet mask. 'My cousins are ashamed to own me, I fear.'

'Oh no! I find it agreeable, my lord. Your cousins must be teasing you if they say otherwise.'

'Perhaps. Yet my mother was a French woman; I am hardly a credit to her.'

'Your command of the language is excellent, my lord. I fear it would put my English to shame.'

'Did you have no one to teach you how to speak it?'

'It was not considered necessary. I am hardly likely to visit England.'

'That is a pity. I believe you might find my part of the country to your taste. It was very pretty in the spring, and there is some excellent hunting.'

Louise was about to ask him exactly where in England his home was, when the music finished. Since she was immediately besieged by eager suitors for the next

dance, their conversation was brought to an abrupt end.
She experienced a feeling of disappointment as he
bowed and walked away, his mouth curving in a cynical
smile as if he were amused at her popularity. For a short
while, Louise, realised, she had felt completely at ease in
his company. Tonight he had seemed a different person
from the man who had sat with her in the clearing,
entertaining his audience with scandalous attacks on the
morality of women.

Her thoughts were brought back to the present by the
insistent questioning of her new partner. He was pretending not to know her, but Louise was certain he was
aware of her identity. She had recognised the heavy
perfume he was wearing and the huge emerald ring on
his right hand. He was one of those hard-eyed courtiers
she had felt so uncomfortable with the other evening,
though she could not recall his name. This evening he
was bolder, as though his mask had lent him greater
courage. His compliments were too intimate, his hands
too warm and moist; it was with relief that she parted
from him as the dance came to a close, refusing his
request to take her to supper with a sharpness that was
unlike her.

Thus far, Pierre de Guise had not approached her.
Louise was a little surprised at his forbearance, and
wondered if she could have been mistaken. Yet she was
sure she would have known him, despite his mask.

The evening was well advanced: several people were
making their way towards the dining hall, Marie among
them. Seeing her cousin signalling to her, Louise decided to join the group. As she began to cross the room,
a man bumped into her, apologising gruffly as he walked
swiftly away.

Turning to gaze at his retreating back, she saw that his
costume was fashioned of dark blue velvet trimmed with
gold and heavily encrusted with pearls. His face had
been completely hidden by the mask of a satyr, effectively concealing his identity. Yet she thought it must

have been Pierre; for the set of his shoulders was familiar, and the hair curling on his lace ruff was the right shade of gold.

Louise's fingers tightened on the note which had been thrust into her hand in that brief contact with the mysterious satyr. She glanced over her shoulder, wondering if the incident had been observed, but was reassured as she saw that everyone was enjoying themselves far too much to notice her.

Keeping the note concealed behind her fan, she managed to open it. A gasp escaped her lips as she scanned the brief message written in a scrawled hand, as if the writer had been in haste. For a moment the room spun dizzily, and she thought that she would faint. She saw Marie beckon to her impatiently, but her appetite had deserted her and she gave a little shake of her head.

Marie shrugged and left without her. For a moment, Louise was too stunned to think properly. She had imagined the note was a romantic gesture from Pierre, and had been prepared for a passionate declaration of his love. Instead, the few, dramatic words had shocked her, sending cold shivers running through her body. Feeling slightly sick, she read it through once more, to be certain she was not mistaken in its meaning.

'If you wish to save the Admiral's life, come to the south courtyard alone at once,' she read, her lips moving silently.

Surely it must be a trick? The Admiral was His Majesty's friend; she had seen them together earlier this evening, for neither was masked. This was but a cruel jest—and yet, she could not be certain, remembering her father's doubts. Had he not warned against this wedding and all it meant? What if this note were genuine? What ought she to do? The message said that she must go alone to the courtyard—instinct told her it would be foolish to obey the summons, but to whom could she turn?

If her father or brother had been here she would have

taken the note to them; but perhaps the warning was from someone who would speak only to her. She was almost sure it was Pierre who had given her the note; he would know it would be useless to try and talk to her family. They would not listen to him, nor would it be wise for him to approach them; if the Admiral was in some kind of danger, Pierre was running a great risk in warning her. Men who were ruthless enough to plan the Admiral's death would not balk at the murder of an unimportant boy, even if he were a distant relative of the Duc de Guise.

Louise shuddered as she felt the trickle of cold sweat run down her spine. If someone was trying to help her to prevent a murder, she must have the courage to do as he asked and meet him in secret. Obviously, whoever it was could not run the risk of speaking to her in a crowded gallery. It was quite clear what she must do: there was no choice if her kinsman's life was in danger.

She took a deep breath, glancing round the gallery in search of the satyr in blue and gold. There was no sign of him, and she realised he must be waiting for her in the courtyard. Her heart was thumping madly as she walked towards the doorway; she had a feeling she was being very foolish—but what else could she do?

Louise was glad of her mask as she left the ballroom. It protected her from too clearly showing her emotional state, and it would not do for anyone to guess where she was going or why. Fortunately, the courtiers were enjoying themselves too much for her departure to arouse any interest. Even those she met on her way through a succession of crowded rooms gave her only a glance in passing. At last, she was able to slip through a side door into the seclusion of the gardens.

It was much cooler and darker outside. Louise paused for a moment as she adjusted to the light, shivering as she tried to work out exactly where she was. The gardens and courtyards were extensive, and she was not sure she knew just where Pierre expected to meet her. She had strolled in the courtyards earlier in the evening with her cousin, but everything looked so different at night. At the moment the moon was half hidden by clouds, throwing pale shadows across the lawns.

Louise began to walk in what she hoped was the right direction, her heart seeming to beat unevenly as the doubts began to crowd in on her. Should she have shown the note to someone? What if she could not find Pierre? How could she be sure it was Pierre who had slipped it into her hand? Perhaps she herself was walking into a trap!

An owl hooted near by, making her start in fright. She glanced over her shoulder, half glimpsing a shadow behind a tree. For a moment her pulses raced, then she drew a deep breath and took a hold on her nerves. There was no one behind the tree: it was merely a trick of the moonlight. The clouds were beginning to move away, and soon there would be more light. She must hurry if she did not want to be seen from the palace windows.

Her thin satin slippers moved soundlessly over the flagstones as she ran towards the formal gardens. When she turned the corner, Louise could see the dark shapes of statues and a fountain, which she knew played into a fish-pool. She thought she must be nearing her destination; the meeting-place was somewhere here—just beyond that patch of shrubbery. Breathing steadily to calm her nerves, she trod noiselessly on the grass and paused as she heard a man's deep voice just ahead of her. It was coming from somewhere within the bushes.

'Do you think the girl will be fool enough to come?' it asked of an unseen companion.

'If she doesn't, there'll be hell to pay; he's determined to have her. Remember he said she was not to be harmed.'

'What if she screams?'

'Use your cloak to muffle the noise. She'll quieten soon enough when he has her, I'll warrant.'

There was a sneering laugh and then silence, as if the waiting kidnappers had heard something to alert them. Louise stopped dead, hardly daring to breathe. They were—they must be!—talking about her. Her heart jerked painfully and she felt a pounding in her temples. The note had been a trick to lure her out here alone, and she had almost walked into the trap. What a fool she had been! For a moment she was paralysed, too frightened to move lest it told the would-be abductors that she was close. She had heard at least three different voices coming from the dark cloisters of that thick shrubbery. If those men suspected she was near by, she would have no chance against such odds.

She must return to the safety of the gallery as quickly as possible. Turning in haste, she saw the black shadow of a tall figure a short distance behind her. She knew he had seen her as he put out a hand as if in warning, and a cry of alarm escaped her lips. There were not three assailants lying in wait for her, but four—and the fourth must have been following her ever since she left the palace. It was his shadow she had glimpsed behind the tree!

Her cry had warned the men in the shrubberies, Louise realised as she heard a muffled oath and then rustling sounds. There was movement in the bushes, and she knew they were coming for her. Giving a little sob of fear, she began to run across the lawn, trying to avoid the oncoming fourth man. She was vaguely aware that he had quickened his pace, and of the burly figures emerging from the shrubberies. In a surge of panic she caught her foot in the hem of her gown and stumbled, falling face down on the grass.

'There she is!'

The shout came from behind Louise. She glanced back in alarm as she got to her feet, brushing débris from the full skirts of her satin gown. For one moment the scene was like a tableau in the moonlight. She clearly saw three men emerge from the bushes into the open, one of them pointing his arm dramatically in her direction. Even as she prepared to continue her flight, she was aware of the fourth man moving into the set-piece. He merely stood there, caught in the full light of the moon as the clouds rolled back, hands on hips and feet apart in arrogant stance. Yet his arrival was enough to halt the others in their tracks, turning them to silver statues. For what seemed an agonising eternity they were all suspended in time; then, amazingly, the three of them turned and slunk back into the bushes.

Louise stood motionless as the fourth man came towards her. In that moment, when time had seemed to stand still, she had recognised him and the panic in her subsided instantly, though her heart still thumped madly as he drew near. She looked up into his face, catching her breath as she saw the anger in those patrician features.

'Are you so mad for that young fool that you will risk anything to meet him?'

His fury made her gasp, flinching back as if she had been struck. 'What do you mean?'

The black eyes glittered with jewel-hardness as he glared down at her. 'I should have thought this morning's little episode would have taught you never to trust a de Guise. Don't you know the whole Court is making wagers as to how soon he'll have you in his bed?'

'You mean . . .?' Louise's face went white. 'No, I don't believe it. Pierre wouldn't . . .'

'Would he not?' Raphael's mouth curved in an unpleasant sneer. 'Had I not followed you, my pretty innocent, you might have disappeared without trace.'

'No! It's not true,' Louise gasped. 'Why should Pierre de Guise want to harm me? He swore he loved me only this morning.'

'And you were flattered by his attentions!' Raphael's harsh laughter seared her. 'Knowing the family he comes from, you believed his intentions were honourable? You are not such a fool, I think! Do you imagine the Cardinal de Lorraine would allow his kinsman to make a fool of himself over the daughter of an enemy?'

A shiver ran down Louise's spine. If half the stories told of the Cardinal de Lorraine were true, he was both ruthless and a lecher. It was with his direction and encouragement that a large body of Protestants had been murdered at Amboise in 1560. She had heard her father speak of the treachery, and of the tortures to which the Huguenots had been subjected while the entire Court looked on. They, too, had had the promise of a king to protect them. Such a man as the Cardinal would not balk at mere kidnap to please a boy who was dear to him. It was clear that Lord Carleton knew what he was about, yet his scorn stung her. Louise realised she ought to be thanking him for saving her, but his assumption that she had come to meet her lover made her angry.

'You presume too much, m'sieur,' she said haughtily. 'Pierre would never allow his kinsman to harm me.'

'You little idiot!' Raphael said, exasperation making him grab her wrist as she tried to push past him. 'At least let me see you safely back to your friends.'

'Leave me alone!' Louise snapped. 'Why should I trust you more than any other?'

His eyes shone silver in the moonlight as he gazed down at her lovely face. For a moment he seemed as if he would strike her in his fury; then, with a deep sigh, he reached out and drew her hard against him. Louise knew a moment of surprise as his head came down and his lips covered hers in a hungry, demanding kiss that sent shock waves coursing through her tense body.

She stood still within the imprisoning circle of his arms, bemused and startled by what was happening to her. His lips teased and caressed hers, moving from her mouth to the white arch of her throat, and on downward, until they were halted by the stiff silver lace sheltering her breasts from his ravaging kisses. She gave a gasp of dismay as his tongue probed beyond the flimsy material, sending a dart of fire inward from the rosy nipple. The tingling sensation jerked her to full awareness of his intentions. She stiffened in his embrace, pressing her hands hard against the padded doublet as she struggled to hold him away.

'No! I beg you to let me go, my lord.'

'You would have given yourself to that pretty boy,' Raphael growled harshly. 'Yet I'll swear I can please you as well as he!'

Louise trembled, feeling herself in imminent danger from this hard-faced man who looked at her so strangely from eyes that seemed to burn her. His breathing was deep and ragged as if he had been running, and he appeared to be losing control.

'Please, my lord, take me back to my cousin!' she said pleadingly. 'I shall be missed, and my reputation will suffer. If my father hears of it he will have me whipped —God knows, he will be angry enough as it is.'

His arms still held her pressed closed to him, and she could feel the steady throbbing of his pulses, yet there was uncertainty in him now.

'You were willing to risk all for Pierre de Guise?'

She could hear the bitterness in his tone, and shook her head as she looked up. 'It was not for a lover's tryst that I came, my lord.'

'What, then?'

'I was given a note. A warning that I must come alone if I wished to save Gaspard de Coligny's life.'

She saw suspicion and disbelief in his face; then his lean features lost their tightness and his arms slackened their hold, releasing her.

'Show me,' he demanded hoarsely.

Louise gave him the note. He turned away, squinting at it in the moonlight. 'Who gave you this?'

'I don't know. He was masked. I thought it must be Pierre de Guise who was trying to warn me. Now I see it was all a trick.'

Raphael's eyes narrowed. 'I am not so sure. It seems I may have been wrong.'

'You mean those men were not sent by the Cardinal?'

'I cannot be certain . . .' He spoke hesitantly, as if his thoughts were still fluid and unformed. 'You were to be kidnapped, of this much I am sure—but perhaps for reasons other than I thought.'

'Then the note was genuine?'

'Perhaps.' His mouth twisted in a wry grimace. 'I have misjudged you, mademoiselle. Now I must ask you to forgive me and to trust me.'

'Why should I?' Louise asked haughtily. The sting of his kisses was still on her lips, and her breathing had only now returned to a semblance of normality. 'How can I be sure it was not your intention to have me lured out here so that you could . . . could . . .' Her words trailed away as she saw the mockery in his look.

'I am no puling youth to sink to such tricks, nor do I need help to lure you into a trap. Believe me, if I wanted you I would take you when and as I pleased.' He laughed harshly. 'Do not imagine you were in danger just now, my poor innocent. I thought you needed a lesson in the ways of men for your own sake . . .'

Louise's hand went out in sudden fury, but he caught her wrist before she could strike. 'You devil!' she cried. 'Why did you follow me, then?'

She glimpsed the sparkle of silver fire in his deep-lidded eyes, his strong fingers bruising her skin as they dug into her flesh.

'I, too, received a warning,' he said with an odd smile. 'So, when I saw you leave the palace alone, I thought it best to follow you.' He arched his brow mockingly. 'It seems that someone thought I might be interested in your welfare. I cannot imagine why—can you?'

She blinked at the thrust of his question. Why should he care what happened to her? 'No . . .' The admission was forced out of her. 'I—I am sorry. I should have thanked you for being here. I heard those men talking . . . You were right, they had orders to abduct me.'

Raphael smoothed the reddened flesh at her wrist

with his thumb. 'Then let us call a truce—please?' He smiled again as she nodded, but gently now and with a trace of amusement. 'Good. It is important that you should trust me, Louise.'

She glanced up as she heard her name on his lips. 'I—I do not know what else to do, my lord. If Pierre de Guise was trying to warn me, it would be useless to speak to my family; they would not listen to him.'

'I am not sure what all this means.' Raphael frowned. 'If there is to be an attempt on the Admiral's life, to act too precipitately could do more harm than good. I must ask you to let me keep the note—and to say nothing of this affair to anyone. Not even to your father or André.

A tremulous smile hovered on her lips as she gazed up at him. 'I shall do as you say—but we should go back now. It may be noticed that I have left the gallery.'

'Of course.' The mockery was back as he offered her his arm. 'We must think of your reputation. Nothing must stand in the way of the negotiations for your marriage to the Chevalier de Leconte.'

'What do you know of that?' Louise asked sharply.

'I know everything about you,' he said with a twist of his mouth. 'I have made it my concern to learn all I can.'

'Why?' She stared at him in surprise, but he only shook his head.

'You must trust me, Louise,' he said with maddening arrogance. 'When the time is right, I shall tell you all you wish to know.'

'You are presumptuous, m'sieur,' she replied with a toss of her head. 'What makes you think I shall ever want to know more about you?'

His laughter was soft and confident. 'I know it, my pretty innocent—because you are a woman . . .'

CHAPTER THREE

LOUISE SMILED as the maid finished dressing her hair, but her smile faded when the door opened and André came in. Dismissing the girl, Louise waited until they were alone before saying. 'I should prefer you to knock when entering my room, André.'

'Since we must leave in a few minutes, I could hardly have found you still in your petticoats.'

Biting back the sharp retort which sprang to her lips, Louise fastened a pearl bracelet about her wrist, concentrating on the intricate clasp. 'Very well, I am ready now.'

André caught her arm as she moved past him, curling his lip. 'Not just yet, sister. I have something to discuss with you first.'

'Oh?' Louise stared at him, wondering at the odd expression in his eyes. 'I hope it won't take long: I have to join Madame Catherine within the hour.'

'If Father had his way, you would ride with us in the wedding procession, not with the royal party.' His fine brows met in a frown. 'I wonder why the Italian Woman has taken such an interest in you?'

Louise, too, had wondered at the remarkable favour being shown her by Madame Catherine, but she supposed it must be because she was Marie's cousin and an excellent horsewoman. The Queen Mother had modelled her Flying Squadron on a group of ladies who had ridden with King François I; his ladies were all renowned for their beauty and quick wits, and as a young woman, Catherine had admired her husband's father. Obviously, she took pleasure in creating a similar band, and Louise was honoured to be asked to ride with them.

'I do not know why Madame Catherine has singled me

out in this way, André, but it would be rude and also unwise to refuse her invitation.' She looked at him nervously, half expecting him to forbid her to join the royal party at the last moment.

'It is for that reason Father has allowed you to accept,' her brother said, his eyes narrowing suddenly. 'Had he heard you slipped out to meet a lover in the gardens of the Louvre, however, it might have been another matter.'

Gasping, Louise felt her cheeks grow warm. 'Who told you that, André?'

'You were seen.' His look pierced her. 'Can you deny it? Can you deny that you were with that Englishman?'

'No . . .' Louise hesitated, wondering whether to tell her brother why she had gone to the gardens alone. Lord Carleton had particularly stressed that she was not to confide in anyone, but was she wise to keep the warning a secret? If André had been a more understanding person, she would have felt inclined to tell him everything, but he had a habit of sneering at her, and he would probably think she had invented it all as an excuse. Besides, Lord Carleton had the note. 'I was feeling a little faint,' she lied, playing with her bracelet. 'Lord Carleton was kind enough to escort me to the gardens so that I might recover in the fresh air.'

André stared at her for a moment, but seemed prepared to accept her word on this occasion. 'You say his name is Lord Carleton? I had assumed . . . But no matter . . .' His words trailed away and he appeared to be deep in thought. 'Did he tell you why he came to France?'

'No. We spoke only for a short time.' Louise looked at him in surprise. 'Why do you ask?'

'I do not trust him, Louise. I believe he may be in league with the Medici. Perhaps he plots a secret treaty with her. There is something . . . threatening about him.'

'I have felt it myself.' She frowned, struck that André

should have had the same feeling. 'Do you think he's a spy? Was that why he wanted to meet the Admiral?'

'A spy? Perhaps. As an Englishman, he may hope to gain the confidence of our people and then betray us to the Medici. Yes, that may well explain the mystery.' He glanced down at her suddenly, his eyes very bright. 'If you notice anything odd about this man's behaviour, Louise, I want you to tell me at once. Do you understand? Tell me. No one else.'

Confused and bewildered by the conflict of emotions within her, Louise nodded, feeling guilty as she whispered, 'As you wish, André.'

He gave her a look of approval. 'Is that a new gown? It certainly becomes you.'

'Thank you.' Louise bit her lip, wondering at his rare mood of benevolence. 'What do you want from me, André? You did not come here to compliment me on my gown?'

His smile disappeared instantly. 'I came to warn you that Father will tolerate no scandal, Louise. I have heard rumours concerning your behaviour during the hunt yesterday—rumours that would make him very angry if he should hear them.'

'And you will no doubt make sure that he does!'

André stared at her, an expression of annoyance on his face. 'Sometimes I think Grand'mère has succeeded in teaching you nothing, Louise. You deserve to be punished, but I shall not tell Father: he will learn of your disobedience soon enough, I'll warrant.'

Louise averted her gaze, feeling a shiver run through her. When André looked at her like that it frightened her. He seemed so strange sometimes, his eyes taking on a distant expression as if his thoughts were far away. She found herself remembering the day, some years previously, when she had discovered him in the stable beating her favourite horse; he had said the animal had a wicked temper and must be taught to obey its master. He had stopped hitting it when she remonstrated with him, but two days later the horse died in terrible agony. The grooms swore it had swallowed a piece of sharp metal which had pierced its intestines, but Louise had suspected that André was somehow to blame.

Sighing, Louise picked up her fan. Perhaps she was misjudging her brother. Although he was very strict with her, he had never actually done anything to harm her. The incident with the horse was an isolated affair; and when they were both children, he had saved her from drowning when she fell into the stream. André, always a strong swimmer, had jumped in after her without hesitation. The memory softened her, and she felt herself relax. André was an honest man who adhered to the rigid standards he believed right. If he was threatening her, it must be because he wished to protect her reputation.

'It wasn't really my fault, André,' she said, laying her hand on his arm. 'Please don't be angry with me. I do try to behave as you and Father would wish me to.'

André tipped her chin towards him with one finger, a faint smile on his lips. 'Yes, you are usually an obedient girl, though I suspect not as meek as you would have us believe? Well, we must hope Father does not hear the rumours, must we not?' He quirked his brow at her.

Why did she have the distinct impression that he was mocking her? The memory of his gallant rescue faded as others, more recent, crowded in on her. André lost no chance to treat her with scorn whenever he could. She was unable to remember just when his manner towards her had begun to change, but he was certainly not the brother she had once looked up to and admired. Sometimes he seemed almost a stranger to her: a stranger whose moods distressed her.

'Why do you look at me that way, André?' she asked.

'You ask too many questions, sister,' he said, his hand gripping her arm hard. 'Come, we must leave now if you are not to keep Madame Catherine waiting.'

*   *   *

The banqueting hall was overflowing with richly-dressed nobles from every region of France, the noise of their chatter reaching far beyond the massive room to the common folk of Paris below. The people had surged into the palace after the wedding ceremony; determined to join in the celebrations, they were demanding food from the royal kitchens, some of them stealing dishes intended for the noble guests.

Seated with the rest of Madame Catherine's ladies at one of the lower tables, Louise found herself watching the high board where the new Queen of Navarre was seated under a golden banner, in the place of honour beside her bridegroom. Noting the sullen expression on the young woman's face, Louise felt a pang of sympathy for her as she let her mind drift back to the excitement of the past few hours.

Because of Madame Catherine's kindness to her, Louise had ridden with the Escadron Volant in the wedding procession, which gave her an excellent view of the ceremony. A much better view than if she had stayed with André and her father, who had been relegated to the tail end with many of the other minor Huguenot nobles.

The streets of Paris had been decorated with bright banners; they hung from the windows of the houses, streaming from balcony to balcony in gay profusion. People were everywhere, laughing, dancing and drinking quantities of good French wine purchased from the street-sellers. At every corner there were tableaux set up in honour of the royal couple: tumblers performed for a handful of coins at the side of the road, and the miracle plays drew wide-eyed audiences.

At the head of the long, glittering procession were the heralds; the noise of their horns announced the arrival of the King and his nobles long before they could be seen by the eager citizens of Paris, who had dressed in their best clothes to be present at this momentous occasion. How the people had cheered when they finally caught a glimpse of the princess in all her finery, and only a few of the more observant remarked on how pale her face was beneath the elaborate veil.

It was indeed a wonderful sight for the ordinary citizens of Paris: magnificent jewels flashed in the brilliant sunshine, competing with the gaudy colours of the courtiers' rich clothes, which were all the shades of the rainbow. Even the horses were bedecked with cloth of gold, their harnesses jingling with the tinkle of silver bells.

The ceremony itself had taken place on a dais outside Notre Dame so that everyone could witness the marriage. Kneeling on embroidered cushions beneath a silken canopy, the bride and groom had taken their sacred vows, though no one heard the princess speak. When asked if she would take Henri of Navarre as her husband, she remained stubbornly silent; but the King placed his hand on her head, forcing her to nod her assent. Afterwards, the nobles had gone inside the cathedral to hear the blessing.

Now, the banquet was almost at an end and the royal party led the way through to the gallery where musicians had begun to play. The entertainment was only just beginning, for besides the dancing there would be plays, masques and many other delights to amuse the guests. Louise walked just behind her cousin and some of the other ladies, her eyes downcast. For some reason, all the gaiety had begun to pall; her head ached and she found herself wishing for the open spaces of the country-side. At home in La Rochelle, she was used to taking long walks and brisk canters through her father's estate.

'What weighty matters bring such a frown to so fair a brow?'

Louise looked up, a sharp tingling at the nape of her neck as she gazed into the Englishman's eyes. 'You are laughing at me, my lord,' she accused, her eyes flashing quick fire.

'It is a day for laughter and celebration, is it not?'

'Perhaps.' Louise frowned. 'Have you any news for me, m'sieur?'

A shuttered expression came over his face. 'I fear not. Nor would it be wise to discuss the matter here.'

'No . . . No, of course you are right, but . . .' Louise broke off as she saw her brother approaching.

Raphael noticed the look of apprehension in her eyes and followed the direction of her gaze. 'I believe your brother is signalling to you, Louise. I shall leave . . .'

'No, please stay?' Louise glanced up at him, an unconscious appeal in her eyes. 'I—I think he is very angry with me.'

'Why should he be angry with you?' Raphael asked, frowning.

Louise shook her head, saying nothing as André came up to them. One look at his face told her all she needed to know: her father had heard the rumours concerning Pierre de Guise!

'We are going home now, Louise,' he said grimly, inclining his head stiffly in the Englishman's direction. 'M'sieur, you will forgive my sister if she leaves you now.'

'Are—Are we not staying for the entertainment?' Louise's hand trembled and she hid it behind her back, but not before Raphael had noticed her distress.

'I am sorry you must leave so soon, mademoiselle,' he said, giving her a reassuring smile. 'Monsieur de Granvelle, would you please convey my compliments to your father and tell him I shall call on him very soon?'

'As you wish, m'sieur.' André bowed. 'Come, Louise, you should not keep Father waiting.'

Louise moved forward slowly, her face pale as she laid her hand on his arm. 'If you will excuse me, Lord Carleton, I must go now.'

'Of course.' The Englishman seemed to be giving

her a message she did not understand. 'We shall meet again—perhaps sooner than you think.' His face hardened as he turned to André. 'Do not forget to give my message to the Seigneur, m'sieur.'

Their eyes met in a glittering challenge, and André's dropped first. Louise could sense the simmering anger in her brother as they walked from the room.

'What was he saying to you, Louise?'

'Lord Carleton was merely making polite conversation, André.' She glanced at his cold face. 'Is Father very angry with me?'

'You will discover that for yourself soon enough,' André said, and she could not help noticing the distinct satisfaction in his tone.

'Am I to understand that this story is true?' The Seigneur de Granvelle looked coldly at his daughter. 'Answer me, girl. I want the truth!'

Louise brought her uncertain gaze up to meet his, biting her lower lip to stop it trembling as she realised how angry he was. As always, his manner puzzled her, for though there were moments when her father seemed to care for her and was kind and gentle, at other times he vented his fury on her in a way that made her feel he disliked her.

'It is true that I was lost in the forest, and that Monsieur de Guise saved me from being attacked by vagrants.'

'Is it not also true that you deliberately set out to lose yourself in order to keep a secret tryst with this young man?'

'No, Father, that is not true.'

'Don't lie to me!' Incensed by the defiant gleam in her eyes, he struck her across the cheek. 'You disobeyed me. In doing so publicly, you have brought shame on your family. Everyone is laughing behind your back; your reputation is in ruins; and I shall not be surprised if the Chevalier de Leconte refuses to sign the marriage

contract. A man like that will not want a woman who has
disgraced herself as his wife. Tell me, are you not
ashamed of yourself?'

'I have done nothing wrong, Father.' Louise blinked
as he struck her again. 'I give you my word that I did not
meet Pierre by prior arrangement.'

'You convict yourself with every word you speak,' he
growled. 'Since when have you been on first-name terms
with de Guise? Since he dishonoured you, I suppose,
you wanton!'

Louise gasped as she saw the fury in his face. He had
been angry with her before, but never quite like this. He
seized her arm, dragging her towards the bed; then,
taking a leather rope from inside his doublet, he began
to bind her wrists to one of the thick posts. Ripping open
the fastenings at the back of her bodice, he picked up a
long, thin stick and brought it down hard across her
thighs. She hardly felt its sting through the thickness of
her petticoats, but she knew the blow was only a warning
of what was to come.

'Admit your sin, and the punishment will be over
swiftly.'

Louise squeezed her lids tight, vainly trying to hold
back the tear that trickled down her cheek. Despite all
his sternness, her father had never actually beaten her
before, and she felt the humiliation of it keenly. This was
far worse than the punishments meted out by her grandmother over the years.

'I have done nothing to shame you, Father,' she
whispered between stiff lips. 'I swear it on my mother's
grave.'

'Liar!' She heard the scorn in his voice, and it hurt her
almost as much as the first blow on her naked back.
'Since you will not repent, you must be taught to feel
your shame, you slut!'

A second blow and then a third followed in swift
succession. She clenched her teeth, determined not to
cry out. She had known ever since they returned from

the Louvre the night before that this punishment must be borne. Only the arrival of a messenger from the Admiral had saved her then, and a night spent locked in her chamber had merely served to increase her fear of it. She tensed herself as the Seigneur drew back his arm once more, praying that it would soon be over.

It was the loud, insistent knocking at the door that saved her. The Seigneur hesitated, frowning in annoyance.

'Who is it?' he asked testily. 'I gave instructions that I was not to be disturbed.'

'You have a visitor, Father. I think you should come down.'

'Very well, André.'

The Seigneur gave a sigh of exasperation and threw down his stick, his heavy features tight with frustration. He walked round the bed to look at his daughter, tipping her chin so that she was forced to look at him.

'Are you ready to confess now, Louise?'

She shook her head mutely, and his frown deepened. 'Then I shall leave you to reflect on your sins. Do not imagine I am satisfied yet. I shall have the truth from you, and you will be punished for your wickedness.'

'I have not deserved this from you,' Louise said, her face white but proud. 'Why will you not believe me? What have I ever done that you should think so ill of me?'

There was a strange, distant expression in his eyes as he looked at her. 'I cannot believe you because I know the evil is in you—but I intend to drive it out of you if I must beat you every day. I will not allow *you* to humiliate me, Louise.' With that last threat, he strode from the room.

Louise laid her head against the bedpost, fighting the tears that welled up. What had she done to make her father treat her like this? Surely it was not such a terrible crime to meet a young man alone in the forest? As she lifted her head, a look of determination settled over the fine-boned features that were so like those of the mother who had given her birth. She had nothing to be ashamed of, and she would die before she begged for mercy or confessed to a sin she had not committed.

Her back was already stinging from the blows her father had inflicted, though he had taken care not to break the flesh. To ease the pain, Louise forced herself to think about her childhood, when the Seigneur had smiled on her more often. When she was tiny, she had sometimes been taken up on his horse and allowed to ride round the estate with him. Yet, as she had grown to womanhood, becoming more and more like the portrait of the woman who had been her mother, the Seigneur's manner had gradually become increasingly severe. Occasionally, when she caught him looking at her, Louise had thought she saw pain in his eyes, and she wondered if his dislike of her was because she was a living reminder of the wife he had lost.

His coldness towards her had stifled the love she felt for him, but even his cruelty today could not quite extinguish it. More than the physical pain, Louise was hurt by his lack of trust. She had always wanted to be closer to him, but now it seemed that he was ashamed of her. The unfairness of it stiffened her resolve as she heard footsteps outside her door. Her brief respite was over. Her father was returning, and he would finish what he had begun.

To her surprise and alarm, it was not the Seigneur, but André, who came into the room. She closed her eyes for a moment, knowing that her brother would show no mercy if he were to continue her punishment. The shame of standing before him with her bodice ripped and her back naked was almost more than she could bear, yet she lifted her head defiantly as he walked purposefully towards her. Now, more than ever, she was determined not to break. She would not give André the satisfaction of seeing her humbled!

She had cared for him once, following him everywhere like a devoted puppy after he saved her from the stream. Until she was fifteen, he had seemed to tolerate her existence, but then a change had come about in him quite suddenly. She could not explain the difference in his manner, nor could she have truthfully said that he was deliberately cruel to her, yet she had sensed he disliked her. Since André had always worshipped their father, Louise believed he had noticed the growing coolness in the Seigneur's attitude towards her, equating the two as a criticism of her behaviour. She strived to please them both, but seldom received a word of praise. Hurt by what she did not understand, Louise stifled the loving heart within her, learning to hide her feelings as much as she could.

Now, she blinked in confusion as André began to undo the ropes binding her wrists. Seeing her look, he gave her a scornful smile. 'You are to get dressed and come down as soon as you are ready. Your maid will come to you in a moment.'

'Am I not to be punished?'

'Father has decided to spare you further chastisement for the present. If you behave yourself, you may escape a beating.'

'Why?' Louise rubbed her wrists, looking at him curiously. There was a queer gleam in his eyes and he seemed nervous. She couldn't decide whether he was excited or very angry. 'Something has happened, hasn't it?'

'You will find out soon enough. Now, be certain to wear your best gown—and wash the tear-stains from your face.'

'Why?' Louise asked again, her stomach tying itself in knots. 'The Chevalier de Leconte is here, isn't he? That's why you want me to look presentable. That's why I'm not to be beaten!'

'How clever you are, sweet sister.' André's mouth narrowed with spite, and the look he gave her was one of pure malice. 'It seems it is time for you to meet your future husband.'

Louise stared at him uncertainly. There was something very peculiar in his manner at the moment. Although he seemed very tense, he was trying to hide it. But André had no reason to be apprehensive—she was the one who was about to meet her future husband!

'What does the Chevalier look like?'

'His looks are not important. He is an influential man, descended from the *noblesse d'epée*. We need such men to join our cause. Your marriage will unite our families and help to strengthen the movement for more political freedom.'

Why did she feel that André was just mouthing empty words, that he did not believe in what he was saying? She was suddenly seized by the conviction that the Chevalier was a terrible, ugly old man who would keep her in exile in his château until she produced a string of heirs. André was deliberately goading her, taking pleasure from the knowledge that she would immediately hate her husband. She stuck her chin in the air and turned away, avoiding the look of triumph she knew would be in his eyes.

'Why do you hate me, André?' she asked, feeling close to despair.

'Since when have I hated you? Do not ask foolish questions. I have no time to waste in arguing with you, Louise. Just do as you are told and come down as quickly as you can.'

Hearing the door shut behind him, Louise sagged against the bedpost, letting the misery wash over her. It had come at last, the moment she had dreaded ever since Étienne was killed. It was not that she had been desperately in love with the man to whom she was betrothed, but she had known him all her life, and she had liked him. He was a gentle person, and their marriage would have brought her some happiness, despite the big difference in their ages. Étienne had been like another father, but kinder than her own parent. While he lived, she had never questioned the contract made while she was a babe. Now the circumstances were altered and she was suddenly afraid—afraid of the man she had never met. What would he be like, this man who, for the sake of politics, was willing to marry a girl he did not know?

It was so unfair! She was to be given in marriage to a man she did not know simply because it suited her father's politics. Yet even as her mind protested at the injustice, Louise knew there was no escape for her. She would do as her father bade her because it was her duty—and because she loved him enough to want to please him. She would do her duty just as the princess had done hers yesterday, though even *she* had known her bridegroom since they were children in the royal nursery, the young prince having been kept as the French King's hostage against his parents' good behaviour.

Splashing her eyes with cold water from a silver ewer, Louise selected a light grey gown with very little ornament except for the fine lace ruff which framed her pale face. Since she had no choice, she would perform her duty with dignity—but she would not pretend to enjoy it! The Chevalier de Leconte should have no smiles from her.

She hid her hair beneath a squared head-dress encrusted with a design of seed pearls, with a lace veil at the back of her head. Glancing at herself in a small hand-mirror, the girl was satisfied with her sober appearance. She had managed to make herself look almost plain; and by setting her mouth in a prim line, she hoped to give her prospective bridegroom something to think about. If he found her looks disappointing, he might change his mind about wanting to marry her.

At least they could not drag her to the altar, Louise thought as she made her way slowly downstairs. If she found the Chevalier too repugnant, she would simply take to her bed and pretend that she was ill. There were ways of delaying the ceremony without actually defying her father outright, and she would use every weapon in her power, however small it might be.

Defiance had brought a sparkle to Louise's eyes, and she looked lovelier than she knew when she finally reached the front hall where her father was waiting. As her gaze travelled slowly round the large, oblong-shaped room with its lofty ceilings and tapestry-hung walls, she saw that he was alone, and her brow creased in a frown.

'André told me I was to meet the Chevalier de Leconte—is he not here, Father?'

'The Chevalier could not wait. He had urgent business outside Paris, but he will come again in a few days and we shall travel to La Rochelle together. The Chevalier wishes to get to know you a little better before you are married, but he hopes that that will be quite soon.'

'How soon?' Louise whispered, feeling a constriction in her breast.

'Within the month, I believe.' There was a softer note in his voice, and he smiled. 'It was my fault you were not able to greet your future husband. I shall not continue the punishment, since I am now prepared to believe your disobedience was not deliberate—but it must not happen again. Your marriage contract is signed, and I expect you to behave accordingly.'

Louise wondered what had brought about his change of heart, realising it must be because the Chevalier had signed the contract. 'I always try to obey you, Father.' Her gaze held a hint of reproach as she looked at him.

The Chevalier recognised the reproach for what it was, and an odd, regretful expression flickered briefly in his eyes. He patted her hand with an awkward gesture. 'Perhaps I have sometimes been too harsh with you, Louise; but, if so, it was because I considered it in your best interests. I have done what I thought right for you, child. We shall forget this unpleasant incident. In the next few days you will gather all the silks and finery you consider necessary for your wedding clothes. You will not find me ungenerous—and I believe you will like the gift your betrothed has left for you.'

He walked across the room to a long, narrow table, picking up a small casket. Louise took it from him with shaking hands, catching her breath as she saw the heavy gold locket and chain inside. The locket was oval and surrounded by pearls, while the chain was intricately worked with pearls, emeralds and topaz. It was a beautiful thing, and in other circumstances she would have been delighted with such a gift.

'It—is very pretty,' she murmured through stiff lips. 'I had not expected such a valuable gift.'

'The Chevalier has extensive estates, I believe.' Her father sounded very pleased with himself, and Louise avoided looking at him. Despite his unusually kind words to her, the truth was damning. She was being sold to the highest bidder!

'I would like to go to my room,' she said, the misery twisting inside her. 'I have a headache.'

'Then you will have to pray that it goes away.' The Seigneur frowned at her, correctly interpreting the pallor in her face. 'Do not be foolish, Louise. The Chevalier will make you an excellent husband. You are a fortunate girl, and I will not have you sulking. Besides, Madame Catherine has sent a message enquiring after your health. There is to be a grand tournament today, and she particularly wishes you to attend.'

Louise stared at him thoughtfully. 'Madame Catherine has been very kind to me, Father. I cannot imagine why she should single me out from so many others, can you.'

A shadow passed across his face. For a moment he seemed to hesitate, as if he were on the verge of telling her something; then a distant, chilled expression came into his eyes and he turned away to summon a servant, glancing back at her as he reached the door.

'Make haste, daughter. It is time we were on our way.'

CHAPTER FOUR

'I DO NOT trust him, Louise . . . There is something . . . threatening about him.'

Louise lay looking at the moonbeams shining through her bedroom window. She was restless, her mind trapped in a maze of doubt and guilt as she recalled her brother's words. An attack on the life of Gaspard de Coligny had taken place the day before, on Friday 22nd August, and she felt herself in part at fault because she had not told André about the note warning of such an attack.

The Admiral, returning from the council held at the Louvre, was wounded by a musket-shot from the ground-floor window of a house in the Rue des Fossés-Saint-Germain. Fortunately, the assassin's aim had been faulty, and the Admiral was still alive.

'It is clearly a plot between Catherine de' Medici and the Guisards!' Seigneur de Granvelle cried when he heard of the cowardly attack. 'They have discovered a musket belonging to one of Monsieur's favourites.'

Since the Duc d'Anjou was Madame Catherine's favourite son, it seemed clear to everyone that she must have had a hand in the plot, though she was swift to deny it. But it was common knowledge that the Duc hated Coligny, and no one believed the denials from the palace.

The royal wedding festivities had come to an abrupt halt. Louise was confined to the house in the Rue Saint-Denis, while her father and brother hurried to join the other Huguenots gathered at the Admiral's lodgings. They remained there until late that Friday evening, leaving Louise to wait and worry alone. She heard only snatches of their conversation when they returned, but

she knew the situation was desperate. The leaders of the
Protestant faction were asking for immediate action,
and the King had flown into a rage, insisting that the
criminals should be found and punished. The Queen
Mother added her demands to his, but few believed her
to be sincere.

Louise knew her family suspected the Cardinal de
Lorraine to be one of the prime movers in the plot,
because of the hatred he felt for Coligny. Remembering
the warning she had received on the eve of the royal
wedding, she was racked with guilt. She had been
warned of the assassination attempt and had done
nothing. If only she had given the note to her father, or
told André about it when he came to her room!

Getting up from the bed where she had been lying,
still wearing her petticoats, Louise went to gaze out
of the window at the deserted street. André and the
Seigneur had gone back to the Admiral's house early this
morning for a further conference. Surely they should
have returned by now? She sighed, covering her face
with her hands as she tried to sort out the tangled
confusion of her thoughts.

In the days succeeding the wedding, she had looked
for Lord Carleton at the jousts, feasts and masques, but
there was no sign of his commanding figure among the
crowd of courtiers. His absence worried her, and when
Marie told her that Pierre de Guise had also disappeared, she had been on the verge of telling her father
about the note.

Perhaps it was fear of his anger that had prevented her,
or the uncertainty she felt about the Englishman's part in
the affair. Was he really a spy, after all? Was André right
to think he might be in league with the Medici? Worst of
all, had she delivered important information into the
hands of an enemy? In her confusion she had hesitated,
and then it was too late.

Her horror on learning about the attack on her kinsman was very real, and she had been consumed with

guilt ever since. She had been wrong to trust Lord Carleton. He had probably gone straight to Madame Catherine . . . 'No, I cannot believe it,' she whispered hoarsely. 'There must be some explanation.'

Hearing noises below, Louise was suddenly awakened from her reverie. That must be André and her father at last, she thought, feeling relieved. She would dress and go down at once. A loud scream and a crashing sound outside her window made her blood run cold. What was happening?

Louise rushed to the window once more, staring at what appeared to be fighting in the street. She heard a shot and saw a man fall face down in the gutter; then there was more shouting as a crowd of men ran riot down the road, smashing doors and shutters as they tried to force entrance into the houses. A chill went down her spine as she realised that the mob was selective in its choice of houses; she understood why, as the chanting became clearer.

'Death to the Huguenots!'

'Kill them! Kill them all!'

'Drag the traitors out of their beds and show them we'll have no conspirators in our city!'

What were they yelling about? Louise wondered dazedly. There was no Huguenot conspiracy; it was the Guisards and the Queen Mother who had plotted against Coligny, almost causing his death. So why had the citizens of Paris turned on the Protestants in their midst?

Seeing a man fall from a second-floor balcony, Louise shrank away from the window, putting her hands to her ears to block out the sounds of his screams. She pulled on the gown she had prepared earlier, her fingers fumbling with the fastenings of her over-bodice, into which she had sewn the jewels entrusted to her that morning by her father.

'Keep them with you, Louise, and be ready to leave here at a moment's notice,' he had said before he left for

the Admiral's lodgings. 'Whatever you do, do not leave
this house until I myself come for you.'

Louise drew a shuddering breath, smoothing her
skirts with damp palms. There were frightening noises
from downstairs: a woman's scream, shouting, and then
the sound of running feet in the corridor outside her
room. Instinctively she turned the key in the lock, her
heart beginning to thump with fear. She retreated
towards the large armoire which held her clothes, preparing to hide in it. Then she saw that someone was
tugging at the intricate ironwork latch, and she choked
back a scream. How long would the lock hold if whoever
was out there was determined to get in?

Suddenly the intruder began to pound furiously on the
door, and relief spread through her as he shouted,
'Unlock this door, Louise! For God's sake, there's no
time to be lost!'

'André . . .' Louise cried, running to open it joyfully.
She stared at her brother, shocked by his wild look and
the dark stains on his clothing. 'You've been wounded!
What has happened to you?'

He shook his head impatiently. 'It's only a scratch. I
ran into some trouble on my way here, but I managed to
escape. The city has gone mad; we must leave at once.'

'Is Father with you?' she asked anxiously.

'No, he stayed with the Admiral. You must bring the
package he entrusted to you, Louise, and come with me
now.'

She hesitated for a moment, remembering the
Seigneur's strict instructions to wait for him, but her
brother frowned, and she realised he was right. Obviously there had been a change of plan at the last moment. She went swiftly to the bed, picking up her cloak
and a small bag containing personal items she had
packed earlier.

André held out his hand. 'I shall carry that for you.
We must hurry.'

Downstairs, Louise saw that furniture had been over-

turned and that the silver had been swept from the
buffet. She looked at André in alarm, and he shook his
head, his mouth twisted wryly.

'No, we have not yet been visited by the mob. I arrived
to find the servants looting the place. No doubt they
have all fled by now—I told Father most of them were
not to be trusted, but he insisted on taking our own men
to the Admiral's in case of trouble.'

Louise nodded, recalling André having said something similar before. The servants had been hired with
the house, and only a few of their trusted retainers
had been brought from La Rochelle. It had been the
Admiral's wish that his relatives should not appear to
have come with a huge following of armed men, since he
wished to demonstrate his faith in the King's promises.
Now look what had happened!

Hearing a crashing noise at the front of the house,
André gripped his sister's arm, his fingers digging into
her so tightly that it hurt. 'We must escape through the
kitchens while there is yet time.'

They ran through the main hall, leaving by a door
which was half hidden behind a heavy silk tapestry. It led
into a small windowless chamber, and from there they
passed into the dining hall; the kitchens were at the rear,
concealed by a screen of carved wood. From the scene of
confusion that met their eyes, it was clear that the
servants had taken what they could before they fled.

Finding their way into the kitchen gardens at last,
André and Louise paused for a moment, listening to the
screams and shouts that seemed to be coming from every
quarter of the city. The sky was streaked with red from
the fires the looters had lit in the streets, and the smell of
death and fear floated on the breeze.

Louise shuddered, her courage almost deserting her.
What chance had they of making their way safely
through the streets this night? Yet even as she shrank
back, her brother's grip tightened on her arm, forcing
her to go with him. She lifted her frightened gaze to his

face, but saw that there was no comfort to be gained
from André. He himself was sweating with fear.

'We must get to the river,' he said. 'Our only chance is
to find a boat and get away while it is still dark.'

She nodded, stifling the quick surge of panic inside
her. Since there was no choice, she must trust in her
brother and obey his commands instantly. Giving him a
faint smile, she allowed him to hurry her through the
gardens to the street beyond. At the moment it was
quiet, though there was grisly evidence that the mob had
been here, too. She looked away from the broken bodies
lying in the gutter as the sickness churned inside her.

Taking a firm grasp on her nerves, Louise walked
silently at André's side. The smell of burning filled the
air, and the acrid taste of it caught in her throat. She had
never felt so frightened in her life, and when the sound of
shouting and pounding feet suddenly came closer, she
looked at him in alarm. At the top of the street, a large
crowd of men had appeared; they were all carrying
sticks, and appeared to beating someone. As they
surged towards Louise and André, he gave her a push in
the direction of a dark, narrow lane.

'Go on, Louise,' he yelled. 'Run! Run for your life!'

The panic in his voice communicated itself to her and
she obeyed instinctively, gathering up the skirt of her
gown as she fled. At once she knew that it was the wrong
thing to have done. Her flight had attracted the attention
of the mob, and she heard the shouting as they gave
chase. She glanced round to look for André, gasping
with fright as she saw he was not behind her. Even as she
realised he must have gone in another direction, she saw
the mob enter the lane. With a cry of despair, she started
to run again, fleeing blindly through the dark, twisting
streets, her mind totally engulfed in terror.

In her urgency to escape, she lost all sense of direction. Hesitating at the end of an unfamiliar street, she
turned to her right and cannoned into the hard, unyield-
ing body of a man who had suddenly appeared. She

opened her mouth to scream just as his hand closed over it; his other arm went round her waist as he dragged her into a dark porch, trapping her against the wall with his own body.

Louise struggled vainly to free herself, trying to protest at this violent treatment, but her mouth was gagged by the suffocating folds of his doublet as he held her head pressed into it. Scarcely able to breathe, she listened as the blood-curdling yells of the mob grew nearer.

'Be still,' the man's voice was harsh in her ear. 'Do not cry out unless you wish them to find us.'

Trembling, she sagged against him. There was no mistaking that voice, and relief surged through her as she recognised her rescuer. She stopped fighting him, standing stiff and tense in his arms as the mob passed by. Even when the sound of their footsteps died away, she remained where she was until he released her.

'They have gone now, Louise. Hush, do not weep. The danger is past for the moment.'

Louise brushed away a single tear, looking up into the face of the Englishman with a hint of defiance. 'I am not crying,' she said, swallowing hard. 'You—You frightened me, that's all.'

'*I* frightened you?' Raphael's brow went up. 'It seemed to me you were frightened when I found you. There was scarcely time for polite conversation.'

Louise knew his prompt action had probably saved her life, and she felt instant remorse. 'It—It was just that I did not know it was you, my lord. You acted so swiftly that I thought you were attacking me.'

Raphael frowned. 'I saw a woman running, and I decided to investigate. When I saw that it was you, and that you were being pursued by the mob, I had to think quickly. One sword would have been useless against so many. I am sorry if I hurt you.'

'You did not.' Louise looked at him uncertainly, aware that he was angry. 'I am sorry if I have offended you, m'sieur.'

His eyes glittered coldly in the moonlight. 'My feelings are unimportant. What are you doing, wandering about the streets alone? It is madness for a woman to be abroad on such a night. Where are your family?'

A sob shook Louise as his words reminded her. 'André was with me,' she gulped, clutching his arm. 'We were separated when the mob attacked us. Oh, please, my lord, we must go and look for him!'

Raphael stared at her for a moment and then shook his head. 'No, it would be too dangerous. I must take you out of the city before another mob discovers us.'

'No! No, we must look for André!' Louise insisted, trying to push past him. 'I shall go alone if you will not come with me.'

Raphael caught her arm, jerking her round to face him. 'I am taking you with me now. You can come willingly, Louise, or I'll bind and gag you if I have to. No one could find your brother tonight, and I'll not risk both our lives on a foolish whim of yours.'

The girl gazed at him, rebellion flaring in her; then the realisation that he was right made her catch her breath on a sob. 'But he came to fetch me,' she said in a little voice. 'He risked his life to come back for me. How can I desert him?'

Raphael's hard face softened slightly. 'You are not deserting him, Louise. We can do nothing tonight while this madness lasts, but I promise I will try to find him as soon as I can.'

She nodded, struggling to control her tears. 'Very well, then. I shall come with you, my lord.'

'We must lose no time. My cousin is waiting with a boat, but I told him to leave without me if I was not back within the hour.'

Louise made no reply, too numbed to wonder why his cousin should be waiting with a boat, or why the Englishman had returned to the city. She allowed him to take her arm, moving at his direction in a kind of daze as they walked swiftly through the streets. The sounds of screams seemed to be growing less, as though there was a lull in the violence as the first streak of light appeared in the sky.

Now she could see the murky waters of the river ahead of them. She felt a new urgency in her companion as he hurried her towards the quay, and she was relieved when she picked out the shape of a small boat. Then a shadowy figure moved towards them.

'Is that you, Raphael?' a man's voice asked. 'Did you find her?'

'Yes, Jean.' Raphael took Louise's hand, leading her forward so that she was close enough to make out the features of a man in his early twenties. He smiled at her, coming to offer his hand to help her down the steps and into the boat.

'Thank God my cousin was in time, Mademoiselle de Granvelle,' he said kindly. 'You will be safe with us. We are Catholics, but we want no part in this madness.'

Louise hesitated, gazing at him in surprise. 'You were expecting me, m'sieur?'

'Of course. Raphael came to warn you and your family of the need to leave.' He glanced over her shoulder as though looking for someone else. 'Your father is not with you?'

'No. He—He stayed with the Admiral. My brother was with me, but we were separated when . . .'

'I chanced on Mademoiselle de Granvelle in the street,' Raphael said as he climbed into the boat beside her.

'Then God was surely with you this night,' Jean said, taking up the oars as he began to row them down the river.

A fine curl of mist was drifting over the water, muffling the sound of the oars. Louise closed her eyes, struggling to hold back the tears. She knew she was safe enough now, but she felt tired, confused and lost.

'The danger is past, Louise.'

Raphael's soft whisper made her aware of him beside

her. She opened her eyes and looked at him searchingly. 'Were you truly on your way to my house?'

'Yes. A note was delivered to my lodgings earlier this evening, warning me to take you out of the city before the tocsin was rung for Saint Bartholomew's Eve. Unfortunately I had been dining with a friend, and I fear I may have drunk a little too much wine. By the time I read the note, the trouble had already begun. I was on my way to you when we met.'

'If you had not found me, I should be dead now.' She shuddered violently.

'When a mob goes mad, people behave like ferocious animals. Soon the madness will have cooled. Jean and I will search for your family later today, when you are safely with Madame Montpellier.'

'My mother will welcome you to our home,' Jean said, smiling at her. 'You may stay with us for as long as you wish.'

Louise nodded. Jean Montpellier had a solidness about him that reassured her. When he gave her his hand to help her into the boat, she had felt a roughness across his palms that spoke of hard work, and she realised that this was a man who liked to labour in the fields beside his peasants. She needed no one to tell her that he had come to Paris only to witness the royal wedding.

'You are very kind, m'sieur,' she whispered.

'Believe me, mademoiselle,' Jean said gently, 'my cousin is right. It is better that we should wait for a while before searching for your family. I am sure they are safe in some secure place, and they will certainly stay there until the worst is over.'

They were trying to comfort her, she knew, but Louise's heart was aching as she sat stiff and straight in her seat, fighting the pain inside her. The terrors of the night were past, but she knew that they would remain with her for a long time. No one could pass through such an experience and emerge untouched by it. As yet she could only speculate about the fate of her family: she must continue to hope, despite the awful feeling in her heart that they were gone from her, taken by the tide of insanity which had gripped Paris.

The Montpelliers' château was situated a few leagues from Paris. It was a modest house with enough land to make it self-supporting, but not sufficient to supply the wealth that was evident in the luxurious furnishings and in the elegant clothes worn by Madame Montpellier and her daughter Juliette. So Louise was not surprised to learn that they lived for most of the year on a large estate in the Loire valley.

Jean and his mother were kindness itself to her during the two days she spent with them, doing their best to make her comfortable and ease the strain of waiting; and if Louise sensed a certain reserve in Mademoiselle Montpellier's manner, it was nothing to complain of. Indeed, in the matter of providing clothing, no one could have been more generous than Juliette. Louise had gratefully accepted the loan of clean linen, but refused to be parted from the gown into which she had sewn her family's jewels.

'Did you really hunt with the Escadron Volant?' Juliette asked as they were strolling through the orchard on the morning of the third day following the massacre. 'I have heard that the ladies are beautiful, witty—and no better than they should be.'

Louise smiled as she saw the curiosity in her companion's eyes. Juliette was a tall girl and heavily boned like her brother; her features were too coarse for real beauty, but her mouth was generous and her hair so fine and pale that it resembled raw silk. There was a certain earthiness in her manner that must make her attractive to men; and Louise realised that she was a girl of spirit who envied the gay life of Madame Catherine's ladies.

'You should not believe all the stories you hear!' Louise replied. 'My cousin says her mistress is very strict. If Madame Catherine considers a lady's behaviour

has disgraced her, she would not balk at beating her
herself.'

Juliette pulled a face and shuddered. 'Then I do not
want to join the Flying Squadron! My mother has never
once beaten me. Father would never have allowed it
while he was alive—nor will Jean.'

'You are fortunate in your family,' Louise said, a little
enviously. 'It does not surprise me that you are in no
hurry to take a husband.'

An odd expression crept into Juliette's eyes. 'I shall
marry when I am ready.'

'Will your brother permit you to choose your own
husband?'

'Jean knows better than to try to force me to wed a
man I cannot love.' A secret smile lurked about her full
lips. 'Besides, I have already decided whom I want to
marry—and I know that Jean will approve.'

'You are indeed fortunate. My father . . .' The words
stuck in Louise's throat, and tears sparkled on her thick
lashes.

'I am sure Jean and Raphael will find your father,'
Juliette said, placing an arm round her waist. 'Jean has
an army of servants out making enquiries . . .' She broke
off as she saw Raphael coming towards them. 'Look,
here is my cousin now. Perhaps he has news for you.'

Blinking back her tears, Louise was aware of excitement in her companion. Suddenly Juliette's face was
glowing with vitality, her eyes fixed on Lord Carleton's
face. Understanding came in a blinding flash. Of course!
Why had she not guessed it at once? Juliette was in love
with her English cousin. It was probably to arrange their
wedding that he had come to France.

Distracted by the discovery she had made, Louise did
not at first notice the grave look on Lord Carleton's face.
It was only when he spoke that she raised her gaze to
meet his, her heart jerked painfully as she saw his
expression.

'Would you leave us, please, Juliette?' he asked. 'I

wish to speak to Mademoiselle de Granvelle alone.'

Juliette hesitated, then inclined her head graciously. 'Of course. I shall see you later, Raphael—and mademoiselle, naturally.'

'Naturally,' he replied, a hint of mockery in his voice.

Juliette blushed, remaining silent as she turned and walked in the direction of the house.

Louise noted the little exchange between them: it confirmed her theory that there was something special in their relationship, but at the moment her concern for her father was all-important.

'I am afraid what I have to tell you will cause you pain, Louise,' Raphael said, his grave look making her heart stand still for one terrible moment.

'My—My father is dead, isn't he?' Louise looked up at him, her eyes dark with anguish.

'He died bravely . . .' The Englishman's face held compassion as he saw her mouth tremble. 'He tried to defend Coligny when they burst into the house, but he was killed—as were many more of your people.'

'I have known it was so since that night.' Louise closed her eyes, trying to hold back the storm of grief within her. 'He—He was not always kind to me, but he was a good man in his own way, and—and I loved him.'

'Some men do not find it easy to show affection, Louise. I am sure he cared for you . . .' He stopped as she held out her hand in protest.

'No, please do not,' she said chokily. 'You can know nothing about my father. You cannot comfort me with false sentiment.'

'Then I shall not try.'

His voice had gone suddenly cold and she glanced up quickly, seeing the glint of anger in his eyes. 'Forgive me, that was rude, m'sieur.'

'No, it was the truth. I am merely a stranger whom Fate has thrust into your life, mademoiselle. Since I can give you no comfort, I shall do the one thing left to me. I shall take you home to La Rochelle.'

His face wore a closed expression, and she bit her lip, wishing she understood more of this man's character. He had gone out of his way to help her on several occasions, yet she had the feeling that he did so unwillingly, that she was in some way an unwanted burden to him.

'It will not be necessary for you to escort me to my home, m'sieur. I can make some arrangements myself. I have only to send to La Rochelle, and my grandmother will have a carriage come for me.'

'That will take time, however, and I think it would be advisable to leave as soon as possible. Paris is a little quieter now, but there are many who believe it is a temporary respite. You will be safer at home.'

Her eyes sparked with anger. 'I cannot leave yet, m'sieur. You seem to have forgotten that my father is dead. I must stay here to see to his funeral—and I must make enquiries as to the whereabouts of my brother. I shall return to Paris tomorrow.'

'That I cannot allow.' Raphael's tone was hard and uncompromising. 'The Seigneur's body has been decently buried according to his religion. I give you my word that everything was as he would have wished. It was better that you should know nothing until it was done.'

Louise looked at him in horror. 'You had no right to keep it from me,' she cried, launching herself at him in a fury of grief and beating at his chest with her fists. 'You should have let me be there!'

Raphael caught her wrists, holding her still until she calmed. 'Believe me, Louise, I did only what I thought best for you.'

'What you thought best?'

He had unknowingly echoed the words spoken to her by her father a few days previously. For a moment she gazed up at him angrily, then her grief burst through and she began to weep, her body shaking with deep, hurtful sobs.

Raphael's arms closed about her, holding her close as

she wept into his doublet. His hand moved softly in the wine-red tresses, caressing the back of her neck.

'You cannot go back to Paris alone,' he said. 'Your father is dead, and André has disappeared. You told me that the house had been ransacked and the servants were gone. How could you manage on your own?'

Louise lifted her tear-drenched eyes to his, knowing he was right but torn by her desire to find her brother. 'André came back to fetch me,' she said. 'If he had not come for me, he could have escaped earlier. He saved my life. I could not desert him.'

Raphael released her, his mouth settling in a thin line. 'My servant will remain in Paris to search for André. If it is possible, he will find him. Besides, if your brother is alive, he will probably make his own way back to La Rochelle.'

She knew he was right. Everything he said made sense, but he was hurting her terribly by forcing her to go with him. He said he had acted for the best when he hid the fact of her father's death from her until after the funeral, but it would have eased her grief to have seen her father one last time. Now she did not even know where his grave was. She raised her head, looking at him coldly.

'Then I must return to my home; but I do not wish to put you to the trouble of taking me, m'sieur. Perhaps your cousin would send one of his grooms with me?'

'I am sure Jean would be delighted to escort you himself,' Raphael said, a flash of anger in his eyes. 'However, I happen to have business in La Rochelle, so I think we shall not trouble Jean. Besides, he must escort his mother and sister to their home.'

She knew there was no more to be said. He made all her objections sound like petulance, when anyone with a heart would understand her concern for her brother. All André's unkindness to her had been wiped from her mind by his selflessness in coming to fetch her. Now when she thought of him, she remembered only that his

first concern when faced with an angry mob had been for
her.

If her conscience reminded her that Lord Carleton,
too, had risked his life for her, she suppressed the
thought. He was alive, and as arrogant as ever! All her
doubts returned to plague her as she looked at his hard
face, and she wondered again just who he was. Why had
he come to France—and why had he decided to take
such an interest in her?

'Then I must thank you, and hope that I shall not keep
you from your business too long, my lord,' she said with
dignity. 'Now, if you will excuse me, I should like to be
alone for a while.'

Raphael looked at her tear-stained face, feeling a
sharp desire to shake her. She seemed determined to
misunderstand him, whatever he did. He watched in
frustration as she walked away with her head high,
wondering how he had managed to involve himself in
such a coil. It would have been better to have told her the
truth from the beginning. Now it was too late. If he tried
to voice his suspicions, she would only call him a liar and
refuse to travel with him.

His eyes narrowed in thought. He must remain silent
for the time being and see what happened when they
reached La Rochelle.

CHAPTER FIVE

'WHY?' Louise's eyes were bright with suspicion as she looked at the Englishman. 'I do not see the reason for what you are suggesting.'

They were waiting to say goodbye to their hosts in the courtyard of the Montpelliers' château. Raphael had chosen this moment to tell her his plan, hoping she would accept it without making a fuss. Now he sighed as he saw the mistrust in her face.

'It will be easier if we travel as man and wife,' he explained with forced patience. 'The riots have spread beyond the city, and you could be in danger if anyone recognised you as being the daughter of an influential Huguenot. Besides, people will think it odd for an unmarried girl to be travelling with a man who is obviously not a relative.'

Louise blushed, knowing that he was right. Everyone would believe the worst of her if she insisted on travelling as Mademoiselle de Granvelle, yet the thought of pretending to be his wife was disturbing.

'What will people say if it is learnt that I posed as your wife?' She stared at him uncertainly, unwilling to say what was really on her mind. How could she tell him that the very idea set her stomach churning?

'They will accept it as a necessary deception in the circumstances.' He frowned at her. 'Give me your hand, Louise.'

For a moment she kept her hand stiffly at her side, gazing at him with mutinous eyes; then, as she saw a muscle begin to flick in his cheek, she held it out in a gesture of defiance.

'I have other rings, if this will not fit,' Raphael said as he slipped a heavy gold band on her third finger, the glimmer of a smile in his eyes when it fitted perfectly.

A shiver crept down her spine as she looked at the ring. She could not have said why she felt threatened by the sight of it, but it seemed to her to be a symbol of bondage. Formed like a pair of hands clasping a blood-red stone that flashed fire in the sunlight, it felt heavy and uncomfortable on her hand. She wanted to protest, but the expression on his face kept her silent. Then, with relief, she saw the Montpelliers emerge into the sunny courtyard. At least she was not afraid of them!

Madame Montpellier embraced her warmly, wishing her a safe journey home. 'If ever we can be of help, you need only send word, mademoiselle,' she said. 'I know I speak for my son as well as myself.'

'Yes, certainly.' Jean moved forward to offer his hand. 'My mother is right, mademoiselle, we—I— would always wish to serve you.'

A hot colour rose in his cheeks as Louise thanked him, and he turned away swiftly to discuss some details of their journey with his cousin.

Juliette took Louise's arm, drawing her away from the others. 'My brother has fallen in love with you. Had you realised that?'

'No, I am sure you are wrong.' Louise was embar-rassed as she saw the teasing look in the other girl's eyes. 'Jean is a kind man. I am sure his concern for me is no more than he would show to anyone in my position.'

'But he would not look at them in the way he looks at you. Can you not see he is eager for your every smile?'

'You should not say such things.' Louise blushed.

Juliette pouted. 'Why, then, did he ask my mother if you might accompany us here? She agreed, naturally, but Raphael said you were determined to go home at once.'

'Your cousin said that?' Louise frowned, but the other girl did not seem to notice.

'Is there no hope for my poor brother, then?'

Louise averted her eyes from Juliette's curious gaze. 'I'm sure you are mistaken. Besides, I am already betrothed.'

'Are you ready, Louise?' Raphael's question broke into their conversation. 'It is time we were leaving.'

'Perhaps I shall be betrothed before too long.' Juliette sighed. 'You will send my cousin back to me soon, won't you?'

'I have no influence over Lord Carleton,' Louise replied, her voice sharper than it might have been because of the confusion of her thoughts. Why had Lord Carleton lied to his aunt?

She moved away to where the grooms were waiting with the horses. Jean came to help her into the saddle, smiling up at her.

'A safe journey, Mademoiselle de Granvelle. I only wish I could have been of more service to you. I pray you will find happiness soon, and I hope—I hope you will think of us sometimes?'

'I shall never forget your kindness to me, m'sieur.' Louise smiled at him cordially.

Raphael was mounted and ready. He noted the warmth in her manner as she spoke to Jean, contrasting it with the coolness she had shown him, and there was a cynical smile on his lips as he met her gaze. A faint colour stained her cheeks, and he turned away with a curl of his lips.

Louise frowned, irritated by the look on his face. If he thought she had gone out of her way to attract Jean's attention, he was wrong! She liked the young man who had been so kind to her, but she was not a flirt, whatever the Englishman might think of her.

Flicking her horse's reins, she moved off ahead of him, an angry glint in her eyes. Lord Carleton had accused her of stealing out to meet Pierre de Guise in the Louvre gardens, and the way he had behaved towards her that night was disgraceful. He had treated her as if she were a coquette, instead of a lady! Remembering the

foolish way her heart had responded only made her
more annoyed.

His high-handed manner in telling Madame Montpellier she wished to return to her home, without con-
sulting her, rankled. It was typical of the man to assume
that she would be safer in his care than his cousin's. It
was only a small thing, but on top of all the rest, it
contributed to the resentment building inside her.

After all, why should she trust him? It was very
strange that Pierre de Guise had not been seen since the
eve of the royal wedding—since she had given the note
to Lord Carleton! Had someone warned him to stay
away from Court for a while, or had something more
sinister occurred? She could not help remembering
André's suspicion that the Englishman might be in
league with the Medici. Supposing her brother had been
right? She did not believe Lord Carleton was concerned
in the massacre itself, but could he not have given
Coligny a timely warning? Such a warning might have
saved the Admiral's life—and that of her father!

Pain struck at her breast as she recalled that she, too,
could have given that warning. It was no use blaming
Lord Carleton when she was equally guilty.

Glancing at her companion, Louise saw that he was
deep in thought, and judging by his frown, it would
appear that his reflections were no happier than her
own. She sighed, wondering why life must be so compli-
cated. If her father had refused to come to Paris, he
would still be alive, the marriage contract could not
have been signed, and she would never have met Lord
Carleton. Nor would she have this terrible ache in her
heart.

Her sighs roused Raphael. They had been riding in
silence for more than an hour, and he realised it could
not go on.

'Why do you frown so?' he asked. 'Are you sad to be
leaving the pleasures of the Court—or perhaps it is Jean
from whom you are loath to part?'

His mocking question incensed her. How could he show such insensitivity when she was so unhappy? 'You need not tease me about your cousin, m'sieur. If I were free to choose, Jean is exactly the kind of man I would have for my husband, but I am not free.'

'Why is that?' His brows went up.

'My marriage contract was signed the day after the royal wedding. Although my father is dead, I am still both legally and morally bound by it.'

'Ah, I see. And do you dislike your betrothed so much?'

'How can I know?' Louise asked bitterly. 'He was so eager to marry me that he signed the contract and left Paris without even speaking to me.'

'And that distressed you?'

'Yes . . . No!' Louise cried. 'Why should I care what he chose to do? I hate the very idea of marrying him!'

'And yet you will do so?'

'What else can I do? If the Chevalier de Leconte wishes to marry me, I am bound to him by law.' Her eyes flashed with anger. 'Since he wished to make me his wife only because of what I might one day inherit from my father's estate, there is no reason for him to change his mind now.'

'Are you sure it was your father's wealth that he wanted?'

'What else can it be, since we have never met?'

'A man might want many things from the woman he chooses as his wife,' Raphael said, an odd look in his eyes. 'Even if you are right, he cannot force you to marry him.'

'You do not understand,' Louise replied impatiently. 'It is a matter of my father's honour. I have no choice in the matter.'

'That depends on how brave you are.'

'What do you mean?'

'No one but myself and my cousins know you survived

the massacre. You could disappear, and the Chevalier would think you were dead.'

'Where would I go?'

'Anywhere . . .' There was a sudden gleam of mischief in his eyes. 'To England, if you wished. As my mistress, you could have your own establishment, and security for the future . . .'

'How dare you?' She reined in sharply as the fury swept through her.

'You are insulted by the idea?' Raphael's brows lifted as if in surprise. 'Would you not prefer your freedom to marriage with a man who cares only for your wealth?'

'No, I would not prefer it!' Louise yelled, spurring her horse to a sudden gallop. She could feel the angry colour in her cheeks, and wanted only to be free of the tormentor at her side.

Her spurt of speed took him by surprise and he lagged behind momentarily, but her slight advantage was soon overcome as his horse drew alongside. Louise could see him from the corner of her eyes, and she was aware that he was laughing. She felt a fierce desire to beat him at something. He was always so confident, so sure of himself. How dared he ask her to be his mistress? Even to herself she would not admit the way her heart had raced when he first mentioned England. For a breathless moment she had thought he was about to ask her to be his wife.

As anger surged through her once more, Louise was determined to win their race. She flicked her horse's rump with her riding crop, urging it to renewed effort. The sudden burst of speed surprised even her, taking her ahead of her rival, and she laughed triumphantly. Now she could feel the wind in her face and the warmth of the sun; the ground was swallowed up beneath her by the pounding hooves, which were echoed in her head by a ceaseless drumming. She had a sensation of flying, as though she were one with the horse she rode. Trees, fields, hedges became a blur of green, indistinguishable from the cloudless blue of the sky. Nothing was quite real any more, not even the man whose taunts had driven her to this madness. She wanted to be free—free of the doubts and aching misery inside her.

Gradually, sanity returned. She realised her companion was keeping pace with her, his horse matching hers stride for stride; the knowledge brought with it a sense of futility. She could not escape, because what she was trying to escape from was inside her.

As if he had sensed the girl's change of mood, Raphael caught at her horse's reins, jerking the animal's head up as he pulled hard. The horse snorted as it came to a shuddering halt, its mouth flecked with foam and sweating all over.

'We'd best rest the horses for a while—unless you want to ride them into the ground?'

Louise shook her head, feeling foolish now. She avoided his eyes as he dismounted and came to help her down. Her anger had evaporated, leaving her with a deep desire to weep. Only pride kept her head high as she walked swiftly away from the probe of his eyes.

Ahead of her she could see a tiny stream. It ran between moss-covered boulders, tumbling busily beneath the overhanging bushes and trees, to disappear over a steep incline. Drawn by the bubbling, gurgling sound it made, Louise sank to the bank, her skirts fanning out round her like the petals of a flower as she cupped her hand to trap the sparkling water. She splashed her heated cheeks several times, and then drank a few sips. The water had a slightly brackish taste, but it refreshed her, and she was feeling calmer when she turned to meet Raphael's cynical gaze.

'Are you satisfied now?' he asked, his scorn making her flinch. 'I'm sure you know you've cost us an hour of travelling time? Your horse won't last the journey if you carry on like this.'

His words stung her. It was unfair of him to blame her when he had started it all. He had deliberately goaded her. Besides, she had sensed the exhilaration in him as they raced.

'You insulted me!' Louise glared at him as he bent to dip his hands in the water.

Raphael drank his fill before replying. 'It was merely a way of shocking you out of your mood of righteous propriety.'

'My what?' Louise stared at him, stunned. 'I am not righteous!'

She stood up and walked swiftly away from him, her silk gown swishing over the grass. Hearing him behind her, she tried to hurry and wrenched her heel in a rut. He caught her arm, saving her from a fall, but instead of thanking him, Louise pushed off his hand.

'Why will you not leave me alone?'

'I am sorely tempted to do so.'

'You insulted me!' There was a catch in her voice, and he saw he had pushed her almost too far.

'Ridiculous child!' Raphael grabbed her as she began to turn away, pulling her hard against him so that she was forced to look up at his face. 'Is this an insult to your womanhood?'

Before she could reply, he bent his head, grinding his lips hard on hers in a chastising kiss. Louise struggled in his embrace, trying to stop the violation of her defences before it was too late; but he held her fast, caressing her mouth with his own until she felt her limbs turn to boneless supplication, and her lips grew warm, begging for the sweet torture to continue. Continue it did, consuming the whole of her body in a molten tide that seemed to rob her of her senses. She clung to him as his mouth released hers at last, breathless and dizzy.

Raphael caught her chin, forcing her to meet his eyes. 'Believe me, I meant no insult. I have wanted few women as I want you, Louise.'

'You—You really want me as your mistress?'

He saw the uncertainty in her eyes, and it raised the

devil in him. 'If you are asking whether I want to make love to you . . . Yes, I would like to carry you to the shade of that tree and teach you what it means to be a woman. You are a beautiful, desirable woman, Louise.' His eyes gleamed wickedly as he saw the wonder in her. 'Yes, I want to make love to you—but no, I do not want you as my mistress. You are far too troublesome a wench.'

'Oh, you wretch!' Louise cried, torn between laughter and frustration. 'Why did you offer to make me your mistress if you did not mean it?'

His husky laughter made her frown as he said, 'Are you disappointed now that I've changed my mind?'

'I won't listen to this . . .'

She turned away, but he caught her wrist. 'I apologise for that, Louise—but you tempt me so.'

'What can you mean?'

'Can you really be so innocent? I admit I have tried to raise you to anger, but you bring so much of it on yourself.'

'I—I do not understand you.'

His face became serious as he looked down at her. 'I know you are grieving for your father, Louise. It is natural that you should mourn him—but you must not sacrifice yourself on the altar of his wishes out of a mistaken sense of duty.'

'Then you think I should refuse to marry the Chevalier?' She looked at him anxiously. 'But—the contract?'

'If the Chevalier has any feelings, he will release you if you ask him. No decent man would force an unwilling woman to be his wife.'

Louise swallowed hard. 'I don't know what to do.'

'You must give yourself time to think. In time you will know what is right for you.'

She gazed up at him with misted eyes. 'Why should you concern yourself with my affairs, my lord?'

He shrugged. 'I have asked myself the same thing

many times. Perhaps it is because you are such a sweet companion?'

'Devil!' she flung at him, but somehow he had eased the ache about her heart, and she realised that might have been his object from the start in mocking her. She glanced up at him provocatively. 'Maybe I shall come to England just to plague you, after all.'

Raphael laughed, his keen eyes noting the lessening of shadows in her face. 'And maybe I shall take you, if I have a mind to it. Be warned, Louise, I am only a man, and I can be noble for only so long.'

She felt a frisson of unease at the veiled threat in his voice. Somehow she knew that her will was not strong enough to resist him if he really wanted her.

'Oh, I think I have nothing to fear, my lord,' she said, turning away from him. 'You have made yourself my protector, and I think your sense of honour will keep me safe.'

A shudder shook her as she felt the touch of his hands on her shoulders. 'You are safe enough as long as you do not provoke me too far, Louise—but be careful. My patience is wearing thin!'

For most of the day, the two travellers stayed clear of the villages they passed, eating the food they had brought with them and resting the horses from time to time. As dusk fell slowly around them, Raphael began to look for an inn where they could spend the night. Although he knew there were dangers in exposing themselves to curious eyes, he also knew that Louise could not stand the rigours of sleeping rough. Besides, that might prove equally dangerous; there were often vagrants in the forests who would attack unwary travellers under cover of darkness.

As yet, they had seen little sign of the violence reported in the provinces, though they had passed an abandoned coach on the road to Orleans. Its leading pole was snapped in two and the horses were gone; from the broken trunks scattered in the road it was clear that the owner's possessions had been looted, but there were no corpses, so it seemed likely that the occupants had escaped.

Jean had begged him to take some of his grooms with them, but Raphael knew from experience that tongues were apt to wag in the stables of an evening, especially after a tankard of ale. He had considered hiring a band of armed followers, but it was impossible to know who could be trusted in this dangerous climate. Had he brought his own men from England, he could have relied on them in any crisis, and not for the first time he realised how unwise he had been. A sudden whim had brought him to France with just his most trusted servant. Thomas Craven was his body-servant, groom and friend: the one man he could share his secret with. Raphael would have felt happier if Thomas had been with them on this journey, but he had stayed behind in Paris to search for Louise's brother.

The dark eyes narrowed in thought as Raphael wondered at the strangeness of Fate. He had come to this country for two reasons, one of them a half-forgotten promise made when he was a boy at his mother's bedside. After her death, he had thought of nothing else for weeks, but as he grew older, the promise had been pushed to the back of his mind, where it might have stayed but for Helen's betrayal and the letter. A letter he'd first thought to be naught but the hysterical ravings of a grieving woman. He might have ignored Madame Dupont's plea for help if there had not been a sudden, pressing need to leave England.

Raphael stroked the almost healed scar at his temple, his mouth hardening as he remembered what had caused his self-imposed exile. He had killed a man in a duel—a duel that had been forced on him despite all his efforts to avoid it. Unfortunately, it had taken place at Court, and the Queen was very angry with him. She had banished him to his estates for six months.

The letter reached him as he was leaving Whitehall, furious at his dismissal. He made up his mind in an instant, taking the next ship bound for France, though he had intended only a short visit to Madame Dupont on his way to the Loire valley. After listening to her story, however, he had known that her suspicions were more than mere speculations. A man had died in strange circumstances, and since that man was his mother's only brother, Raphael determined that it was his duty to discover the truth.

He had gone first to his cousins. Madame Montpellier could tell him little, for she had not seen her brother in years; but she welcomed her older sister's only child warmly, inviting him to travel to Paris with them for the royal wedding. He had accepted the offer because it suited his plans. He had little dreamt that in doing so he would stumble on a deeper mystery, nor that he would find himself the self-appointed protector of a beautiful, wilful girl.

A grim smile curled his lips as he looked at her. After he learned the extent of Helen's betrayal, he had sworn never to be swayed by a woman's tears again—so why had he risked his life to bring this girl out of Paris during the riots? And what would she do when they reached La Rochelle, and he was obliged to tell her the truth?

'I'm tired!' Louise's words broke the pattern of his thoughts. 'Can we not rest for a while?'

'I came this way some days ago,' he said, hearing the weariness in her voice. 'There is a small inn not far ahead where I think we may safely stay for the night.'

Louise nodded, past caring now why he had passed this way. She drew a sigh of relief when he reined in and pointed to a shadowy building at the bottom of a dip.

'There is the inn,' he said. 'Come, we shall have supper, and bespeak a room for the night.'

She looked at him in alarm. 'We shall need two rooms. You are not expecting me to share a bed with you?'

The suspicion in her face angered him, and he frowned. 'Then it seems I must make shift on the floor, for I'll not trust you to sleep alone. I should very likely wake to find you had gone.'

He had planned this all the time! If he had told her at the start, she would never have agreed to masquerade as his wife. She could not—dared not—share a room with him.

'I will not agree to this, my lord,' she said, her heart racing wildly.

'Then you may sleep in the stable.'

'W-What?' Louise gasped as she saw his un-compromising look. 'You don't mean that?'

He shot her a scornful glance, but did not answer. They had reached the inn and he gave his horse a sudden kick with his heels, riding on ahead of her into the stableyard. Louise watched as he dismounted, waiting for him to help her down as he usually did. She felt a spurt of panic as he strode towards the inn without a backward glance. Surely he would not really let her sleep in the stable?

She accepted the clumsy ministrations of the ostler, standing undecided for a moment as the horses were led away. She would have loved to ride off and leave her arrogant companion to his own devices, but her whole body was aching, and she was so tired that she craved the softness of a bed. Gathering the hem of her gown with one hand, she ran after Raphael. She was just in time to hear the innkeeper greeting him, and waited breathlessly for his reply.

'I want a room for tonight,' Raphael said, pausing as he looked at her. 'My wife is weary. We will have supper served in our chamber, if you please.'

'Certainly, m'sieur.' The fat landlord bowed, wiping his greasy palms on his jerkin. 'You shall have the best room in the house, if you will kindly follow me.'

'Louise!' Raphael held out his hand to her with that imperious gesture she had seen several times before.

She went to him, eyes downcast so that he should not see how angry she was.

Louise sighed, and stirred in her sleep. She was dreaming—a dream so pleasant she did not want to wake up.

'It's time we were on our way.'

Raphael's words shattered the illusion of peace, forcing her to face reality. She opened her eyes, looking into his frowning features.

'Is it morning already? I ache all over.' She groaned as she sat up, her limbs feeling stiff from the day before, throwing off the coarse blanket beneath which she had lain fully clothed all night.

'If you had slept where I did, you might have cause to complain!'

Louise looked at the pillow and crumpled coverlet on the floor, and her lips twitched. 'I trust you slept well, my lord?'

A muttered oath escaped his lips as he turned away to gather up the offending articles, tossing them on to the bed as she left it.

'Have a care, mademoiselle. You have not seen the worst of me yet!'

'Sleeping on the floor does not seem to improve your temper,' Louise agreed sweetly. 'Perhaps you will bespeak two rooms this evening?'

'Belike I shall break your neck before this journey is done.'

'Oh, I do not think so, my lord.' Louise pouted at him, her eyes sparkling with mischief. 'I do not know why you have chosen to appoint yourself as my protector, but I am sure I may rely on your honour as a gentleman.'

'Certainly you can rely on me to conduct you safely to your home,' Raphael told her. 'But unless you behave like a lady, I shall treat you as you deserve!'

The smile died out of Louise's face as she saw his murderous expression. She had intended only to tease him a little, to pay him back for frightening her the previous evening.

'I—I meant it only as a jest,' she faltered.

'Like all your kind, you take advantage of your womanhood,' he replied savagely. 'You protest your innocence, while your eyes tempt a man to acts of madness.'

'No . . .' Louise gazed into his black eyes and shivered at what she read there. What could she possibly have done to make him so angry? 'I—I am going down to the parlour. I am hungry.' She lifted her chin, brushing past him as she left the room.

Raphael made no attempt to stop her. He knew what she could not, that his anger was directed more at himself than at her. Her face had looked so lovely while she slept; he had found himself wanting to gather her up in his arms, to kiss her awake and tell her they were leaving for England this very day.

A wry smile lit the dark eyes. He was wavering like a fool—and over a woman! He had sworn never to trust a beautiful woman again, however innocent she might look in her sleep. He must not be swayed from his purpose; the girl was an integral part of his plan. They must go on to La Rochelle, no matter what.

'What fools women make of us,' he muttered, his voice harsh with bitterness. 'Damn her! Damn all her kind!'

Picking up his sword, he buckled it on before leaving the room.

Louise had almost finished her breakfast when Raphael joined her. She looked up hopefully as he entered, but seeing the coldness was still in his eyes, the determination to make him pay for his harsh treatment of her grew steadily stronger. Why did he act as though she were somehow a threat to him? She was hurt by the look of dislike she had seen on his face when she had attempted to tease him. He was always taunting her, but when she responded in like manner, he was angry with her. The man was impossible, and she would be glad when this journey was over.

'I shall take a walk outside,' she said. 'Pray continue with your meal, lord.'

'You will wait here until I am ready.'

'I am not your prisoner!'

'Nevertheless, you will wait.' Raphael touched the napkin to his lips. 'I do not trust you, Louise.'

'You do not trust me?' she said incredulously. 'You —You are beyond belief, m'sieur!'

Turning on her heel, she stalked out of the parlour. Raphael swore as he pushed away the remains of his breakfast. He refused to run after her like a lackey. Besides, she could not go far in the few minutes it would take him to settle with the host, even if she did ride off in a temper.

A little to his surprise, however, Louise was waiting meekly in the courtyard. She made no comment as he helped her to mount, nor did she answer as he pointed out the direction they must take. He permitted himself a smile. Obviously, she had decided to retreat into a dignified silence. Well, so be it. At least they could not quarrel if they were not talking to one another. He began to whistle a tune as he rode, his bleak mood easing as he felt the warm breeze on his face. If it was to be a contest between them, he would not be the first to break.

In the event, it was Raphael who spoke first, but only because he was forced to rest the horses by a convenient stream. Louise was riding slightly ahead of him, but she halted when he called to her, dismounting without waiting for his help. Her wide skirts hampered her, and she felt a twinge of pain in her ankle when she landed too heavily. She pressed her lips together, determined not to let him guess she had hurt herself.

In total silence they ate the food Raphael had purchased earlier at the inn. Louise took the bread and cheese offered her, trying hard to avoid touching his hand as she did so. A dark look from him was matched by a glare from her, both of them equally convinced that the other must apologise first.

Early in the day they had made a detour to avoid the royal estate at Blois. In doing so, they had come close to a small village, and there they had seen signs of the violence. The ruins of two cottages built on the outskirts of the hamlet were still smouldering after the fire that had destroyed them. The Huguenots who had lived in them were clearly regarded as outsiders, and the villagers had taken their chance to wreak havoc in the name of religion.

Louise dared not imagine what had happened to the occupants, and her face was pale as she averted her eyes. Passing a labourer driving a team of oxen, she was aware of the odd look he gave her, and her heart contracted. Was it possible for a stranger to guess she was a Huguenot just by looking at her? At that moment she would have given anything for a comforting word from her companion, but he merely continued to ride just behind her as they passed more of the villagers.

To have attempted reassurance at such a time was perhaps the worst thing Raphael could have done, but Louise thought he was still angry with her. Her own anger had long since faded, but she dared not let him see how hurt she was by his unreasonable behaviour this morning.

Awaking to find him bending over her, she had thought it was a continuation of her dream. Her cheeks flushed as she recalled just how sweet that dream had been. Raphael had been kissing her again, but not in the way he had kissed her yesterday. In her dream he had held her tenderly, whispering words of love that made her whole body tingle. Her foolish hopes had soon evaporated at the expression of disgust on his face when she teased him.

As the day progressed, Louise grew annoyed with

herself. She was a fool to indulge in such dreams. The Englishman was a rake by his own admission. He wanted a woman for only as long as she pleased him, never giving anything himself. He had said he wanted to make love to her, but she was the one who would suffer if she gave in to his whim. It could only bring her heartache. No, somehow she must keep a distance between them, because if she did not, her own weakness would betray her.

It was very late when they finally found a small inn. Having passed a much larger house in the evening because it looked too busy, Louise had begun to think they would have to sleep beneath the stars. She was too relieved when they were at last shown up to their chamber even to think of arguing, and it surprised her when Raphael turned to leave.

'W-Where are you going?'

'The host will bring you supper in a moment. I shall eat in the parlour tonight. I shall not disturb you if you leave the door unlocked.'

'As you wish. Please knock if you return within the hour: I should like to take this opportunity to wash.'

'You need not concern yourself, mademoiselle. It will be late before I come . . . If I come at all.'

Louise averted her head, holding back her tears. She knew it was better that it should be like this, but she had not expected it to hurt so much. She brushed a single tear from her cheek as she heard footsteps outside the room, her heart thumping. Had Raphael changed his mind? Was he coming back to apologise to her? Her disappointment was sharp when the innkeeper's wife knocked and requested entry.

The woman was bright-eyed and curious, her thin nose quivering like a terrier's as she took in every detail of Louise's appearance. She stayed talking for several minutes, while the girl's supper turned cold on the plate.

'Have you come far, madame?'

'We—We travelled from Blois today.'

'Then you've not come from Paris?'

Was it imagination, or was there suspicion in those hawklike eyes?'

'No. We've been staying with my husband's cousins the Montpelliers.'

'Ah, then you did not see what happened on Saint Bartholomew's Eve. We've heard there were thousands killed.' The woman crossed herself.

'So many?' Louise dug her nails into the palms as she fought to control the tide of sickness inside her. 'We —We were told it was nearer eight hundred.'

'Oh no, it was many more,' the woman said with relish. 'Do you think it was the Italian Woman's doing?'

'Was it not done on the King's orders?' Louise asked, feeling faint. She could not stand much more of this.

'That's as maybe—but we all know Madame Serpent was behind it, don't we? I remember the way the young Dauphin died so mysteriously when he stood in the Medicis' way to the throne. It was her servant who poisoned him, make no mistake about that!' The woman chuckled suddenly. 'Well, for once I say good luck to her. We don't want these heretics in our midst. I say good riddance to the Huguenots! What do you think, madame?'

Louise met the woman's challenging look, a cold chill trickling down her back. 'I do not understand these things, madame. My husband does not consider it fitting for a woman to discuss politics.' She smiled confidentially and lifted her hands in an expressive gesture. 'You know how men are, madame—they are all the same, are they not?'

Her little ruse was successful: the woman was diverted into a long tirade on the selfishness of men in general, and of her husband in particular. Louise listened patiently, sympathising with her, and sighing when she was asked how long she had been married.

'Too long, madame. My—My husband is not kind to me.'

'Ah, I knew it was so, my poor little one! I could see what kind of man he was as soon as he came in.'

Louise had to struggle to hold back a smile as she saw the gleam of battle in the woman's eyes. It would serve Raphael right if he looked in vain for his supper tonight, she thought.

The woman looked set to talk all night, but an irate shout from below recalled her to her duty at last. She pulled a face.

'Men! they are the scourge of many a good woman's life.'

Louise relaxed as the door closed behind her. Although the woman had seemed friendly enough in the end, there was no doubt of where her sympathies lay, and the girl shivered at the thought of what might happen if she guessed she was sheltering beneath her roof a fugitive from the atrocities.

Any appetite Louise might have had deserted her as she picked at the congealing mess of stewed meat on her plate. She nibbled a piece of bread, washing it down with a mouthful of the strong ale; then she picked up the tray and deposited it outside her door, locking it carefully after her so that she should not be disturbed.

It was good to remove her gown and petticoats, and to feel the cool water on her skin after two days of hard riding. She washed her whole body, enjoying the sensation, and wishing she could do the same for her hair. Unfortunately, she must wait until she was safely home before she could indulge in that luxury.

Thoughts of home and of the terrible news she carried brought tears to Louise's eyes. Her grandmother was old, and had been unwell for some weeks before their departure for Paris. That was why she had remained at home, and now perhaps the shock of learning about the Seigneur's death might prove too much for her.

Life was so cruel! Louise had struggled to control her

grief, knowing that she had a long journey before her, but now it washed over her, and her body began to shake with uncontrollable sobs. Suddenly she felt desperately alone. Her father was dead, and for all she knew, so was André. There was only the hard-eyed Englishman to stand between her and the wrath of the people who had turned against the Huguenots. Yet how could she trust him when she knew so little about him?

She felt that he resented her in some way, that she was somehow preventing him from doing what he wished to do. He looked at her so strangely sometimes that it sent prickles of fear shooting all over her—but when he had held her in his arms, she had wanted to stay there for ever. He haunted her dreams, and he made her days a living nightmare. She was afraid of him when he looked at her with anger in his face, while he could melt her limbs with just one smile. She was so confused that she almost wished he had left her to the fury of the mob.

Leaving her petticoats lying on the floor, she slipped hurriedly beneath the coverlet, her body trembling. With her face in the pillows, she wept as though her heart would break. She wept for her father and her people—and for herself.

Remembering she had promised to leave the door open for Lord Carleton, Louise sighed. She was so weary that it was too much effort to get up again. In a little while she would dress, and then she would unlock the door . . .

CHAPTER SIX

RAPHAEL STARED moodily into his tankard. He had already drunk more than was wise in the circumstances, but his anger at the world had turned inwards, and his only consolation was at the bottom of a pewter pot. He drained it and signalled to the innkeeper's wife, frowning as he saw the odd look she gave him.

The woman refilled his tankard from her ewer, slapping it down hard on the table so that it spilled over the sides and splashed Raphael's velvet jerkin.

'Have a care, woman,' he growled, rubbing at the stains.

'Your good wife awaits you upstairs, m'sieur,' she replied with a scowl. 'You have drunk enough this night, I'll swear. Drinking strong wine addles a man's brain, and it's we women who suffer the consequences.' She cast a sullen look in her husband's direction.

'What say you?' Raphael looked up, startled.

'Ah, I know you for what you are, m'sieur. You should be ashamed to treat that sweet child upstairs so cruelly.'

Astonished, Raphael was lost for words, and could only stare after her as she moved away to serve another customer. A man had just entered, taking a seat by the window, his face turned from the Englishman's bewildered gaze.

Uninterested in his fellow-traveller, Raphael got abruptly to his feet as the meaning of the woman's remarks drove home. He was scowling as he strode from the room, his eyes narrowed in thought. What had Louise been saying to their hostess to bring on her verbal attack? And, in God's name, why?

Anger flickered in the black eyes. Louise had done

nothing but insult him since he had risked his life to save
hers; the injustice of her behaviour rankled, adding to
the balance of his aggrieved feelings. What had he done
that the girl should complain of him to a stranger? If
there was one thing he could not abide it was falseness in
a woman! Helen had lied to him, blinding him to her
treachery with honeyed smiles; she had wept on her
knees before him when he finally discovered the extent
of her schemes. All women were liars: a man would be a
fool to believe otherwise.

Reaching the door of the bedchamber he had reserved
for the night, Raphael tried the latch and found it
immovable. His mouth tightened with temper. The
wench was impossible! Surely she must know that he had
insisted on sharing her room only so that he could
protect her in the event of a sudden attack? Did he
imagine he liked sleeping on the floor?

'Open this door at once, Louise. You are behaving
like a foolish child!' Receiving no answer from inside,
he banged loudly on the wooden panels. 'Let me in
immediately!'

The noise Raphael was making finally roused Louise.
She had drifted into an uneasy sleep, awaking suddenly
as she heard the banging outside. For a moment she
could not think what was wrong; then she realised she
had forgotten to unlock the door. She must have been
asleep for ages! Rising swiftly, she caught up her shift
and slipped it over her head, neglecting in her haste to
put on the several layers of petticoats she normally wore
beneath her gown.

'I'm sorry! I forgot to leave it unocked,' Louise apolo-
gised as she opened the door. 'I lay down for a while,
and . . .' Her words trailed away as she saw his face.
'W-What is the matter?'

Raphael was staring at her oddly. He had been angry
when she opened the door, but now his eyes had begun
to burn with an inner fire that brought a strange silver-

white flame into being. His skin was pale in the candle-light, its fairness accentuated by the raven-black of his hair. He moved his tongue slowly over dry lips, a queer, blind look on his face as his gaze travelled over her.

'Why do you torment me so?' he asked harshly. 'What have I done that you should hate me?'

'I—I do not understand, my lord,' Louise whispered, backing away from him in sudden fear. 'I do not hate you. Why should I?'

Something about the way she looked at him then sent Raphael's senses reeling. Her breasts were clearly out-lined beneath the thin silk she wore, drawing his hungry gaze to the rose-dark shadows of her nipples. Anger and desire fused into one overpowering emotion: the need to possess her body became all-important, blotting out everything else. He moved towards her like a man in a dream, his breath ragged and tortured.

'You are so beautiful,' he groaned, the words torn from him unwillingly. 'Yet that beauty is naught but an illusion to trap a man's senses. Beneath it lies a heart as false as any . . .'

'No!' Louise cried, stung by the whiplash of his accus-ing words. 'Please do not say such things, my lord. Do not . . . look at me so strangely.'

'How else should I look at you? Have you not sought to drive me to madness? It is always a woman's way to taunt a man with smiles and promises until he loses control—you use your arts to make slaves of us all for your amusement.' Raphael reached out for her, his hands catching her shoulders as she drew away from him, pulling her tight against his chest. 'You have pushed me too far, Louise. I want you, and now I mean to have you!'

Louise could smell the bitter-sweetness of wine on his breath as his mouth reached hungrily for hers. The harshness in his voice seared her, making her recoil from his feverish kisses. This was not how he had kissed her before. There was a hardness in him now that frightened her, making her eyes open wide as she gazed up at him.

'Please do not,' she begged as his ravaging mouth moved down her throat to the pulsating swell of her breasts. 'I beg you to stop this, my lord!'

'You will beg me not to leave you before I have done with you,' he threatened, his hand moving to cup one firm breast. 'Save your tears for others who may believe in them, Louise; they will not help you now.'

'No! I shall not permit this, m'sieur,' she said fiercely, catching at his invading hands.

'You will not permit?' Raphael laughed scornfully, brushing aside her protesting fingers. 'If you will not give, I must take, for I shall not be denied. I saved your life. Therefore, it belongs to me! Resist no more, Louise, you are mine, to do with as I will!'

Louise gave a cry of anger, beginning to struggle wildly as he bent down to sweep her up in his arms. She beat at him with her fists as he strode towards the bed, tossing her carelessly on to it before starting to unbuckle his belt.

'You devil!' she shrieked. 'I hate you, Raphael. I hate you! Do you hear me?'

'How sweetly you speak my name,' he murmured mockingly, moving swiftly to prevent her as she tried to roll across the bed away from him. 'Say it again, my lovely wanton, whisper it gently as you give yourself to me, and I'll not complain that you have whispered a dozen others as sweetly.'

'I am no wanton, I swear it on my father's grave!' Louise looked up at him, her eyes smoky with distress. 'Do not take me thus, my lord, I beg you.'

'How should I take you then—with love?' His hand caught in her tumbled tresses, letting the strands run through his fingers like burnished silk. 'Oh, yes, you would like that, wouldn't you? You would enjoy seeing me humbled at your feet, begging for the favour of a smile . . . Well, that is something you will never see. Raphael Carleton begs for no woman's favours!'

'No!' Louise cried, her heart contorting with pain as she saw the tortured carving of his features. 'What cause have I given you to scorn me so, my lord? I have not asked for your love—nor do I want your kisses. What you have taken was taken by force!'

'You were willing enough, yester morn, I'll swear!'

His hand moved to her breast, smoothing the soft flesh with the tip of his thumb. Louise gasped as the sharp, tingling sensation shot through her, and he laughed as he looked down into her face.

'Not so unwilling, my sweet.'

Anger flared in her then. He was mocking her weakness, laughing at her because she could not control her betraying body.

'I hate you,' she hissed. 'You sicken me, coming to my bed like a drunken fool! Force me if you will, m'sieur, but know that I shall always despise you for it!'

Raphael's face hardened. His hand encircled her slender throat and there was murder in his eyes as he looked at her. 'You say you hate me, yet I could have taken you that night in the Louvre gardens had I wished, just as I could take you now. You might fight me for a while, but then you would beg me to possess you.'

Louise closed her eyes as his lips touched her throat. She clenched her hands as she tried to resist the surge of desire his nearness aroused in her. Even now, when she should hate him, there was a part of her that cried out for him. She fought back her tears, knowing she must not give in.

'You would not dare to treat me so wickedly if my father had lived to defend my name . . .'

Raphael flinched as though she had struck him. 'Do you call me a coward? No man could name me thus and hope to live!'

'Kill me, then!' Louise cried. 'Where is the honour in deflowering a defenceless maiden? Are you so fallen that you must force an unwilling woman to your bed?'

He stared at her, seeing her clearly for the first time

since he had entered her room. The white heat died out of his eyes and he blinked, as if he were just beginning to realise what he had been about. A muscle flicked in his cheek, and his nostrils flared as if he struggled for control.

His fingers entwined in her hair, the reluctance to let go stamped on his features. Yet she could see that her words had reached his heated brain.

'Please, Raphael,' she whispered. 'If I have hurt or angered you these past few days, I am sorry. Do not seek to take your vengeance on me in this way.'

Slowly, his fingers uncurled, and he shook his head as if to free it from the wine fumes. 'If you are truly a maiden, it would be coward's work to take you thus,' he said uncertainly.

'I have known no man,' Louise said, meeting his gaze. 'Nor shall I willingly until I go to my husband's bed.'

His mouth curved mockingly. 'The Chevalier de Leconte does not know what a fortunate man he is.'

Louise made no reply, but an odd, shamed look came into his eyes. He turned away from her as he rose from the bed.

'It seems I have misjudged you, mademoiselle.'

'Perhaps I was partly to blame, m'sieur. I have not behaved well towards you.'

Raphael stood with his back to her, his voice sounding hoarse as he said, 'The fault was mine. I have drunk too much of wine and bitterness . . .' He was silent for a moment, then, 'I was blaming you for another's vices.'

'She must have hurt you very much, my lord.'

He swung round to face her, and his eyes were dark with anger. 'I do not wish for your pity, Louise.'

She shrank away from him. 'It—It was not pity.'

His mouth tightened as he saw the apprehension in her face. 'Fear not, mademoiselle, this will not happen again. Tomorrow we shall resume our journey—and in future you will have your own room.' He bowed stiffly. 'Good night. I advise you to lock your door when I have

gone—not against me, you have no more to fear on that
score, but in case of a surprise attack. Our hosts have no
love for Huguenots, I fear.'

Louise nodded, wondering if she should tell him what
the landlady had said to her, but it was too late. Even as
she hesitated, he went out, closing the door behind him.
For a moment she stayed where she was, then she got up
and locked it. Returning to the bed, she sat on the edge,
hugging her arms round her as she began to tremble.

How could Raphael come to her like that? she asked
herself miserably. He had meant to use her like a harlot.
His drunken state was no excuse for such behaviour. He
was a rake, and she despised him. She hated him! No,
that wasn't true. Even though he had used her so cruelly,
she loved him. At last she admitted the truth to herself.
She had loved him from the very beginning.

It was a painful discovery. She was in love with a man
who thought all women were whores, a man who could
never love her as she needed to be loved. And she did
desperately need love. Her nature had been starved of it
for years, the loving woman within her stifled for lack of
human warmth.

It would be better for her if she were never to see him
again, Louise thought. A wild surge of panic rose in her
and she was tempted to run away from him now, this
very minute. It died as soon as it was born. She could not
run away from herself. All she could do was to hide her
true feelings from him and pray that the pain would go
away.

They had been riding for ever, or so it seemed to Louise
as she reined in to survey the landscape before them. At
first they had travelled in a silent world broken only by
the faint twitterings of the birds, but for the last few
miles they had seen peasants at work in the fields or
driving their swine to feed in the woods.

As yet Raphael had spoken to her only once, when he
came to tell her it was time to leave. From time to time

she had dared to glance at his profile, but the hard lines of his face offered no comfort. She sensed he was very angry, but she did not know whether it was with her or himself.

For some time they had been following the river, and she remembered that this was the way she had come with her father and André some weeks ago. In time the road should bring them to the forest of Chanelais, and from there they could go on to Saumur. On their way to Paris, her father had pointed out a fourteenth-century castle built on a sheer cliff, telling her it was a Huguenot stronghold. Surely there they would be among friends and this nightmare journey would soon be over.

It should take another hour to reach the forest, Louise calculated, looking up at the position of the sun in the cloudless sky. By then it would be mid-morning. She was beginning to feel hungry and regretted that she had not touched the breakfast brought to her chamber before they left.

Seeing that Raphael had moved on some way ahead of her, Louise flicked her horse's reins, urging it to a brisk canter. If she lagged too far behind, he would think she was being difficult, and she couldn't bear yet another quarrel between them.

The sun had reached its zenith when Raphael decided it was time to rest the horses. The woodland road dipped sharply at one point, and a sluggish stream had slowed to a mere trickle between the protruding roots of encroaching bushes.

Louise dismounted, allowing the Englishman to help her, and whispering her thanks. The feel of his strong hands about her waist brought a quick flush to her cheeks, and she turned away, leading her horse to the stream. While the animal drank the brownish water, she contented herself with wetting her lips. It was cooler beneath the trees than on the open road, and she was glad of the shade, for the day had become hot despite the cool air of early morning. Perspiration clung to her brow, making the strands of wine-red hair straggle wetly across her forehead and in the nape of her neck.

When she turned to look, she saw that Raphael had spread his cloak on the ground and was lying stretched out with his eyes closed. The parcel of food and wine was opened beside him, and she thought that he was probably waiting for her to join him before eating.

It had clearly been his intention; but as she approached, she saw that he had fallen asleep, and she realised that, like her, he had slept very little last night. In his slumber, Raphael's face had lost its sternness and he seemed to look younger and even a little vulnerable, though perhaps that was only in her mind.

She knelt down beside him, feeling a surge of love for him. How handsome he was! Impulsively, she touched her lips gently to the scar at his temple. He stirred, and murmured something that sounded like a name. She wondered if he were dreaming of her, and like many women before her, she began to make excuses to herself for the behaviour of the man she loved. Perhaps it was her fault that he had drunk too much wine last night. She had let their quarrel go on too long, when a smile from her would have eased the tension between them. What did it matter if he arrogantly assumed that he knew what was best for her? All that really counted was that he had cared enough to want to help her. She smiled and sat down, preparing to wait for him to wake up. As she did so, he flung out an arm and jerked violently, calling out in his dream.

'Helen . . .' he muttered, his features contorting with anguish. 'Helen . . . No, don't! In God's name, I beg you . . .'

The smile left Louise's face. As he had spoken in English, she could understand only that he was troubled and that he called for a woman. All at once she knew why he spoke so bitterly of the female sex. There was one special woman in his life, and she had hurt him so badly that he dreamed of her. It was not Louise he loved, or even his cousin Juliette, but a woman he had left in England.

Standing up, Louise walked swiftly away. Tears were blinding her, and she was afraid he would wake to find her crying. The tears she had not shed after he left her last night came now as she stood looking at the stream.

The future stretched bleakly before her. She was in love with a man who thought of her merely as an unwanted burden, and when she reached La Rochelle she would have to marry a man who cared only for her inheritance . . .

Suddenly, Louise's thoughts were interrupted as she heard the sound of horses' hooves. Glancing up, she saw two riders approaching through the trees, and fear trickled through her. She had wandered away from Raphael and was not sure how far she had come.

'Good afternoon, mademoiselle,' the first man said. 'It is a pleasant day, is it not?'

'Yes, indeed,' Louise replied, staring at him uncertainly. She immediately distrusted the men, who, judging by their appearance, were merchants of some kind. She had seen hard-eyed men like them before when they came to the château to offer their wares; then they had always smiled and bowed to her father, but she had sensed their dislike. It was these men who hated the Huguenots the most because their industrious ways had made so many of her people wealthy. Instinct told her that these men were her enemies. By the way they were looking at her, she was sure they had guessed she was a Huguenot, and that they believed she was alone in the forest.

One of them had dismounted and was coming towards her. Giving a cry of alarm, Louise backed away from him, knowing she must somehow get back to Raphael.

'Why do you look so scared?' the man asked with a

knowing leer. 'Come here, my pretty little Huguenot. I want to talk to you.'

'Why do you call me that?' she said, licking her dry lips with the tip of her tongue. 'I am Lady Carleton, and I am travelling with my husband.'

'Indeed?' The man grinned his disbelief. 'And where's your husband, then?'

He made a threatening move towards her, stopping as his companion called a warning. His gaze shifted to the figure of a man who had just appeared, and Louise sighed with relief as she saw Raphael.

'Here is my husband now, m'sieur,' she said.

Raphael walked slowly towards them, his hand resting lightly on his sword. He halted after a few paces, a cool smile on his lips as he took in the scene.

'Good afternoon, gentlemen,' he said, in a deceptively pleasant voice. 'I see you have already met my wife.'

'We'd better go, Henri,' the man who was still mounted called, but his companion remained where he was, his eyes narrowing.

'We have reason to believe this young woman is a Huguenot, and a criminal fleeing from justice. There's a reward for her capture, see?'

'No, I do not see,' Raphael said, his mouth tightening as he noted the greed in the other's face. 'You have made a mistake, m'sieur. This lady is my wife, and we are travelling through France under the protection of the Queen Mother. I have a pass signed by Madame Catherine herself.'

'I'd like to see that . . .' Henri began, but he was interrupted by an agitated shout from his companion.

'Come on, Henri, we don't want no trouble.'

Henri hesitated for a moment, then shrugged his shoulders. 'Your pardon, m'sieur. It seems we made a mistake.'

'It seems you have.' Raphael moved his hand impatiently on his sword-hilt, standing where he was until the man climbed into the saddle and rode off with his companion. Then he went to join Louise, who had not dared to move.

'I think we should leave now,' he said when the two had disappeared into the trees. 'It is more than likely that they will come back with their friends.'

She shivered, recalling the malicious look in the merchant's face when he had thought her alone. 'Did you really have a pass signed by Madame Catherine?'

'No.'

'What would you have done if he had insisted on seeing it?'

'I should have had to kill him.'

The colour drained from her face. 'It was my fault for wandering away like that. I am sorry to have put you to the trouble of searching for me.'

The unusual meekness in her voice made Raphael look at her quickly. Noticing the tear-stains on her pale cheeks, he asked, 'Are you ill? They have not harmed you?'

She shook her head. 'No. It is merely that I know I have been a burden to you, and—and I am sorry.'

'You have been crying.' His eyes glittered beneath the half-closed lids. 'Was it because of what I did last night, Louise? I have given you my word that it will not happen again.'

She could not tell him that she had been crying because he had called for another woman in his sleep, and that it was breaking her heart because she loved him.

She turned away as she lied. 'I—I was thinking of my brother . . .'

'Ah yes, the gallant André.'

There was something in his voice that made her look at him sharply. 'It was brave of André to come for me,' she said defensively as she saw the mocking gleam in his eyes.

'Perhaps.' He looked at her intently. 'Have you

considered that your brother might have had reasons
of his own for returning to the house that night?'

'That's a despicable thing to say! What other reason
could he have had?'

Raphael shrugged. 'I thought perhaps you would
know?'

'No. No, I don't . . .' Louise faltered as she recalled
something André had said when he came to fetch her.
The suspicion that he might have been worried about the
jewels entrusted to her by the Seigneur entered her
mind, but she crushed it at once as unworthy. André had
come for *her*!

Her eyes glinted angrily as she swept past the Englishman, and she barely thanked him as he helped her to
mount. It was unjust of him to question André's
motives, and she wouldn't entertain such a thought.

'I am ready,' she said. 'Let us waste no more time.'

'Good,' Raphael replied coldly. 'Keep up with me. I
intend to put as much distance between us and this place
by nightfall as I can.'

Louise looked down into the face of the man who came
to help her to dismount, looking for some sign of warmth
or understanding. There was none, and she had nothing
to help her to guess what was in his mind. It seemed that
he was still angry, though her own temper had cooled
long ago. She sighed, wishing that she could reach
through the barrier he had erected between them.

'I shall tell the innkeeper you are tired,' Raphael said,
his eyes moving over her pale face. 'I believe you are in
no danger now, but it would be best to go straight to your
room and lock the door. I shall bring your supper
myself . . .' He smiled wryly as he saw her eyelids
flicker. 'Do not fear, Louise! I shall be quite sober.'

She nodded dumbly, wanting to tell him that after her
encounter with the merchants in the wood, she would
feel safer if he shared her room, but she did not know
how to begin. Following Raphael into the inn, she

listened as he made arrangements for the night, explaining to the innkeeper that his wife was unwell and that they would require two rooms for the night.

'Yes, m'sieur.' The man bowed low before Raphael, his manner respectful. 'I shall prepare your supper myself, and Michelle will conduct madame to her room.' He beckoned to a young serving-wench, telling her to show Louise to their best chamber.

The girl curtsied to her, asking if she would follow her upstairs. Louise agreed, her eyes dark with exhaustion. It was no lie to say she was unwell, she thought ruefully: her head was aching and she felt weak from lack of food. It was an effort for her to answer the girl's cheerful chattering as they walked up together, and Louise could only be grateful that she was not faced with her suspicious hostess of the previous evening.

Pausing at the top of the stairs to glance back as the front door opened, letting in a sudden gust of cool air, Louise saw a man enter. He stood for a moment beneath the light of a hanging lantern, and she stiffened, feeling a prickling sensation in the nape of her neck. There was a familiarity about the set of his shoulders that made her think she had seen him before, yet she could not remember where or when. He was not one of the men who had been waiting for her in the gardens of the Louvre, she was reasonably certain of that. But she had seen him recently.

The man moved away into the parlour and was lost to sight. Louise hurried after the serving-girl, telling herself she must have been mistaken. Having been through so much these past few days, she was starting at shadows. And yet she was sure she had seen the traveller somewhere . . .

'Here is your room, madame. I hope you will be comfortable here?'

Louise glanced around the chamber; it was clean and well furnished. 'Yes, I am sure I shall.' She made an effort to smile at the girl. 'Thank you. I shall tell my—my husband to give you something for your trouble.'

The girl curtsied and went out. As the door closed behind her, Louise sank to the edge of the bed, feeling too weary to remove her cloak.

She was still sitting there when Raphael arrived with her supper tray. He stood for a moment in the doorway, regarding her with a frown. Then he came into the room, setting his burden down on the table beside the bed.

'Take off your cloak, Louise. You must eat, and then you may rest.' He absorbed the signs of strain in her face. 'What is troubling you? Did those men frighten you so much?'

'No . . .' she whispered, biting her lower lip to stop it from trembling. 'It is only that I am tired, my lord. I shall try to eat a little if you will stay with me for a moment.'

'You must not be afraid,' he said, a tiny pulse beating in his temple as he saw the dark shadows beneath her eyes. 'Our host is sympathetic to your cause, so you can sleep safely in your bed tonight.'

'I am not afraid,' Louise repeated. She looked up at him suddenly, her eyes full of a silent appeal. 'I know you are angry with me, but I cannot bear it when you look at me so coldly. I—I do not want to quarrel with you, my lord.'

'I am not angry with you, Louise.' Raphael gently untied the strings of her cloak, pushing it back so that it fell from her shoulders. 'It is I who should apologise to you for my behaviour last night. I swear it shall never happen again.' He placed one finger beneath her chin, tipping it delicately towards him. 'Do you believe me?'

'Yes . . .' She blushed. 'I fear I was in part to blame for the way you behaved as you did last night. I had been cold to you for no true reason.'

'Indeed, your obvious distrust has angered me many times.' Raphael raised his brows. 'What had I done that you should complain of me to that virago?'

She looked at him in surprise. 'I am sorry if she burnt

your supper, my lord. It was but a ruse to distract her
from asking about the troubles in Paris. I told her my
husband was not kind to me; I did not need to say more.'

'Ah, now I understand.' A gleam of mockery lit his
eyes. 'If I were in truth your husband, I should beat you
for telling tales to that sharp-tongued scold. I vow I
thought she meant to take a broom to me!'

A ripple of laughter ran through her. 'I believe she
frightened you, m'sieur!'

'I ran in terror from her outrage,' Raphael retorted,
thinking how beautiful she looked when she laughed.
Her hair shone like burnished copper in the candlelight,
and her skin was as soft as silk. He ached to take her in
his arms and feel the cool satin of her naked flesh pressed
against his, but now was not the time. He was not sure
that that day would ever come. There was blood between them, and more blood must be shed if justice were
to be done. The laughter left his face and he was
suddenly serious. 'I willingly forgive you—if you will
forgive me? Have I forfeited all right to your trust,
Louise?'

Her startled eyes flew to his, and she quivered to hear
the softer note in his voice. 'I want to trust you, my lord,
but—but I cannot forget that I gave you a note and
you did nothing to prevent the murder of my kinsman.
How can I believe in you, when I do not understand
this?'

'I spoke to the Admiral myself before I left Paris,' he
said quietly. 'I am unable to prove what I say, Louise. I
can only ask you to believe me.'

She looked up into his face. 'Yes, I do believe you,'
she said at last. 'Why did he not heed your warning and
leave the city at once?'

'The King had given him his personal protection.'
Raphael shrugged his shoulders. 'I think perhaps he did
not believe me. I tried to locate Pierre de Guise in order
to discover if he had sent the note, but there was no trace
of him . . .'

He paused, and Louise drew a sharp breath, instinctively knowing that he was keeping something from her. 'Marie told me that Pierre had not been seen for several days at Court. Do you know where he went?'

His eyes narrowed. 'I had hoped to keep it from you until you recovered from the shock of your father's death . . .'

'Pierre is dead?' Louise gasped as she guessed what he was about to say. 'Oh no! Why? Was it because he tried to warn me?'

'I did not want to give you this anguish, but I have known it since before we left my cousin's house. His body was found beneath some bushes in the woods outside Paris. I believe he was murdered as he waited for you that night, and his body carried away to conceal the crime.'

Louise felt the tears choking her as she recalled the sweetness of the young courtier's smile. He had loved her, and because of his love he had tried to help her. Now he was dead. She covered her face with her hands, close to despair as she thought of all those who had died in the past few days.

'Why did they kill him?' she whispered. 'He was only a boy . . . Who would want to do such a terrible thing?'

Raphael did not answer at once. If the half-formed suspicion in his mind was correct, he knew he could never tell her the truth. They were both of them caught in a mesh of lies, and as yet he could not see how either of them could ever be free.

'I cannot answer your question,' he said at last, 'because I do not know where the truth lies. All I can be sure of is that Pierre died that night—and we know someone tried to abduct you. Those men in the forest today were looking for someone in particular, and I believe it may well have been you. I think someone is offering a reward for your capture.'

'But why?' Louise stared at him, her eyes dark with anguish. 'Who would gain by abducting me? I know my father was wealthy—but I have a brother who will inherit most of the estate . . .' Louise gulped as she realised she did not know whether André was alive or dead.

'I wish I knew. I shall not feel secure until you are safely home.' He was not certain that the danger would be over then, but he could not speak until he had proof of his suspicions, and, even so, she might not believe him. He could only hope that his decision to take her to La Rochelle had been the right one. It had been a gamble, but not one he had taken lightly, for both their lives could hang on the turn of a card.

'So whoever it was could try again?' Louise raised her anxious eyes to his. 'I—I saw someone this evening . . .'

'You saw someone you know here?' Raphael looked at her sharply. 'Why did you not tell me at once?'

'I—I wasn't sure.' Louise twisted her hands nervously in her lap. 'A man came in as I paused at the head of the stairs. I feel I have seen him somewhere before, but I don't know who he is or where I saw him.'

'Describe him to me.'

'Tall—but not as tall as you.' She wrinkled her brow as she tried to remember the details. 'His hair is brown, and he wears a cloak of wine-coloured velvet—and his left shoulder is slightly lower than his right. That was what made me notice him tonight.'

Raphael stood up, his face grim. 'I shall discover if our friend is still here. Lock your door after me, Louise.' He walked to the door, pausing to glance back at her. 'I promise no harm will come to you—you may sleep in peace.'

There was something she had not told him. Louise thought of the jewels concealed in her bodice, and wondered if she ought to have confided in him. However, no one could know she was carrying a fortune on her person, and it could have nothing to do with the abduction attempt in Paris.

Sighing, Louise began to eat her supper. It was a

simple meal of cold meat, cheese, fresh bread and wine, but it was wholesome and she was hungry. She ate it all and drained her wine cup; then she lay down on the bed, feeling too tired to undress.

Louise slept until late in the morning, her whole body feeling rested when she awoke. Having washed in cold water and tidied her hair, she looked down at her creased gown with distaste. Once she reached her home, she would never wear it again!

A discreet knocking at her door announced the arrival of the serving-girl who had looked after her the previous evening. She smiled and curtsied as Louise opened the door, telling her that a meal was awaiting her downstairs in the parlour, where Lord Carleton would meet her.

Thanking her, Louise picked up her cloak and went out. She did now know why it was, but her heart felt much lighter this morning, as if the terrible ache had begun to ease at last. Raphael was standing by the parlour window, seemingly absorbed in the view, but he smiled and came to greet her as she entered.

'You look as if you slept well,' he said. 'I let you rest a little longer this morning. We have only one more night on the road. Tomorrow you will be home, Louise.'

'Yes.' She looked at him anxiously. 'Did you see the stranger I told you of last night?'

He nodded. 'Briefly. He stayed for a meal, and then left. I think you must have been mistaken in believing you had seen him before.'

'Perhaps I was.' Somehow it did not seem to matter this morning.

'We must be on our guard, nevertheless,' Raphael said. 'This man could be cleverer than we imagine. If you see him again, you will tell me at once?'

'Yes, of course.'

He smiled and came to place a chair for her at the table. 'Our host has provided a goodly feast for us. Will you not try some of this delicious ham—or perhaps a little fruit?'

She glanced at him shyly, not quite sure what to make of his courtly attentions. This was a different man, quite unlike the one she had become accustomed to. His hand brushed hers as he offered her a cup of wine, and a shiver of delight went through her. It was almost as though he had decided to court her! A faint blush brought a pretty colour to her cheeks. She had always known he would be irresistible if he chose to use his charm to seduce her, and already her heart was racing wildly. Casting down her eyes, Louise told herself she must not let him guess how much his attentions pleased her. She must remember that he was by his own admission a man who used women for his pleasure, discarding them as soon as they no longer interested him.

She looked down at the table, concentrating on her breakfast as Raphael began to make polite conversation, describing his home to her. As he talked, her curiosity was aroused and she glanced across the table.

'Where exactly is your home in England, my lord?'

'My estates border a great forest in the county of Hampshire. At this time of the year the trees are a rainbow of colour; the leaves beginning to turn bronze, purple and gold before they fall. In the winter, the deer come nearly up to the house in search of food. While my mother lived she would never allow us to hunt them, so they have become almost tame. For myself, I prefer to fly the hawks—there is more skill in the sport.

Louise laughed. 'I have never dared to admit this to anyone, but I hate to see a stag killed. The thrill of the chase is exciting, but I take no pleasure from watching a magnificent beast being slaughtered.'

'My mother would have approved of you,' Raphael said, and something in his tone made her look at him curiously.

'You loved her very much, didn't you?'

'Adored her—hated her.' The lazy lids veiled his eyes

from her. 'She was an exceptional woman. After my
father died—when I was perhaps five or six—she took a
succession of lovers to satisfy her lust, but she never
married again. In her own way, I think she believed she
was faithful to his memory.'

The bitterness in his voice hurt Louise. She longed to
go to him and put her arms round him, but she knew she
dared not. 'Would you have preferred her to marry
again?'

'No, I suppose I wanted her to remain on the pedestal
my father had built for her. I remembered how much he
worshipped her.' Raphael almost seemed to be mocking him himself. 'I was an idealistic youth, you see—
but I learned my lessons well. She was a woman, not a
goddess. I expected too much of her.'

It was there again, the hard core of bitterness inside
him that had made him the man he was. For a short while
he had appeared to have forgotten his past; he had let
down the barriers, speaking of his home as though he
would like to take her there one day. Now the shutters
were in place, a look of self-mockery again in his eyes.

Pushing away her plate, Louise felt the pain deep
inside her. There were things in this man's past of which
she could know nothing. Something—some woman—
had hurt him badly, making him incapable of love, so
how could she hope for anything from him? Even to let
herself dream of a future with him was to lay herself
open to pain, and yet the dream was with her constantly.
She got to her feet, walking to the window to gaze out
blindly as she fought her tears.

'It is time we were on our way,' she said in a muffled
tone. 'I should like to reach La Rochelle as soon as
possible.'

'Yes, we should be leaving,' Raphael agreed. 'Excuse
me. I must settle with our host.'

Louise did not turn as he left the room. Brushing her
hand across her eyes, she cursed her own weakness. No
matter what happened, she must hide her true feelings

A DIAMOND ZIRCONIA NECKLACE ABSOLUTELY FREE!

Dear Susan,

Your special introductory offer of 12 FREE BOOKS is too good to miss. Please will you also reserve a Reader Service Subscription for me so that I will receive 12 brand new Mills & Boon Romances each month for £14.40, post and packing free. If I decide not to subscribe, I shall write to you within 10 days. The free books and necklace will be mine to keep in any case. I understand that I may cancel or suspend my subscription at any time. I am over 18 years of age.

Yours FREE this beautiful
diamond zirconia necklace

Name_____

Address_____

_____ Postcode_____

10A6TB

Offer applies in the UK and Eire, overseas send for details. Mills & Boon Ltd. reserve the right to exercise discretion in granting membership. Should a price change become necessary you will be notified. You may be mailed with other offers as a result of this application. Offer expires 31st March 1987.

Susan Welland
Mills & Boon
Reader Service
FREEPOST
P.O. Box 236
CROYDON
Surrey CR9 9EL

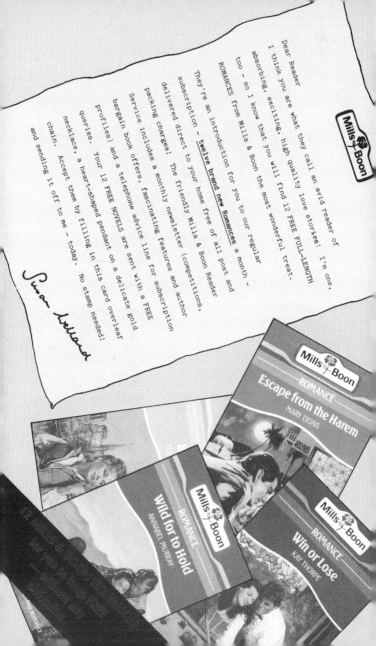

Mills & Boon

Dear Reader

I think you are what they call an avid reader of ROMANCES from Mills & Boon the most wonderful treat. absorbing, exciting, high quality love stories! I'm one, too - so I know that you will find 12 FREE FULL-LENGTH

They're an introduction for you to our regular subscription - **twelve brand new Romances** a month delivered direct to your home free of all post and packing charges! The friendly Mills & Boon Reader Service includes a monthly newsletter (competitions, bargain book offers, fascinating features and author profiles) and a telephone advice line for subscription queries. Your 12 FREE NOVELS are sent with a FREE necklace, a heart-shaped pendant on a delicate gold chain. Accept them by filling in this card overleaf and sending it off to me - today. No stamp needed!

Susan Welland

Mills & Boon
ROMANCE
Escape from the Harem
MARY LYONS

Mills & Boon
ROMANCE
Wild for to Hold
ANNABEL MURRAY

Mills & Boon
ROMANCE
Win or Lose
KAY THORPE

from him. Pride came to her aid. Their journey was almost over; she could hold out for another two days, and after that the temptation would end. Lord Carleton would return to England, and she would honour her father's promise to the Chevalier de Leconte.

Lifting her chin proudly, she went out into the courtyard.

CHAPTER SEVEN

RAPHAEL SIGNALLED ahead, pointing towards the small inn almost hidden among the trees. Louise stared at it with mixed feelings, smothering a sigh. It was late in the evening and she was tired, but there was an air of neglect about the place that made her feel uneasy.

'Do you think it wise to stay here for the night?' she asked doubtfully, reining in to look across at him.

'It has a seedy appearnce, I grant you, but we might travel for hours and find nothing better,' Raphael said, glancing quickly over his shoulder. 'Besides, I have felt for some time that we are being followed . . . No, do not turn round, Louise. He cannot be far behind us.'

She looked at him, her eyes widening with fright. 'How do you know?'

'I think it is the man you told me of the other evening. I have three times caught a fleeting glimpse of him through the trees since it began to grow dark. He has kept a distance between us during the day, but now he becomes careless.'

'Why does he not attack us openly if he means us harm?'

'Perhaps he has heard I have some skill with the sword. Last night we were protected by our honest host: I believe that is why he went away as he did. Tonight we must both be on our guard.'

'What shall we do?' She shivered.

'Do not be afraid, Louise.' Raphael smiled at her grimly. 'I shall kill him before I let harm come to you—but I think we must try to discover why this man is following us. It may be that he is merely a common thief hoping to catch us unawares—or he could be concerned in the plot to abduct you.'

They had ridden into the inn courtyard by now, and Louise gazed into his face as he came to help her to dismount. 'Tell me what to do,' she said earnestly, 'and I shall do it.'

His gaze softened as he saw the brightness of her eyes. 'Trust me, Louise, no matter what I do. We shall take our supper in the inn parlour tonight. Try to act naturally. If this man comes in, do not let him suspect we know he has been following us. Remember always that we are travelling as man and wife.'

She felt the reassuring pressure of his hand on her arm as an ostler came reluctantly from the warmth of the stables to take their horses. He was yawning and had obviously been sleeping in the straw, pieces of which still clung to his hair and clothes. His face wore a sullen look, but his manner became instantly more amenable when Raphael pressed a silver coin into his dirty palm, promising more in the morning if their horses were well cared for.

'Yes, m'sieur. I'll tend them as if they were my own,' the man promised, bowing low before leading the horses into the stables.

'We must be prepared to leave at any time,' Raphael said as they walked towards the inn. 'Sleep in your clothes—and do not be alarmed if I appear to drink more wine than is wise at supper. If I quarrel with you, it is a signal for you to go at once to your room and lock the door. Open it only if I ask you to. Do you understand?'

'Yes. I shall do exactly as you say.' She gave him a tremulous smile. 'I am not afraid when you are with me.'

Raphael smiled down at her but made no comment. They walked into the inn, and Louise's nose wrinkled as she smelt the odour of stale wine. Glancing about her with distaste, she saw that the floor was unswept and some of the wooden tables were strewn with dirty pots.

'Forgive me for bringing you to such a place, but I had no choice,' Raphael murmured. 'We are safer here than on the road, I think, though I dare swear the beds are crawling with vermin.'

'Tomorrow I shall burn my clothes,' Louise replied with a grimace. 'Do not concern yourself—vile though it is, it will suffice for tonight.'

Raphael chuckled. 'It is well for me that you are not as ill tempered as some ladies of my acquaintance—most of whom would refuse to step inside such a house.'

Like Louise, he was disgusted by all he saw, but he managed to hide his feelings as their host approached, bowing in a servile manner.

'We shall dine in your parlour, m'sieur,' he drawled, his eyes half-closed as if in boredom. 'Be so good as to have your best room prepared for us.'

'Certainly, your honour.' The landlord regarded him from bright, close-set eyes. 'You shall have everything of the finest, your lordship. There's a fat goose on the spit, and pigeons dressed with wine and herbs.'

'You keep a good table here,' Raphael replied, a little surprised. 'I trust your wine will do the food justice?'

The man's eyes gleamed with greed, scenting a fat profit from his wealthy customer. He bowed low as he led the way into the parlour, which was empty save for a cat sleeping by the hearth.

'Sit here by the window, your honour,' he said. 'Supper will be ready soon—and I shall bring you a jug of my best wine to ease your thirst while you wait.'

'See to it.' Raphael waved his dismissal. 'My wife is tired. She will retire as soon as we have eaten.'

The man assured him that all would be ready. After he had left the room, Raphael set a chair for Louise so that her back was turned to the doorway, taking up a position on a bench exactly opposite. Hearing voices outside, he gave her a warning look.

'They are coming,' he said quietly. 'Do not look round . . . And remember what we arranged earlier.'

Louise nodded, feeling a tense knot form in her stomach. The sound of footsteps drawing nearer heralded their host's arrival, together with the new-comer. It took all the girl's will-power to keep from turning round to stare at the man she suspected of following them.

'Make yourself comfortable, m'sieur,' the innkeeper said, his tone a trifle less respectful than it had been when speaking to his first customers of the evening. 'I shall take your order in a moment.' He came to where Louise was sitting, setting a jug of wine and two pewter cups on the table. 'Your supper will be here soon, your honour.'

Raphael nodded. He poured wine into both cups, draining the contents of one with a flourish and instantly refilling it.

'Your wine is good, landlord,' he commented. 'You may bring more later.'

'Yes, your lordship, certainly.'

The landlord went off to serve his other customer. For a moment, his bulk blocked any view of the stranger. In that instant, Raphael winked at Louise and tossed the contents of his wine-cup out of the open window, raising the empty vessel to his lips as their host hurried off to the kitchen. He refilled his cup again and drank half the wine, topping it up at once as if he could not wait to finish the jug off and call for more.

By watching their fellow-traveller from beneath lowered lids, Raphael was able to dispose of some of the wine he was supposedly drinking by tipping it into a crevice where the oak bench adjoined the wall. Thus he was able to empty the jug by the time the host returned with their meal.

'You were thirsty, your honour,' the landlord remarked as he set down a full jug. 'Will you require more wine?'

'Certainly.' Raphael waved him away, turning his eyes to Louise. 'Eat your supper, wife, and do not look at me so reproachfully.'

Louise blinked at the suddenness of his attack, eating

a few mouthfuls of the goose before replying. 'You are imagining things, husband. Why should I reproach you?'

'I saw the way you pulled up your mouth just now.' Raphael scowled at her. 'Surely a man is entitled to a little pleasure at the end of a weary day?'

Louise was glad that her back was turned towards the stranger, for she was sure he would have read her mind with ease. Her eyes danced with laughter as Raphael appeared to drain his wine-cup once more.

'Pleasure is one thing, husband,' she said in a severe voice. 'You drink too much wine for my comfort.'

'Your comfort, madame! You have done nothing but complain all day: the sun is too hot, the wind too cold—and now I am drinking too much! I vow you try my patience sorely . . .'

'Then I shall do so no more.' Louise pushed away the remains of her supper. 'I wish you good night, husband. Pray do not disturb me when you come to bed—if you come to bed!' She stood up and swept from the room, a picture of outraged dignity.

Raphael conquered the urge to laugh, scowling into his wine-cup as if he were truly the hen-pecked husband he made himself out to be. 'Women,' he muttered moodily. 'I vow they are the devil's own invention. Do you not agree, m'sieur?' Raising his head, he looked across at the stranger.

The man started, seeming at a loss for words; then he shrugged his shoulders, saying gruffly, 'I have never married, m'sieur—nor am I like to do so.'

'You are wiser than I,' Raphael shook his head ruefully. 'It is not worth the loss of freedom—a wife's scolding tongue lasts longer than her beauty.'

'As you say.' The stranger frowned, as if he did not wish to continue the conversation. At the landlord's approach with his supper, he turned his head aside, giving all his attention to the food in front of him.

Raphael's eyes glinted with a cold anger, then he snapped his fingers imperiously. 'More wine,' he said, slurring his words as if his brain was already affected by the drink he had taken. 'And be quick about it, landlord.'

Louise opened her eyes to find it was still dark. She had meant to stay awake until Raphael came, but her lids had grown heavy as the hours passed and she had at last fallen into an uneasy slumber. Now, for a moment, she lay staring into the gloom, wondering why her heart was beating so fast. What had caused her to wake with a start?

Suddenly she heard a faint sound from somewhere at the foot of her bed, and her limbs froze in terror. There was someone in her room! She was about to cry out and ask if it was Raphael, when instinct stopped her. She recalled quite clearly locking her door, and she knew from experience that he would have found a way to wake her if he wanted to enter.

Her eyes strained towards where she had last heard a sound, and as her vision accustomed itself to the semi-darkness, she could just make out the figure of a man. He was moving stealthily about the room, as if trying not to disturb her, and he appeared to be searching for something in the saddle-bags Raphael had sent up to the room when they arrived.

Louise lay absolutely still, hardly daring to breathe as she watched the man pick up her cloak and examine it. She was sure it must be the same one who had been following them for the last two days—and she believed she knew what he was looking for. Somehow he had learned that she was carrying a fortune in jewels. How could he know? She was sure her father had told no one else—and she had taken great care that none of the servants should see her sewing them into her bodice.

A rush of cold air from the open window drew Louise's attention. The intruder had neglected to fasten it after forcing his entry, and she could see beyond the moving curtains to the balcony. They had been tightly drawn when she was shown into her room, and she had been so tired that it had not occurred to her to make sure the windows were securely fastened. How careless she had been!

A spurt of fear shot through her as the man suddenly stopped moving about the room and stood still, as if listening intently. Had she made a sound without realising it? Her nails clawed at the sheets as the intruder turned deliberately towards the bed. He was coming for her! Caution fled as she recalled the terrible attack she had experienced in the woods. She could not bear to go through that again!

She sat bolt upright in bed and screamed as loudly as she could. The shadowy figure beside her was immobilised by the suddenness of her action. As he hesitated, uncertain, another figure burst through the open window, launching itself at him.

The intruder reacted instinctively. Turning swiftly, he ran for the door, fumbling with the key in his haste to get away, obviously not wanting to get involved in a fight. He was brought down by a flying leap from his pursuer, grunting and cursing as he put up a belated struggle.

Louise jumped out of bed, watching the fight in the gloom as the two men went crashing about the room, bumping into a wooden stool and sending it clattering across the floor. Muffled groans and thuds reached her ears as she strained to discover who was winning the contest. Recalling the candlestick beside the bed, she struck a tinder and lit the flame just in time to see Raphael land an almighty blow on the skull of the stranger. The man gave a cry, and slumped unconscious beneath him.

'Damn, I hit him too hard!' Raphael said ruefully, looking as if in surprise at the edge of the stool with which he had struck the blow. 'I think I may have killed him.' He knelt on the floor by the still figure, feeling for a heartbeat. 'No, I was wrong: he still lives.'

He unbuckled the stranger's belt, using it to bind his

hands behind his back. 'I would take him with us, but probably he is just a common thief. I'm not sure what he expected to find—or why he thought it worth while to follow us all this time.'

Louise blushed, holding out her hand to him. 'Lend me your knife for a moment, my lord.'

'My knife—why?' He looked puzzled, giving it to her reluctantly.

'I want to show you something . . . Something I should have told you about from the start.'

His eyes narrowed, and he watched in silence as she removed her velvet over-bodice, slitting the thick lining with a deft stroke.

'I have remembered at last where I saw this man,' she said, inserting her fingers into the opening to pull out a necklace of large white diamonds. 'It was one morning after you had left Paris, and he was talking with a groom in the courtyard of the house in the Rue Saint-Denis. I had thought no one knew I was carrying these—but one of the servants must have been listening when my father entrusted them to me.'

Raphael took the necklace from her, his brows lifting as he saw their size and clarity. 'These are worth a great deal of money, Louise!'

'Yes, I know. I have more besides. My father gave them to me before he left to meet the Admiral that last morning. I wondered why he should have asked me to hide them, but I think he must have realised there was a danger of something happening to him. I hid them in my bodice so that I could carry them and no one would suspect I had anything of value with me.'

'No wonder you insisted on keeping your own gown when my cousin offered you a fresh one! I think you are right: this man must have learned of the jewels and decided to follow you. Perhaps it was only by chance that he met us on the road—or he may have seen me when I went back to the house the day after the massacre.' Raphael looked thoughtful. 'I did not tell you that the house had been ransacked because I thought it would distress you unnecessarily. I had intended to fetch some of your belongings—but everything had been ripped to pieces. Now I see why. It was not the work of the mob, but of someone who was looking for something in particular.'

'Yes. That is a relief! Then his appearance here tonight can have nothing to do with what happened in the Louvre gardens?'

'If I thought he was concerned with that, I would have to question him before I killed him.'

'Oh no!' Louise looked at him in horror. 'You do not mean to kill this man, my lord? He is merely a thief; you said so yourself. He cannot harm us now. Tomorrow we shall reach my home, and the jewels will be restored to my father's strong-room. Please, I beg you, spare him for my sake.'

Raphael hesitated as he saw the whiteness of her face. He knew she had been greatly shocked by what she had witnessed the day before, and he was almost convinced that the intruder had been after the jewels. He believed his own ruse in allowing the stranger to believe he was slumped on the bench in the parlour, a pitiful victim of strong wine, had given the man the courage and opportunity to force an entry into Louise's room. He had waited a few minutes after the man had left the parlour, shadowing him as he made his way out of the inn and through the dark courtyard. He had seemed to know which window he sought, an indication that their landlord might have had a hand in the villainy. Watching from below, he had seen the intruder climb up to the balcony and pry open the shutters. He had followed silently and swiftly, a witness from the balcony as their friend made a thorough search of the room, wanting to discover just why he had thought it necessary to go to such lengths. It was only Louise's scream that had brought him crashing through the open window a little too soon. Now he could not be sure just what the

stranger had been after, and he thought it best to kill him
in case his intentions had been other than mere robbery.

As he remained silent, Louise went up to him,
touching his arm. 'There has been enough killing, my
lord. I beg you not to shed this man's blood. He has done
me no real harm, and his death would weigh heavily on
my conscience.'

'Very well.' Raphael allowed himself to be persuaded.
'We must leave here before he wakes and causes us more
trouble. It will soon be light, and if we leave now we shall
be sure of reaching La Rochelle by midday.'

'Thank you.' Louise replaced the jewels in her bodice
and handed it to him. 'Will you forgive me for not telling
you about these before?'

He smiled oddly as she held the bundle out to him.
'Does this mean you have decided to trust me at last?'

'I was foolish to doubt you. Without your help, I
should have died in Paris!' She smiled up at him, and
for a moment her eyes glowed with love. 'Will you
keep these for me, please? I shall feel safer if you have
them.'

'As you wish.' His hand touched hers briefly, and she
saw a spark of fire in his eyes. It died swiftly, to be
replaced by a rueful expression she did not understand.
'Come, we must go quickly. I think I hear our host
stirring below, and I do not trust him. We shall pay him
what we owe—but say nothing of our uninvited guest. I
think we shall let him rest in peace until he is discovered.
We want no more surprises from him!'

The sky was streaked with the first fingers of a rosy dawn
as they rode away from the inn. It was the last stage of
their journey, and Louise knew she should be feeling
relieved, but her heart was heavy. She was sure Raphael
would leave for England as soon as he had seen her
safely home, and she did not want him to go.

At first the roads were quiet, but as the light
strengthened, they passed several riders and carts drawn

by oxen, piled high with vegetables. Now Louise could see the landmarks she recognised.

'We shall soon reach the city, my lord. My father has a house there. We should perhaps call in for any news before we go on to his estate.'

'You might be wiser to remain within the city walls. I suspect that your people will demand satisfaction for the recent outrages: it will mean war, unless I am mistaken.'

Shadows clouded her face and there was a suspicion of tears in her eyes as she looked at him. 'I fear you are right,' she whispered chokily. 'Will there never be an end to it all? France has already suffered three civil wars in the name of religion—how long must it go on?'

'As long as men use intolerance as a means of holding others in a subservient position. Power is the real cause of France's troubles. The Catholics deny the Huguenots the right to hold important office in the land, and this leads to jealousy and dissension. While both sides struggle to achieve superiority, there will be constant strife. The Admiral was murdered because those who rule feared his influence on the King. Charles is a weak boy, who is prone to fits of insanity. Only a strong king could control the opposing factions sufficiently to bring peace. It is a pity that Navarre was not born to be France's ruler. I believe there is strength in that young man.'

Louise stared at him, respect mixed with wonder. He had answered her questions fully, speaking to her as though she were a man, and his equal. It was the first time in her life that anyone had taken the trouble to listen and explain what she wanted to know. Her father would have ignored her question, or told her not to worry her pretty head over things that did not concern her, while André would have sneered at her. She listened attentively to Raphael as he continued speaking.

'In the event of a war, you should try to reach the city, Louise. La Rochelle is a stronghold the royalist armies will find difficult to breach. If the burghers stand firm, you need never surrender.'

'I—I shall remember what you have said, my lord. Thank you for your advice.' She could not look at him as she fought to contain the tide of emotion that swept over her. How could she bear to part from him now that she had at long last realised how much he meant to her? 'How—How soon will you have to leave for England?'

He was silent for a moment, then, 'I have some unfinished business in France that may keep me here for a while. Certainly, I shall not leave until I know you are settled with your grandmother.'

Was he saying he would stay with her for a time? Louise glanced at his face, trying to understand the strange expression she saw there. Despite all that had happened between them on the journey, she was no closer to understanding this man. He was a creature of moods, often changing as swiftly as a wilful breeze in the treetops; but she knew he could be both kind and gentle, and his smile set her heart racing like the white horses on the sea which swirled about the cliffs beneath La Rochelle.

The stronghold of the Huguenots was a maritime city, and for some time now the travellers had caught glimpses of the ocean. Glittering in the sunlight, the foaming water was suddenly before them as they rounded a curve in the road; there in the distance was the place of her birth, and Louise smiled excitedly as she leaned forward over her horse's neck to point towards the towers and spires of the ancient walled city. A new urgency stirred in her and she gave her mount a little flick with the reins. She was almost home!

Understanding the girl's nostalgic mood, Raphael spurred his horse to keep pace with hers. Soon they were riding through the open gates of the city. Now Louise was leading the way, pointing out buildings she thought might interest him. Their horses' hooves clattered on cobbled stones, becoming part of the general noise and bustle. Carts rumbled by, crowding the narrow streets and adding to the general confusion. Everyone seemed to be in a hurry, and men stood in large groups at the corners of the streets, gesticulating and talking loudly. It was quite clear that the news of the massacre in Paris had reached the citizens of La Rochelle long before the two of them.

Louise heard the names of other cities on the lips of passers-by; but it was not until Raphael questioned some of the burghers that she learned of the terrible killings in cities such as Rouen and Bordeaux. It seemed now that what she had imagined to be a spontaneous uprising in Paris had in reality been an act of war, for the other massacres had taken place almost simultaneously.

The news took away any pleasure Louise might have found in returning to her home. She realised that Raphael was right: the citizens of La Rochelle were bitterly angry at what had been done to their brethren. Talk of war was everywhere, and she knew it was merely a matter of time. The good people of La Rochelle were already intent on raising the militia.

It was clear that with both her father and André dead, her duty would be to Madame de Granvelle and to the estate. Alone, she would find it difficult to survive the hardships of war. For the sake of her grandmother, she must marry as quickly as possible. Since the Chevalier de Leconte had left Paris before the murders began, it was highly likely that he had survived. No doubt, Madame de Granvelle would know where he could be reached if he did not immediately come forward to claim his bride.

Had André lived, Louise was certain the bulk of her father's estate would have passed to him as the only son. She was not sure what provisions the Seigneur had made in his will for the unlikely event of his son's early death. In any case, the marriage contract bound her to the Chevalier as tightly as if she were already his wife. It appeared that she was trapped in the meshes of a web from which she could not honourably even try to break free. Any hopes of future happiness died in her with the realisation.

Her face was white and strained as she turned to Raphael, pointing towards an imposing building at the end of the street. 'Our journey's end, m'sieur: that is my father's house.' She smiled at him, but her eyes reflected the sadness inside her. 'I fear I have been a troublesome charge to you, and I do most sincerely thank you for your care of me. Without your help, I know I would never have come this far.'

'Your safety is all that concerns me, mademoiselle.' Raphael's eyes seemed to avoid hers. 'Whatever I have done was by my own choice, without thought of reward or gratitude. I beg you to remember that.'

Louise studied his profile in a vain attempt to read the unreadable. The Englishman sounded odd, almost unsure, except that it was impossible that he should be less than completely confident. His arrogance, she saw now, was part of his strength. If she thought she noticed a fleeting uncertainty in his face, it was her imagination. It would be foolish to let herself believe that their parting might cause him some grief.

Reaching the small archway which opened out into a sheltered courtyard at the back of her home, Louise led the way through. She was immediately struck by the quietness, and a shudder ran down her spine. Where was everyone? The courtyard was normally a hive of activity as the servants bustled about their work. She looked worried as Raphael dismounted and came to help her: this was a strange homecoming.

Glancing anxiously about her, she said, 'I fear something must be wrong. The courtyard looks as if it has not been swept for several days, and there are no servants to greet us.'

'Perhaps Madame de Granvelle has gone to the château,' Raphael suggested. 'She may have realised a war was imminent, and decided to make what arrangements she could to safeguard the estate. It would be wiser to transport what stores you have inside the city to ensure that you have enough food in the event of a long siege.'

Louise nodded. 'You may be right, my lord. Yet it is strange that the house should be so quiet. Come, we should discover if anyone is still here.'

They walked up to the back entrance, which would normally have stood open to reveal the inner door beneath the portico. Today the iron grille was in place, securely locked from within. Louise stared at it in frustration, a growing unease making her hands tense into tight fists.

She tugged furiously at the bell-rope, setting off a loud clanging noise within the hall. 'My father has never closed the house like this,' she said. 'I cannot understand it.'

'Perhaps Madame de Granvelle has heard that your father was killed,' Raphael said gently, his hand resting on her arm as he saw the pain in her face. 'In her grief she may believe you, too, are dead, Louise.'

The colour drained from her cheeks. 'Oh, poor Grand'mère, how distressed she must be! I must find her quickly!'

She pulled the bell again sharply, sighing with relief as the sound of bolts being drawn told her that someone was at last coming to answer her summons.

The door swung open at last, and an old man peered out at them. He blinked in disbelief, then hurried to unlock the gate, apologising for his slowness.

'Is it really you, Mademoiselle de Granvelle? The saints be praised! We heard you were dead.' The weary eyes were suddenly bright with tears, and he kissed the hand she held out to him. 'And the master—is he with you?'

'No, Martin, I am afraid the Seigneur was killed in the massacre. We—We have seen his body laid to rest . . .' She paused as he crossed himself. 'But we have no news of my brother. Have you heard from André?' She looked at him eagerly.

The old man shook his head, standing back respectfully to allow them to enter the cool hall. Louise saw him glance curiously at Raphael, and smiled.

'This is Lord Carleton, Martin. He saved my life on Saint Bartholomew's Eve and brought me safely home.'

'God bless your lordship.' The old man bowed low before Raphael. 'The house was closed by the Seigneur's steward after—after we heard the news; but I can fetch wine if you wish it?'

'Yes, bring wine, Martin,' Louise said. 'But stay a moment . . . Can you tell me if my grandmother is at the château?'

The servant's lined face crumpled with grief. 'That I should be the one to give you such news, mistress . . .'

Louise caught his trembling hand, looking anxiously into his face. 'What news? Is my grandmother ill?'

'Forgive me,' Martin gulped, tears escaping from the corners of his eyes. 'Madame de Granvelle died five days ago. She was found in her bed when the maids went to wake her—at least she cannot have suffered. They say she looked peaceful . . .'

'Dead?' Louise whispered, feeling faint as the room spun round her. 'That cannot be!'

Raphael moved swiftly to support her as she swayed. Bending down, he took her up in his arms, holding her close to his heart as she swooned.

'Lead me to your mistress's chamber,' he barked at the old man. 'She has suffered too much, and must rest.'

'Yes, your lordship.' Martin looked worriedly at the girl's white face. 'I meant no harm to the mistress.'

'Yours is not the blame,' Raphael said as the servant hurried through the shuttered house. 'Mademoiselle de Granvelle would have had to learn the truth in time.'

The old man hobbled up the stairs at a surprising pace, throwing open the door of a room half-way along the gallery. He hesitated, looking uncertainly at Raphael.

'Shall I bring wine, m'sieur, and goose-feathers to burn under mademoiselle's nose?'

'Yes—as quickly as you can.'

As Martin hastened away, Raphael laid the unconscious girl gently on the silken covers. He untied the strings of her cloak and loosened the waist of her gown. Smoothing back the hair from her damp forehead, he touched his lips to her closed eyelids.

'It has all been too much for you, my little one,' he murmured softly. 'So you are alone in the world now, Louise.' His hand traced the pale curve of her cheek. 'Shall I risk your hatred and tell you the truth? Or shall I carry you off to England before it's too late? I wonder . . .' He had spoken in his native tongue, mystifying the servant, who had returned with the wine.

Standing up, Raphael unbuckled his sword and removed his cloak, assuming command of the household. 'I want a heated pan to air the sheets. Your mistress will need the services of a maid, and the house must be opened up again. Do you know anyone who can be trusted?'

Martin nodded eagerly, obviously thankful to have a master again. 'Yes, my lord. My granddaughter and her husband will be pleased to help—and there are others who will return as soon as word reaches them. We did not know what to do when the mistress died.'

'Good. You have been a faithful servant, Martin, and your service will be rewarded. Give me the wine and the goose-feathers, then go to your granddaughter's house. You may trust me to care for your mistress.'

Raphael lit a tinder, setting alight the feathers Martin had brought. Blowing out the flame, he waved the acrid smoke beneath Louise's nose. For a moment or two it had no effect, then she moaned, moving her head restlessly on the pillow. She suddenly choked, opening her eyes with a start.

'W-What happened?' she whispered, looking bewildered.

'You fainted.' Raphael smiled at her. 'Don't try to think about it, Louise. You are in your own room. I carried you here and I shall stay by your side until Martin's granddaughter comes to act as your maid.'

Tears filled Louise's eyes, spilling over to run down her cheeks. 'My—My grandmother is dead.'

Raphael stroked the hair back from her wet cheeks. 'She did not suffer: Martin said it was a peaceful death. Perhaps it was better for her, Louise. She did not live to learn of her son's murder.'

'Yes, it is selfish of me to weep.' Louise blinked her tears away. 'Grand'mère was a good woman. I—I believe she truly loved me, despite her stern manner. She used to cry when she punished me, though she tried to hide it.' She choked on her emotion. 'What shall I do, my lord? I—I expected Grand'mère to guide me . . .'

Raphael looked down into her frightened eyes, and mentally cursed himself for his stupidity. None of this need have happened if he had told her the truth long ago. He hesitated, wanting to banish the shadows from her eyes, but knowing that to do so at this moment might hurt her more than all the rest.

'For now you must relax, Louise,' he said, a little smile easing the lines of strain round his mouth. 'You have endured too much these past days. Soon we will talk about the future. I shall not desert you, I give you my word.'

'You will stay with me until the Chevalier de Leconte comes?' she asked hopefully.

'If that is your wish.' Raphael looked grim. 'Do you intend to marry him after all?'

'I am alone now . . .' Her lips quivered with suppressed emotion. 'What else can I do?'

Raphael was silent for a moment, and she saw a tiny pulse flick in the base of his throat. 'You could come to England with me,' he said at last.

'As—As your mistress?' Louise's eyes were wide as she gazed at him from the pillow, and something tightened in his stomach, wounding him. 'Is that what you are asking, my lord?'

'No . . .' His lids snapped down, hiding the black eyes from her. 'You would live in my house as . . . as an honoured guest. I told you once before, Louise, we should not suit. I could not dishonour you by making you my mistress, and you know my views on marriage.'

'But would my reputation not be lost if I lived in your house? Everyone would think me your mistress even if I were innocent.'

'We would tell the curious that you are my cousin. Under the circumstances, I believe no one would question your decision to leave France for the safety of England. I am sure many of your countrymen will do so. Who knows, we might even find a rich husband for you at Court . . .'

'If I leave France with you, I shall never marry,' Louise said fiercely, her cheeks flushed.

Could he not see that he was breaking her heart? She closed her eyes, holding back the tears that threatened to disgrace her.

'You are tired,' Raphael said. 'I believe I hear voices below. I shall leave you to the ministrations of your maid. We shall talk of this again another day, when you are feeling more yourself.'

Louise nodded miserably, longing for him to go so that she could weep into her pillow. Everyone would think she was grieving for her family: no one—no one!—must guess she was crying because she had given her heart to a man who could never love her.

Louise bent to lay her flowers on the fresh grave. There was sadness in her face, but she did not cry as she straightened up and looked at Raphael. She was empty of tears. The past was gone, and she knew she must begin to look to the future.

She was wearing a gown of pale lilac silk, and the colour brought out hidden highlights in her hair. Raising her clear eyes to Raphael's, she smiled. 'I fear my weakness these last few days has kept you from your business, my lord.'

'I have none of any consequence.' He offered her his arm as they left the churchyard and began to walk across the park towards the château. 'I came to France to discover the truth about something—and to keep a promise I made long ago. I have kept my promise, and the other no longer matters.'

She looked at him curiously. 'Why? If it brought you from England, it must have been important.'

'It was a whim, no more.' Raphael paused as they entered the formal gardens to look down at her. 'Shall you return to La Rochelle now that you have seen your grandmother's grave? Your steward is capable of running the estate himself—and you would be safer in the city.'

'Perhaps, in a few days.' Louise sighed. 'I prefer the freedom of the château, but—but I know your advice is good, my lord.' She licked her lips nervously. 'When —When do you leave for England?'

'Soon.' Raphael stared at a point in space somewhere above her head, knowing that the time had come to make his decision. He must tell her the truth now, or risk her hatred if she should ever discover it for herself. He took her hand gently in his. 'I have something I must say to you, Louise . . .'

Seeing the grave look in his eyes, she clutched at him desperately. 'You have heard from your servant? Oh, please do not tell me André is dead!'

At that moment, Raphael knew that he could never burden her with his suspicions. 'No, I have not heard from Tom,' he said, raising his brows in an attempt at mockery. 'I am sure your sainted brother is on his way home, Louise. I meant only to say that I would take you with me to England if you wish.'

Hurt by his sudden change of mood, she turned her face aside. 'I cannot go to England with you until I know what has happened to my brother.'

'It need only be for a few months—to help you to recover from all you have suffered. We could leave word for André if he returns. You would be safer in England if your country is embroiled in civil war.'

With all her heart Louise longed to throw herself in his arms and confess the love she bore him, but pride forbade it. He was offering to take her to England because she was alone and unhappy. He said she would be an honoured guest in his house, but how long would it be before she became his mistress? Every time he looked at her, her will seemed to melt in the heat of her love for him, and in the end it would crumble. Yet, if she sent him away, her heart would break.

She looked up into his handsome face, searching it for she knew not what. If only he would give some sign that he cared for her as a person, that she was not just another woman to him. His eyes wore that lazy, amused look she had seen so often, effectively hiding his thoughts from her.

'You must give me a little time to consider, my lord,' she said at last.

He nodded. 'As you wish, Louise—but remember I am not a patient man.'

It was nearly midnight as Raphael passed the stables. He stopped for a moment to glance up at the bright, moonlit sky. It was warm for late the summer, and he had felt trapped in the house. Louise had retired over an hour ago, and the thought of her lying alone in her bed, so close and yet so far from him, made him restless. His loins ached with the desire to claim her as his own, and it was straining his will-power to keep from going to her even now. He had the right: she was his if he chose to say the words. With one sentence he could sweep away the barriers between them and ease this burning in his guts. Yet in taking what was his, he might lose the greater prize.

He cursed aloud, angry at the way Fate had twisted their lives. If he followed his instinct, he must tell Louise the truth, but to do so would cause her pain, and she had suffered enough. He must continue to lie to her unless he wished to see hatred in those beautiful eyes . . .

Raphael stiffened as he saw a shadow move from behind the stables. A man was making his way stealthily towards the château. Sensing danger, Raphael took a short-cut through the shrubberies, which led to the back of the house. Keeping close to the walls, he moved silently towards the spot where he had last seen the man, halting as he saw a burly figure intent on forcing the lock of a door leading into the buttery. Drawing his sword, he advanced purposefully.

'May I be of help, m'sieur?'

The stranger turned with a muttered oath, his hand flying to his own sword-hilt; then his mouth fell open in astonishment, just as Raphael started to laugh.

'By God, Thomas! Your face was a picture, man.'

'You scared the life out of me, my lord.' Tom Craven's indignant tone brought a gleam of mockery to his master's face.

'So you deserve, you rogue. What do you mean by creeping about the place at this hour?'

'I might say the same of you,' Tom replied gruffly. 'I wanted to speak to you—and I did not wish to be seen.'

'So you intended to break into Mademoiselle de Granvelle's home and search for me . . .' Raphael's smile disappeared as he saw his servant's grim look. 'What is so important that you felt the need for such secrecy?'

'I found him, my lord.'

Raphael's eyes narrowed, and his voice was hoarse as he said, 'Alive or dead?'

'He is alive for the moment.'

The way Tom stressed those last words was not lost on his master. 'So—you have discovered something important.' Raphael frowned. 'You had better tell me everything.'

Tom nodded. 'I've followed him every step of the way from Paris, my lord, just as you instructed me. At first I thought his odd behaviour was just that of a man frightened for his life.'

'What do you mean, odd behaviour?'

'He took care not to be seen, travelling by night and using only the country roads, buying his food from isolated farms.'

Raphael nodded. 'Yes, that could be the behaviour of a frightened man. We chose our way carefully, to avoid suspicion.'

'Ay, that's what I thought at first, my lord.'

'So what changed your mind?'

Raphael listened intently as his servant described what he had seen. As Tom's tale went on, a dangerous gleam came in his dark eyes as it drew to its close.

'You are perfectly sure of what you heard, Tom?'

'Quite sure, my lord. I followed him here to this very house. They met in a deserted wine-cellar—the place looked as if it hadn't been used for years. They were arguing; he called his servant a fool, and he said that there was no choice now but to kill you and the girl.'

'The devil he did!' An angry pulse started to throb at his temple. 'I can't believe any man could be so cold-blooded.' His brow furrowed with concentration. 'Do you know what they plan for us, Tom?'

The servant shook his head. 'No, my lord. They were shouting at each other at the start, but then they began to whisper, and I could hear no more.'

'And when did all this happen?'

'Two days ago, my lord.'

'Just before we arrived. You know what this means, Tom?'

'You'll have to kill him first.'

Raphael shook his head. 'That's the one thing I can't do. After what happened in Paris, she thinks of him almost as a saint. No, I must take her to England at once.'

His servant frowned. 'After what he's done?'

'I have no proof—and even if I had, I could not use it now. She has suffered too much, Tom.'

Tom looked at his face and saw something that surprised him. 'If that's the way it is, I could kill him for you?'

Raphael placed his hand on the man's shoulder. 'No, that would be murder, and I shall not ask that of you, my friend. Perhaps, if I take her to England, there need be no more bloodshed.'

'Ay, mayhap you're right.' Tom gazed at him. 'But what will you tell her?'

Raphael's lip curled. 'I shall invent some story to satisfy her. What can one more lie matter, when there have been so many already?' He paused. 'We shall leave tonight, Tom. Even one more day might be too late. See to the horses, and we shall join you within the hour.'

CHAPTER EIGHT

LOUISE AWOKE as someone touched her shoulder, shaking her gently. Gazing up into the face of the man who had filled her dreams she sighed, smiling sleepily.

'You came to me . . .' she murmured, so softly that he could not be sure he had heard the words. 'Raphael . . .'

She looked just as he had imagined her on his walk, when fevered thoughts of possessing her had almost driven him to an act of madness. Seeing the flushed softness of her skin and the moist sheen of her lips, he felt a sharp surge of desire. It coursed hotly through his body, making him want her, tempting him to take her even now. The saner side of his nature asserted itself, and he fought back his longing with an iron will.

'You must get up and dress at once,' he said. 'We are leaving for England on the tide. There is no time for you to pack or to summon your maid. Bring only a few possessions, and be ready to leave within half an hour.'

Louise was wide awake now, tingling with alarm. 'Why?' she asked. 'What is wrong?'

'Your life is in danger every moment you stay here. I have received a warning of a plot to kill us both.'

The urgency in his voice made her realise he was in earnest. She sat up, throwing back the bedcovers as he handed her a silk wrap. 'Then I must come with you, my lord. But what of André?

'I have already left a letter for your steward, telling him that I have taken you to England for your own safety. If André returns, he will know where you are to be found.'

Louise clutched her wrap round her, shivering. 'Who are these men who wish to kill us?'

'My informant was unable to tell me that,' Raphael lied. 'Yet, since I believe this warning to have come from someone at Court, I think it probably was the Cardinal de Lorraine.'

'The warning must have come from Madame Catherine,' Louise said. 'I'm sure it was she who told you to take me out of Paris on Saint Bartholomew's Eve. For some reason, she was very kind to me when I was at Court.'

'Then perhaps it was from her.' His voice sounded odd, and she looked at him. He saw the uncertainty in her face and he grasped her shoulders. 'You must come with me, Louise. You have no alternative. Neither of us has a choice now.'

Louise met his gaze and found it compelling. He meant her to go with him tonight, and she sensed that he would brook no refusal from her. He had once threatened to carry her off by force if she did not go with him, and she did not doubt that he would have done it had she refused. Fate was taking control of her life, forcing her to go with this man to that cold, grey country across the sea, yet even now her pride would not let her admit to him that it was what she wanted more than anything else in the world.

'Yes, I shall come,' she said, keeping her voice cool. 'Give me a moment to dress and to gather a few trinkets. I shall take the jewels my father entrusted to me. I have kept them close by me since you returned them to me, my lord.' Running swiftly to an iron-bound chest in the corner of the chamber, she took out a small casket and gave it to him. 'Will you take care of these for me once more?'

'Of course.' Raphael caught her hand as she would have moved away. 'Before you trust yourself to me, I want you to know that I shall make no demands on you. I once teased you about becoming my mistress, Louise, and I would have you know that you have naught to fear. I shall treat you as if you were in truth my cousin.'

'T-Thank you,' Louise whispered, turning her face aside swiftly so that he should not see the pain his words had caused her. She did not want to be his cousin. She wanted to be his wife!

'I shall wait downstairs,' Raphael said, his voice harsher than he knew. 'Be as quick as you can. The sooner we are on board a ship bound for England, the better.'

Louise blinked back the rush of tears as he left. This was foolishness! Because of his kindness to her of late, she had begun to dream that he would one day ask her to marry him. It was her own fault if she was hurt now by his careless words. He had meant only to reassure her; he could not know that his indifference was breaking her heart—that she would rather be his mistress than an honoured guest who meant nothing to him!

Dashing the humiliating tears from her cheeks, Louise dressed hurriedly in a simple black gown, adding a warm cloak to protect her from the sea breezes. She must accept Raphael's kindness for what it was and be thankful he cared enough to be concerned for her. She had no claim on him, no right to ask for more than he wished to give. She had always known he did not love her. He was incapable of love because another woman had hurt him too badly. A woman he called for in his sleep.

Letting her long hair hang loose on her shoulders, she pushed a few personal trinkets into a bag and snatched up her riding-crop. There was no time to waste. With one swift glance round the room she had known all her life, she went out, closing the door behind her.

Raphael was waiting for her at the foot of the stairs, cursing beneath his breath as he saw her white face. All his plans had gone awry, and for the first time in his adult life he felt powerless to direct his own fate. The frustration made him angry, his lean face hardening into a granite mask as he took Louise's bag from her, slinging it across his shoulder.

'Come.' He held out his hand. 'We must go now.'

'Yes,' she said, her eyes proud and distant as she struggled to forget the ache inside her.

'If we ride hard, we should catch the tide. With a fair wind, we shall be in England within two days.' He saw her mouth tremble. 'Do not be afraid, Louise. You will learn to like your new home, and soon all the pain will go away.'

She nodded, making no answer. She knew he believed her distress was because she was forced to abandon her home and live in a strange land; he could not guess that she would have gone willingly, eagerly, if only he loved her just a little. And he must never know. All she had left now was her pride.

Louise stood looking at the receding shores of France. Overhead, the sky was bright blue without a cloud to dim the sun. A fair breeze was filling the sails as the ship sped over the water.

She breathed deeply of the salty tang, her hair clustering about her oval face as the wind whipped her curls into little tangles. She was leaving her homeland, perhaps for ever, but surprisingly she was not frightened by the prospect. It was an adventure: a new life. Besides, she would be with the man she loved, and that was all that really mattered to her. To be able to see him and hear his voice—to hope that he would one day turn to her with love in his heart—it was all she needed.

A little smile curved her mouth as she watched the sea-spray rise high into the air, sparkling like diamonds as it hung there momentarily before it was lost. She was a little like that spray, Louise thought; her life had been tossed into the storm by Fate, and she could go only where the wind carried her.

'You should go below to the cabin,' Raphael said, placing his hands lightly on her arms from behind. 'It is cold on deck, and you must be weary.'

Louise leaned back against his chest, closing her eyes as the warmth of his body sent her senses reeling. Here in his arms she was at peace, secure and protected from the pain she knew would come when she was alone.

'Let me stay here for a while,' she whispered, her heart beating wildly as she felt his strong arms enfold her, sheltering her from the wind with his body.

Raphael's lips touched her hair, inhaling the scent of her as he buried his face in the rich tresses. He, too, was reluctant to end this moment and break the spell that bound them. He held her close to his heart, the rhythm of it echoing the pounding of the waves against the ship. Tomorrow was time enough to think of the future and his duty.

They stood together unmoving and silent until the sun began to fade from the sky. Then the man took the girl's hand and led her below.

It was growing dark as the coach rattled into the long tree-lined driveway. Glancing out of the window, Louise could see the sprawling shape of a Tudor manor house a short distance ahead. She felt a little tingle of excitement as the horses began to slow their pace and she heard the coachman give the order to halt. At last they had arrived at the house which was to be her new home.

On reaching England, they had stayed in Portsmouth for a few days. Raphael had taken over a floor of the largest inn, sending Tom Craven on ahead to announce the arrival of Lord Carleton and his French cousin. Then he set about providing Louise with a maid and a new wardrobe.

'We shall go to London soon,' he told her when she protested that she did not need the half of the finery he insisted on buying her. 'These trifles will do until we can purchase more suitable attire for my cousin. Besides, it will give your maid something to do.'

Louise smiled. She was beginning to understand his dry humour at last. Having seen him with Thomas Craven, she realised that what she had thought of as mockery was often merely amusement.

'I wish you would allow me to pay for my own clothes, my lord,' she said. 'I cannot live as your pensioner.'

Raphael frowned. 'You are my guest, not my dependant, Louise. While you reside beneath my roof, I shall provide for your comfort as I think right. You will please not insult me by offering me money.'

Finding her protests fell on deaf ears, Louise gave herself up to the pleasures of choosing reams of pretty laces, silks and satins. She managed to persuade Raphael to let her make most of her own clothes, wrinkling her nose as she saw the stiff, unbecoming gowns presented to her by the English seamstresses.

'I can fashion my own gowns,' Louise said, 'and my maid will help with the sewing. The English have no sense of style.' She draped a pale yellow silk seductively against her, her eyes provocative as she gazed up at him. 'Do you not think this would suit me, my lord?'

'You know very well it does,' Raphael retorted, as she continued to preen herself in front of him. 'You are in England now. It is time you began to learn our language and our ways. If you wear your bodice too low at Court, the ladies will say you are a French harlot.'

Louise pouted at him. 'Yes, m'sieur. I vow you are worse than Grand'mère ever was!'

The dark eyes glinted with anger. The last few days had brought about a marked change in her. It was as though she had cast off her old self when they left the ship. It was good that her eyes no longer wore that haunted look, but her flirtatious manner was something he found difficult to understand. Was she deliberately provoking him? he wondered. Could she be unaware of the effect those pouting lips had on his pulses? More likely she had taken it into her head to punish him for some slight, Raphael decided, remembering the tricks Helen had played to catch his attention. He had no idea what he had done to upset Louise, but he felt instinctively that something was wrong.

She was behaving like the sophisticated women of the

Court he had taken as his mistresses and then discarded when he tired of their false ways. If he had not promised himself he would not lay a finger on the girl, he would be tempted to answer those wanton looks she was giving him with the punishment they deserved. As the chastisement he had in mind conjured up delicious but forbidden pictures of her lying naked in his arms, it required all Raphael's determination to banish them. Consequently, his temper grew shorter by the hour.

It was a relief to them both when Tom returned with the coach and a retinue of servants. Raphael was determined that Louise should be conveyed to her new home in style. He meant to make it clear from the start that she was to be received at Carleton Manor with the respect due to her as his cousin. There should be no scandal to harm her reputation—even though she was a tiresome minx who was slowly driving him out of his mind!

Unaware that Raphael's black looks were brought on by her attempts to flirt with him, Louise kept a bright smile on her lips while the pain settled into a tight knot about her heart. Pride was all that she had left to her now, and she was acting out her own little masquerade so that he should not see how much his indifference was hurting her. Let him believe her a heartless flirt if he wished: he thought all women were harlots anyway. She could not fault his generosity in material things, or the polite deference he showed her, as though she were indeed his cousin, but she looked in vain for a sign that she meant more to him than a burden he had decided to shoulder because Fate had thrust it on him.

Such were Louise's thoughts as she gazed at the huge, rambling manor house spread out before her in the gathering dusk. It was larger by far than her father's château, the east wing half-timbered and newer than the rest, which was built of grey stone and looked as if it had been designed as a fortress. A tentative enquiry brought a smile from Raphael as he told her she had guessed correctly. He explained that his ancestors had been

feudal lords, who built their stronghold to resist attack
from warlike neighbours.

'Before Henry Tudor wrested power from the
Plantagenets, England was constantly at war,' he said, as
they stood together in the dusk, looking up at the
crenellated battlements of the west tower. 'The Tudors
are a strong breed—and I'm damned if our Bess isn't the
best king England ever had!'

Louise heard the pride in his voice and smiled. She
had heard stories of the fiery-haired English Queen, and
she knew that Elizabeth's skill at diplomacy was both
feared and respected by her peers. She had kept France,
Spain and Holland dangling on her string, holding the
dazzling prize of her throne before her suitor's eyes like
a golden apple. There were Catholics and Protestants
living side by side in her realm, and the struggle for
power was as constant as in Louise's own country, yet
the English Queen held her subjects' love and loyalty in
the palm of her hand. And her people lived in peace.

Already the French girl had noticed the prosperity in
her adopted country. There was a vitality about the
people, as if they knew it was the golden age. New
horizons were opening up for those with the courage to
seek their fortunes on the high seas. Merchant-
adventurers were sailing further than ever before, bringing back the treasures of the earth to England's shores. It
was a time when the humblest in the land could rise to
dizzy heights simply by daring to reach out and take what
others feared to touch.

Coming from a country torn by repeated civil wars,
Louise envied the English their way of life. She sensed a
freedom of thought in the country that was not yet in
France, and it seemed to her that even the beggars were
less miserable. The divide between the nobles and their
peasants was not as deep as in her country. In fact,
Raphael had told her that his people were all freemen.
They served him for the wages he paid them, and were
free to leave his estate if they so wished, though it was

seldom that a man born to the land chose to seek his own way.

Listening to Raphael talk as he led her into his house, Louise felt an intense happiness. This was her new home, and she felt it welcoming her, as if its spirit reached out to embrace her. She gazed up at Raphael, her smoky eyes glowing with excitement.

'Your house is beautiful, my lord.'

'I am glad you find it so, Louise. It is as it was when my mother was alive, but you must feel free to make what changes you wish.'

Her eyes moved slowly over the heavy oak furniture, which gleamed with beeswax, liking the dark sheen of its satiny surface that reflected the years of loving care. Rich silk tapestries covered the walls, except where they were hung with portraits of long-dead Carletons, and polished armour of another age caught the glow of a fire burning in the huge open hearth.

In the great hall an intricately carved buffet was set with silver plates and tankards; matching silver-gilt candlesticks stood guard at either end of a massive table, with a magnificent salt at its centre. An impressive boxed chair stood at the head of the table, another at its foot; but what caught Louise's eyes was a beautiful gilt table clock set on six clawed feet and decorated with medallions of hunting scenes carved in precious stone.

Everywhere she looked there was some new treasure to delight her, the equal of which she had seen only at Court. It was clearly the house of a wealthy family who had found pleasure in collecting beautiful things around them.

'Come, Louise.' Raphael held out his hand to her as an elderly woman dressed in a sombre grey gown came quietly into the room. 'This lady was my mother's maid and companion. She has acted as my housekeeper for many years. You will find that Mistress Beacham understands French very well. She will show you to your rooms, and you may ask her for anything you need.'

'Thank you, my lord.'

Louise felt suddenly shy. Raphael was no longer the man she had travelled with through France. He had become a great lord, master of what was obviously a vast estate. Somehow she had never expected such riches. Unlike the men she had known at the French Court, he seldom wore jewellery, and though his clothes were of the finest cloth, he made little show of his wealth. His arrogance was a natural part of the man, and Louise knew it came from a belief in himself and not pride in his possessions. Indeed, from what he had told her these past days of his ancestors, he seemed to feel his position more a burden he must carry for the sake of his people rather than a vehicle for his personal pleasure.

She was a little in awe of him. He had somehow withdrawn from her, his manner scrupulously polite but cool. It was almost as if they were strangers, and she turned to the waiting housekeeper. The woman curtsied, replying to her greeting with a friendly smile.

'You must be tired, mademoiselle,' she said, her perfect French accent sounding like music to Louise's ears after all the harsh English voices she had heard of late. 'Please follow me. Your rooms are prepared as his lordship commanded, and I believe you will find them comfortable.'

Louise thanked her. Mistress Beacham's quiet manner was reassuring, banishing any fears she had harboured that Lord Carleton's servants might resent a Frenchwoman in their midst.

The attention that had been given to the suite of rooms on an upper floor was apparent when they entered. Fires were burning in both the reception and the sleeping chambers, making Louise feel immediately welcome. As she looked round the spacious apartments, she saw that nothing had been forgotten. Everything she could possibly want was ready and waiting for her: even a beautiful writing-desk made of a pale, silky wood inlaid with intricate panels stood open on a table by the window. Near the fire was an embroidery frame, and there were several musical instruments.

'This was Lord Carleton's mother's chamber, was it not?' Louise looked questioningly at the housekeeper.

'Yes, mademoiselle.' Mrs Beacham touched a silk tapestry with reverent fingers. 'This was my dear mistress's own work. Is it not beautiful?'

'It is very lovely,' Louise agreed, admiring the perfect stitching. 'I am honoured to be given the privilage of using these things—but are you sure Lord Carleton intended me to have these rooms?'

'Oh yes, his orders were quite clear. I was a little surprised at first . . .' Mrs Beacham hesitated, then, 'As you can see, nothing in here has been moved since Lady Carleton died. His lordship has never allowed Lady Helen to use these rooms, even though she frequently complains they are the best in the house.'

The colour left Louise's cheeks. That was the name she had heard on Raphael's lips when he was dreaming. Helen: the woman she called for in his sleep!

'Lady Helen?' she whispered. 'Who is this woman?'

A faint colour stained the housekeeper's cheeks. 'Forgive me, mademoiselle, my stupid tongue ran away with me. Please, I beg you, do not tell the master I mentioned her name.'

'Please tell me who Lady Helen is,' Louise said. 'I have to know.'

She gave a slight shrug. 'We all thought she would marry the master. Her family have lived near by for many years, though not as long as the Carletons, of course. His lordship's ancestors came to England with the Conqueror, you know.'

'You are fond of your master, are you not?'

Mrs Beacham smiled. 'We all respect his lordship.'

'You were telling me about Lady Helen. Is—Is she betrothed to your master?'

'Oh no, mademoiselle. She married his cousin Richard.' Her mouth settled in a thin line. 'Please don't ask me to tell you any more, mademoiselle. His lordship will tell you himself if he wishes you to know.'

Louise sensed that there was much more Mrs Beacham could have said had she wished to, but she had already heard enough. Now she understood why Raphael called for Helen in his sleep. He was still in love with her even though she had betrayed him by marrying his cousin.

'Is Lady Helen very beautiful?' Louise asked, turning away to toy with a silver dish on the table.

'Oh yes, mademoiselle. She has hair like pale silk, and her eyes are as blue as sapphires. She's pretty enough.' Mrs Beacham sniffed loudly, and Louise realised that there was disapproval in her tone.

A little more prompting might have brought the whole story tumbling out, for she was obviously eager to gossip, but Louise decided she had heard sufficient for the moment. Tears were stinging her eyes, and she wanted desperately to be alone.

'Thank you for preparing my room so thoughtfully,' she said, forcing herself to smile at the housekeeper. 'I am a little tired, and I would like to rest for a while before dinner.'

She curtsied. 'If there is anything more I can do for you, you have only to ring.'

Louise inclined her head but made no reply. She could not trust herself to speak. Her heart felt as if it were split in two, and the rooms was spinning. Now, at last, she had her answer. She knew why Raphael could never trust again.

Louise glanced at herself in the small silver-backed hand-mirror, frowning as she saw there was still a trace of redness about her eyes despite all her attempts to hide it. She had spent a long time dressing for her first evening at Carleton Manor, and was reasonably pleased with her appearance. Her gown was fashioned in the English style, with a high, stiff ruff, but she had altered the neckline so that it dipped enticingly to reveal a tantalising glimpse of her breasts.

Glancing once more at her reflection, she sighed and handed the mirror to her maid. A knock at the door made her look up, expecting the housekeeper who had promised to show her the way to the dining hall. A tiny shock went through Louise as she heard Raphael's voice requesting entry, and she lifted her chin a little higher, determined not to let him see her distress.

'You may go,' Raphael dismissed the servant with a nod of his head. He regarded Louise with disapproval as he saw the pallor of her cheeks.

'Are you warm enough?' he asked. 'It is chilly this evening, and you have been used to a warmer climate.'

Was that all he could say when she had taken so much trouble to please him? 'I am quite warm, my lord. I have a headache, but I am sure it will soon pass.'

'You look tired. You must rest and recover your strength, now we are home.' His expression lightened, and he smiled at her. 'Perhaps my small gift will bring the sparkle back to your eyes, Louise.'

'You have already given me too much, my lord.' She looked at the ring on her left hand. 'I should return this to you—but it will not easily come off.'

'Leave it where it is—I like to see it there. Besides, it was a gift. You should not refuse a present unless you wish to sound churlish.'

'You know I am grateful for all you have done for me.'

'Then wear my gift tonight. I have a special reason for asking you, Louise.'

She looked at him curiously but he shook his head, merely handing her a small velvet-covered casket. Opening it, she saw a string of magnificent pearls. Each bead was perfect, with a pinkish lustre, and the necklace was long enough to wind twice round her throat and still reach to the deep V at the waist of her gown.

'They are magnificent, my lord!'

'I'm glad you like them. They belonged to my mother:

she brought them with her from France when she came to this house as a bride. I know she would have wanted you to have them.' He came to her, lifting the necklace from the box and placing it over her head. 'Yes, that is better. Come, supper awaits you, Louise—and our guests are anxious to meet the new mistress of Carleton Manor.'

'Our guests?' She stared at him in surprise: this was the first she had heard of any visitors. 'I am but a guest myself, my lord. Surely you do not expect me to assume the role of châtelaine?'

'This house has been too long without a mistress. It is time there was music and laughter—and the sound of woman's footsteps to send the maids scurrying about their work.' Raphael glanced down at her. 'It will not be too arduous a task. I hope it is not too much to ask?'

'No, of course not.' Louise bit her lip. Could he think her so ungrateful for all he had done both in France and since they arrived in England? It was only that she was surprised by his request. 'It will honour me to act as mistress in your house, my lord. At least, until—until you marry . . .'

'Ah, but you know I do not wish for a wife, do you not?' His brows rose lazily. 'It will suit me very well to have my French cousin as my hostess.'

Louise could not answer him, so she merely smiled and took his arm. Her heart was fluttering as they walked together along the gallery towards the main staircase. For the moment she could pretend that she was truly the mistress of this great house, and that the handsome man at her side was her adoring husband. Oh, if only that were so, she thought, sneaking a glance at his profile and noticing the pulse throbbing at his temple. She had noticed that it happened whenever he was disturbed about something, and she wondered what he was thinking at this moment. He looked down at her and she turned away quickly, giving her attention to the portraits lining the oak-panelled walls. Then she gave a

little gasp and stopped walking as she saw the picture of a
striking woman with black hair and dark eyes.

Raphael noticed her interest and frowned as he
studied the portrait. 'Yes, it is a good likeness of my
mother,' he said as Louise turned to look at him. 'I see
you have noticed the resemblance between us.'

'She was very beautiful,' Louise said, recognising the
same pride and arrogance in the mother that she had
seen in the son.

'Beautiful, passionate—and sometimes cruel. She
was the kind of woman who can uplift or destroy a man's
soul.'

A slight smile curved Raphael's sensuous mouth as he
looked down into the girl's anxious eyes. 'You will bring
a woman's warmth back to this house, Louise. It has
been sadly lacking since she died.'

His words brought a glow to Louise's face. He really
wanted her here: she was not simply a fugitive he was
helping out of a sense of duty. The knowledge eased the
pain in her heart, making her feel that the future held a
promise of happiness. After all, she had never known
what it was like to feel really loved; as she had borne her
father's stern indifference and André's scorn, so she
could bear the pain of Raphael's rejection of her love.
Perhaps, in time, she might even win some true affection
from him.

Louise could have no idea of how magnificent she
looked as she paused at the head of the stairs, her hand
resting lightly on her companion's arm. She was no
longer the innocent girl who had watched the dancing at
the Louvre with a child's delight. A subtle change had
taken place over the past weeks, and it had served only
to enhance her beauty. Her slightly olive-toned skin
was warmed by the fiery tints in the thick hair she had
chosen to wear in shining coils this evening, and her lips
had the sheen and softness of a rose-petal. The deep
blue of her brocaded gown made her eyes seem darker
and more mysterious, as if she were somehow apart

from ordinary mortals: the eternal woman, gentle yet calm, proud yet compassionate, cool yet full of a loving warmth.

She turned her head to glance up at Raphael, and in that moment her love shone like a beacon from her eyes, though she herself was unaware of it. Yet no one else who saw her at that moment could have doubted it. Unfortunately, Raphael was staring at the two people in the hall. Jealousy sparked in the fair-skinned woman watching from below. Her wide mouth tightened with anger, and the sapphire eyes narrowed in spite as she saw that Louise was wearing the pearls she had long coveted.

'By God! she's beautiful,' said the man at her side. 'I think you've lost him, Helen. You should have stayed in London, and looked for a husband there.'

'Damn you, Edward,' Lady Helen muttered at her brother, her eyes glinting with anger. 'Richard is scarcely in his grave, and I am in mourning. You know I couldn't stay at Court after—after what happened. Everyone was talking about me.'

A slightly malicious smile twisted the pale lips of her companion. Several years younger than his sister, Lord Edward Ross was an effeminate youth, his thin face yellow-tinged from years of ill-health. Tonight he was dressed in puce and silver, his doublet thickly padded and sewn with pearls. He wore a large diamond stud in one ear, and his fingers were crammed with precious rings of all shades.

'Yet you dared to come here tonight.' Edward glanced at her with a flicker of admiration. 'You've got courage, Helen, I'll say that for you. I expected Raphael to throw us out.'

'That's because you don't know him as well as I do.' Helen's eyes sparkled with temper. 'I could always get him to do what I wanted. He belongs to me—that French slut has no hold over him. When I snap my fingers, he will come running back . . .'

'Be careful,' Edward warned, knowing how recklessly his sister could behave. 'They will hear you.'

He moved forward to the foot of the stairs, bowing low as Louise reached the bottom. 'Mademoiselle de Granvelle,' he said. 'Raphael is a selfish fellow to keep you hidden from us all this time. I swear I would have come to Portsmouth had I known what a rare prize he had brought back from his travels!'

A mocking smile lingered on Raphael's mouth as he observed the youth's gallantry. 'Louise, this is a close neighbour of ours—Lord Edward Ross, the Marquis of Rosslayne. Do not be fooled by his smooth tongue —Edward seldom exerts himself for anyone.'

'You are unfair to poor Edward.' Helen glided towards them in a haze of distinctive perfume, holding out her hand to Raphael so that he was forced to carry it briefly to his lips. 'Please, Raphael, won't you introduce me to this lovely creature?' Her hard blue eyes surveyed Louise with a dislike she could barely hide.

'Of course.' His smile faded, as he looked at her and saw the provocative challenge in her face. 'Louise, this is Mistress Carleton . . .'

'I am Lady Helen.' The blue eyes snapped with anger. 'I chose to keep my title when I married, since my husband had none of his own.'

'Ah yes, I had forgotten,' he said coldly. 'Forgive me, but I think of you as my cousin's wife.'

'His widow now.' Helen's eyes accused him. 'Or had you forgotten that, too?'

'How could I forget?'

The sharp exchange between them was in English. Louise could understand only a few words, but she knew that Raphael was disturbed by what had been said. She saw his jaw harden, sensing the tension in him. She was filled with a sudden, terrible hatred for the beautiful woman who could rouse such strong emotion in Raphael, and she would have liked to slash those sapphire eyes with her nails. The pulse was beating wildly at his temple now, causing her to seek desperately for something to say that would avert the storm.

'You are both welcome visitors,' she said nervously. 'It—It was kind of you to call on my very first night here. I do hope you will feel free to come whenever you wish. I shall enjoy getting to know my neighbours.'

Her speech astonished them all. Helen's eyes narrowed dangerously and she looked at Raphael, as if demanding that he should put this upstart cousin in her place.

'You are very gracious, mademoiselle,' she snapped, as both men remained silent. 'But I have considered Carleton Manor my second home for as long as I can remember.'

Pride came to Louise's rescue, and her chin went up. 'Then I urge you to continue to do so,' she said, every inch the grand lady. 'The servants will have instructions to receive you, should I be absent.'

Respect flickered in Edward's eyes. It was amusing to see Helen bested for once—and by a girl several years her junior!

'Raphael always was a sly one,' he said. 'You may expect me to dine with you almost every night until I leave for London, mademoiselle. Your cooks are far superior to my own. Besides, I shall have another reason to come here now.'

Relief flooded through Louise as she heard Raphael's soft laugh. She glanced at him and saw the danger had passed. He was in control once more, his eyes amused beneath the lowered lids. She felt a surge of triumph, like a she-wolf who has successfully defended her den against invaders. Raphael had made her the mistress of his household, and no one would deny her her position here—not even that silver-haired enchantress who had broken his heart!

Raphael's fingers smoothed the soft flesh at Louise's wrists, sending delicate shivers through her. She lifted her eyes to his, her pupils dilating as she saw the sudden shaft of fire in those dark orbs and felt the warmth of his breath close to her ear as he leant closer.

'Bravo, sweet protector,' he whispered, so softly that she was not sure she had heard correctly. 'Surely I acted wisely when I chose you as the mistress of my home.'

He had spoken softly and in her own tongue, but his gesture had been noticed, and Louise could not miss the look of hatred on Helen's beautiful face. In that instant she knew that the older woman meant to have Raphael for her own—and that she herself would use every weapon in her power to stop her!

CHAPTER NINE

SUNBEAMS WERE filtering through the tiny leaded windows, creating multicoloured patterns on the wall. Louise laid aside her sewing with a sigh. It was much too nice a day to waste indoors, and she was missing her usual morning ride with Raphael. He had gone with his steward to inspect some labourers' cottages that needed repair before the winter, and had told her he would not be back until the evening.

She got up to gaze out of the window at the gardens, admiring the smooth lawns and formal walks that led to the park beyond, and then to a large wood that stretched on as far as the eye could see. The view only made her more restless, and she decided to go for a walk. Soon enough this bright spell would pass and then it would be too cold for exercise outside.

Paying a quick visit to the kitchens, where she found the servants busily engaged in plucking some plump geese for supper, she begged some bread from Mrs Beacham and tied it into a linen napkin, laughing as the housekeeper anxiously enquired if she was hungry.

'I noticed some swans on the lake when I was out riding,' she explained. 'In France, I often fed the wild birds as they flew in for the winter. Some of them would even take the food from my hand.'

Mrs Beacham smiled and shook her head. 'You remind me of my dear mistress. She was always finding some creature to be fussing over.'

Louise strolled leisurely towards the small artificial lake, noticing how prettily it had been landscaped with trees and bushes. She liked this part of the estate far more than the formal gardens, and she knew that she would come here often in summer.

To her delight, she saw the family of swans feeding on a patch of weed at the far side of the lake. She began to make her way steadily round the bank, taking care not to step on the muddy patches here and there. She had taught the swans at home to take bread from her hand, and she hoped that these birds would become as tame in time.

The male swan raised his head warily as she approached; but when she began to throw pieces of bread into the water, he became curious and led his family towards the unexpected feast. They came gliding across the water like a stately armada, sending little ripples across the surface.

Absorbed by the soft hissing noises made by the cygnets as they competed for the bread, Louise failed to notice the other woman's approach. She jumped as she heard a harsh laugh behind her, and spun round to find Helen watching her.

'I was told I would find you here.' Helen gave her a look of dislike. 'I should have thought you could find more gainful employment.'

Louise frowned as she saw the sneer on the other woman's face. She knew Helen resented her presence at the manor: it was obvious every time they met, but Helen usually kept up a pretence of friendship, limiting herself to the occasional, barbed remark. She had not had it all her own way, however, for Louise was well able to protect herself from Helen's arrows.

'I do not understand you,' she said. 'I am at liberty to do as I please in my cousin's house. I am not a servant.'

'Cousin?' Helen laughed disbelievingly. 'Raphael only ever had one French cousin that I knew of—and her name was not Louise.'

Louise's chin went up. 'Are you saying that Raphael is lying?'

'I don't care whether Raphael brought you here as a glorified housekeeper, a poor relation, or just another of his whores!' Helen's eyes glittered dangerously. 'Just remember that, when I am mistress here, your presence will not be tolerated.'

'You are not yet Lady Carleton,' Louise replied, digging her nails into the palms of her hands as she struggled to maintain her dignity. 'When that day comes —if it ever does—you may be sure I shall not stay in this house. Until then, I would ask you to remember your manners.'

'Why, you little slut!' Helen cried furiously. 'How dare you speak to me like that?'

Incensed, Helen lunged at her as if to claw at her face. Louise threw out an arm to protect herself and caught Helen off balance. She slipped on a muddy patch and screamed as she fell into the lake.

The sight of her floundering in the shallow water and hampered by her full skirts brought back to Louise memories of a similar unpleasant accident. She gave a cry and knelt down, offering her hand to Helen as she struggled up on to the bank. Her help was angrily refused, and she could only stand by as the other woman hauled herself up to safety. Although Helen had been in no danger, she was soaked from head to foot, her gown stained with mud and slime. Noticing a piece of weed caught in her straggling hair, Louise tried to remove it, but Helen struck her hand away with a glare.

'Don't you dare to touch me!' She glanced down at her gown, and gave a howl of rage. 'You've ruined my dress. You pushed me deliberately. Just wait until I tell Raphael how his precious French cousin behaves!'

'It was an accident,' Louise protested. 'Besides, he will not believe you. He will know I would never do such a thing.'

Helen's eyes narrowed. 'You think not? Do you really imagine he will take your word against mine? Raphael is in love with me. He has loved me for years.' She smiled triumphantly. 'He killed a man in a duel because of me. Do you think he would do as much for you?'

Louise gasped, her face draining of colour. 'I don't believe you!'

'No?' Helen laughed. 'Ask him, then. Ask him how Richard died, if you dare.' With that, she turned and walked swiftly away.

Louise watched as she mounted the horse she had tethered near by, unable to move from the spot. She felt stunned, her stomach churning as the sickness rose in her throat. Raphael had killed his own cousin in a duel over Helen? No, it could not be true! If he had killed Helen's husband out of a jealousy that amounted to murder . . .

Suddenly, Louise realised she had to know the truth whatever it might be, but she could not ask Raphael. There was, however, one other person who might be persuaded to tell her how and why Richard Carleton had died.

'You sent for me, mademoiselle?' Mrs Beacham stood just inside the door with her hands clasped in front of her. 'Is something wrong?'

'No, indeed, you look after me wonderfully, Mrs Beacham.' Louise smiled at her, indicating a glass flagon and two dainty drinking-cups. 'I thought you might join me in a cup of wine. Since my cousin is away, it is an ideal moment for us to get to know one another better.'

'Why, that's very thoughtful of you, mademoiselle. My dear mistress sometimes invited me to sit with her for a while. You are very like her in many ways.'

'Thank you.' Louise smiled. 'I am honoured by the compliment, for I think she was a worthy mistress of this house.'

'Oh yes—she would turn in her grave if she knew . . .' The housekeeper's cheeks flushed. 'But I shouldn't gossip, mademoiselle.'

'Is the wine to your liking?' Louise tipped a little more into her cup. 'I sense you have something on your mind, Mrs Beacham. Will you not tell me about it?'

'I don't see how she has the boldness to come to this house after what happened. I don't like it, mademoiselle, I can tell you. And I can't understand why the master receives her in the way he does.'

'You are speaking of Lady Helen, I believe?' Louise leaned towards her, touching her hand. 'You may speak freely to me. If I am to live here, I must know what this woman did to hurt my cousin. I must know . . .'

'You love him, don't you? I saw it in your eyes the first night you came here. You cannot know how much I have prayed he would find happiness with a good woman.' Her lips tightened with anger. 'I could kill her for bringing shame on my master's good name.'

'Then she was to blame for what happened?'

The housekeeper nodded, holding her hands to the flames from the fire as her eyes took on a strange glow.

'They played together as children, the three of them. Lady Helen, my master and Richard Carleton. Even when they were young it was always a contest between the two boys—and *her* watching them with that look on her face, as if she knew it was because of her they fought. Richard could never quite match his cousin in anything. The master could ride faster, run swifter and learn everything his tutors asked him. When they fought, it was ever Master Raphael who won, though sometimes he would let Richard best him—but even when he did, the lad knew it was not really a fair fight . . .'

Her face wore a wistful expression. 'My mistress used to watch them, and smile. She told me that Helen was an enchantress who had snared them all with her beauty. We all knew she was naughty—but she could charm the birds from the trees with her smile.'

Louise twisted her hands in her lap. She could imagine the scene, and as the other woman talked, the pictures of Raphael's childhood seemed to come to life in the flames of the fire. She saw him as a boy, then a youth, growing to manhood filled with a pride in his own strength.

'We expected Lady Helen to marry his lordship.

Nothing was said, but it was understood from the beginning. She was everything a man could want—the perfect mistress for his house . . .' Mrs Beacham faltered, and her face crumpled. 'God forgive her for what she did, for I never shall!'

Louise felt a cold shiver run down her spine. 'What did she do?'

The housekeeper clasped her hands together tightly as if to stop them from shaking. 'When she married Master Richard, his lordship was very quiet. He acted as if he expected it, but he spent a lot of time out riding or locked away in his library—he's always been a great reader, has Master Raphael. Well, for a few months nothing happened, then one day Lady Helen came here and there was a terrible quarrel between them. Don't ask me what it was about, for I cannot tell you. She rode away like the fury, and the next day Master Richard turned up. He was shouting at the master and saying terrible things. They came to blows, and his lordship threw him out of the house; then he went off to London . . .' She shook her head, muttering in a low voice.

'Yes, what happened then?'

'I've only heard rumours, but—but Master Richard forced a sword-fight on his lordship, and my master killed him. He killed a man who was like a brother to him, mademoiselle. And it was because of her!'

Louise closed her eyes as the room seemed to spin. So it was true. Every word Helen had told her was true! Raphael had killed his own cousin because of a quarrel over the woman they both loved.

'Are you ill, mademoiselle?'

Louise opened her eyes to find Mrs Beacham bending over her in concern. 'Forgive me, I shouldn't have told you. I did not want to upset you like this.'

'No . . . No, you were right to tell me.' Louise looked up at her. 'I had to know.'

She frowned. 'Forgive me for asking, mademoiselle, but when is the wedding to be? Between you and his lordship, I mean,' she added, as Louise stared at her in surprise.

'There is to be no wedding between us,' she said. 'What made you think there was?'

'You are wearing the Carleton betrothal ring. I . . . We all assumed you would marry the master.'

Louise glanced at her left hand. She had become so used to wearing the ring that she had forgotten it was there. She twisted it nervously on her finger, knowing she had no right to wear it.

'Lord Carleton lent it to me. We are not betrothed.'

'I am sorry, mademoiselle. I should not have asked.'

'You have not offended me.' Louise smiled, despite the ache in her heart. 'I am in your debt for telling me this, and I give you my word that I shall never speak of it.'

'You are a great lady, mademoiselle. I shall pray that my master realises your worth before it is too late.'

'Thank you,' Louise whispered, tears springing to her eyes. 'I should like to be alone now.'

'Yes, my lady.' Mrs Beacham curtsied and went out.

Louise stared into the fire, feeling cold, despite its warmth. It was the end of all her hopes. How could she hope to compete with the woman Raphael had loved all his life?

Louise looked up as Raphael came into the room. She got to her feet, struggling to hide her distress behind a smile, but it faded as she saw the anger in his face.

'Louise, I must talk to you.'

'Yes, my lord. I am listening.' She stood quietly in front of him.

He looked grave as he studied her, wondering at her pallor. 'You know what I have to ask you, don't you? Is it true that you pushed Lady Helen into the lake?'

Anger flared in her. How could he ask such a question? Surely he must know she would not stoop to such a petty act, even when severely provoked! She lifted her chin defiantly, her eyes cold.

'You must believe what you wish, my lord.'

'And what does that mean?'

'I am not prepared to defend myself against Lady Helen's accusations. If you wish to believe her, you must do so.'

'I would believe you if you told me it was a lie, Louise.'

'Would you?' she laughed bitterly. 'You are like all men. My father would not believe I did not arrange to meet Pierre de Guise in the forest that day. He beat me because I would not confess my so-called sin. I shall tell you nothing.'

He looked at her stubborn face, and sighed. 'I have no intention of beating you, Louise, but I must ask you to apologise to Lady Helen. Her gown is ruined and she was very distressed.'

'No! I shall never apologise to her,' Louise cried. 'Send me away if you wish, but I shall not apologise.'

Raphael's face hardened. 'You disappoint me. This is not the behaviour I had expected from my cousin.'

'I am not your cousin,' Louise snapped.

'No, you are not.' Suddenly he took hold of her shoulders, shaking her. 'You are a stubborn, proud wench, and one day you will push me too far.'

'Then send me away,' Louise repeated.

His eyes narrowed thoughtfully as he looked at her. 'Was Helen lying, Louise? What did she say to make you hit her?'

Louise set her lips and looked straight ahead, refusing to answer.

Raphael stamped his foot in frustration. 'I swear you will drive me to madness!' he said. 'Was I wrong to believe her? I know you do not like her.'

'Even if I hated her, I would not push her in the lake.'

'Would you not?' His voice softened, and he smiled wryly. 'No, I do not believe you would. Forgive me, Louise. I should have known.'

She looked up at him, choking back her emotion. 'It was an accident.'

Raphael reached out and touched her cheek. 'I should not have accused you, but . . . I was angry about something else. Please forgive me, Louise, and do not think of leaving. I want you to stay here.'

Louise swallowed hard, not wanting him to see how his words had affected her. 'Then I shall stay,' she whispered. 'For the moment . . .'

She would stay until Lady Helen became mistress of Carleton Manor, and then she would go.

'His lordship asks if you will come down at once, mademoiselle,' the maid said, sounding as if she had been running. 'He is waiting for you in the hall.'

The message seemed urgent, and Louise's heart began to jerk painfully. What had she done now? Remembering Raphael's anger only a few days ago, she felt sick with apprehension as she left her room. Helen had visited the house again the day before, but though they met in the grounds, they had scarcely spoken. Could she have complained to Raphael of his cousin's further rudeness?

Straightening her back in an attempt to hide her misgivings, Louise hurried downstairs, halting as she saw Raphael standing with his back turned to her. His thick hair clustered above the delicate lace of his ruff, and she felt a sharp desire to run her fingers through those shining locks. How much she loved him! How could she bear it if he was angry with her again? Perhaps Lady Helen was insisting that she be sent away. The thought gave her a stab of swift pain, making her gasp.

The pounding of her heart brought a flush to Louise's cheeks as the man turned to greet her, his steady, serious gaze causing her to clench her fists; then he smiled, and she felt the blood surge through her veins with the power of a spring tide as he came striding over, hands outstretched to grasp hers.

'Louise,' he said, his cool fingers winding possessively about hers. 'Hurry, I have something to show you.'

There was an air of suppressed excitement about him. Gazing up into his face, Louise caught the impish gleam in his eyes, and drew a sharp breath. Only once or twice before had she glimpsed that expression, and it set her pulses racing as she took his mood.

'What is it, my lord?' she asked, her mouth curving as he tugged impatiently at her hand, hurrying her through the long room and out of the house. 'What is so important that I must come at once?'

'You will see in a moment.'

Within a few seconds of leaving the house, Louise guessed that he was taking her to the stables. She glanced at his profile, wondering at that almost boyish look of pleasure. The stables were full of thoroughbred horses, she knew, but perhaps one of the mares had given birth to a particularly fine foal. Happiness swept through her at the thought. The successful birth of a foal was always cause for celebration, and it pleased her that Raphael should choose to share his triumph with her.

'Wait here, Louise,' he instructed as they reached the cobbled yard. 'Close your eyes, and do not open them until I tell you.'

Laughing, she did as she was told, feeling like an excited child.

'You may look now.' His voice was curiously apprehensive.

Wondering at the sudden tension in him, Louise opened her eyes, and gasped. There in front of her was not a new-born foal, as she had expected, but the most beautiful creature she had ever seen. The mare was snowy-white, its eyes as bright as black diamonds, and a mane of flowing silk gleamed in the autumn sunshine.

'Oh, you lovely creature!' Louise cried, reaching out instinctively to stroke the mare's velvet nose.

The horse snickered softly, nuzzling her hand gently and pawing at the ground with its delicate forehoof.

'I'm glad you like her,' Raphael murmured. 'She's yours, Louise—a small gift to make your stay here more enjoyable.'

'For me?'

She looked at him in amazement. Raphael had already told her that she might ride any suitable horse in his stables, but she had not expected him to buy her a mount of her own. Tears stung her eyes, and she felt her lips tremble.

'You are too kind, my lord,' she whispered. 'The mare is beautiful. I—I love her.'

'Yes, she is lovely,' Raphael replied, an odd, strained note in his voice. 'But not as beautiful as her mistress. I'm glad you are pleased with the mare, Louise.'

Something in his face made her hold her breath, her heart contracting as an iron band seemed to tighten round it. For a moment she thought he would say more, and her lips parted slowly as she waited. He was looking at her in that special way, almost hungrily, as though he wanted to take her in his arms and make love to her. Louise swayed towards him, longing to feel the warm sweetness of his mouth on hers, but as she did so, one of the grooms came out of the stables and Raphael turned away abruptly.

'I'll have my horse saddled,' he said. 'We'll ride together, Louise.'

Disappointment pierced her. Raphael had not looked at her like that since before they left France. For one brief instant she had believed that he still wanted her, but the moment had passed.

Blinking back her tears, Louise lifted her chin a little higher. 'You must excuse me, my lord,' she said, sounding much calmer than she felt. 'I am not dressed for riding. I shall return to the house and change my gown —if you will wait for me?'

Raphael nodded, his face now strangely grim.

Turning swiftly away, she began to walk in the direction of the house, knowing she must be alone for a while.

In her pleasure at receiving such a wonderful gift, she had nearly betrayed herself. All her instincts had told her to throw her arms round Raphael's neck and thank him properly, but to behave so immodestly could only disgust a man who thought of her as his cousin—unless she had not imagined that look in his eyes! Yet if he wanted her, surely he would just reach out and take what he desired? He must know by now how vulnerable she was!

Feeling confused but faintly excited, she ran quickly up to her room. A tiny seed of hope had begun to take root in her heart and she was suddenly anxious to return to Raphael. After all, he had bought her the mare and she was sure she had not mistaken that look in his eyes. So perhaps there was a chance for her. A chance that he would not marry Lady Helen too soon . . .

Louise sipped the delicious concoction from the delicate milk glass posset-cup, sighing with contentment.

'You will spoil me, Mrs Beacham. It is not for you to wait on me. My maid could have brought this.'

'I made it for you myself. It will soothe your throat. The wind has been cold of late, and we can't have you taking a chill before tonight.'

'No,' Louise agreed, feeling a tingle of excitement. 'Everything must be perfect for Lord Carleton's friends from London; he tells me this is the first time he has invited mixed company to stay.'

'Yes, my lady. His lordship usually asks only one or two gentlemen for the hawking—the master is very fond of his falcons, as you know.'

The girl nodded and smiled. She had seen the wonderful patience Raphael had when training his precious hawks to fly after the lure. There was something noble about the sport, and she had already spent several hours watching him with the kingly birds.

'Will you get up now, my lady?'

Louise inclined her head but did not move at once.

Mrs Beacham now insisted on addressing her as if she were truly the mistress of the house, and she was beginning to feel assured of her position. All the years of strict training by Madame de Granvelle had served her well these past weeks: she knew instinctively how to win the respect of her servants, and she had quickly taken up the reins of the household without offending Mrs Beacham. In fact, the housekeeper was her staunchest ally in the continuing battle with Lady Helen. Of late, Helen's manner had been a little subdued, but she still lost no chance to criticise where she could, and had several times tried to make Louise look a fool by countermanding her orders or complaining that the changes she made were unacceptable.

Throwing back the bedcovers with a spurt of determination, Louise pulled on a heavy silk wrap. The days were growing steadily colder, and she was finding the climate harsh, despite the huge fires kept burning day and night for her benefit.

'Where is Lord Carleton?' Louise asked. 'I want to ask him something about the musicians he has engaged for this evening.'

'He went riding earlier, my lady,' the housekeeper said, wrinkling her brow. 'Shall I give Lord Edward and Lady Helen their usual rooms? The best guest-chamber should really be for the Earl of Harland.'

'That would mean moving Lady Helen, I suppose?' Louise nodded decisively. 'We must not offend the Earl—move Lady Helen to the Green Chamber.'

'Yes, my lady.' Mrs Beacham's eyes gleamed with satisfaction. 'Will you make your inspection of the kitchens this morning?'

'I think I shall ride first,' she said. 'The air is cool, but it will refresh me.'

The housekeeper went away and Louise dressed swiftly, a tingle of anticipation running through her. It was a bright, crisp morning and she felt in need of exercise after several days of rain. It would be pleasant to ride in the park. Besides, she might meet Raphael. Of late she had scarcely seen him except in company. All the local aristocracy had called, and it seemed the house was always filled with people. Raphael went hawking most mornings with his neighbours, leaving Louise to entertain the ladies.

Walking through the great hall, Louise smiled at the servants who were busily preparing for the evening, acknowledging their bows and curtsies with a little nod. She had requested greenery be brought inside to give the chamber a festive air, and she appreciated the pleasant scent of fern and the last of the roses from the formal gardens. She knew the servants thought it a strange custom to bring flowers indoors, but she had always loved their scent, and Raphael, too, seemed to enjoy it.

Now that he had given her the beautiful snow-white mare for her own use, she seized every opportunity to ride, often completely alone after that first morning when Raphael had accompanied her. If she had hoped for some sign from him that day, she had hoped in vain. He had been polite, charming, but distant. Since then, she suspected him of avoiding her.

Mrs Beacham must have sent word to the stables, for Louise's groom was waiting in the courtyard with her horse. He stood back respectfully, having helped her to mount. She was an experienced rider, seldom taking a groom with her unless she wished to leave the estate. This morning she intended a brisk gallop through the park. There was a busy day ahead of her, and she would need to rest in the afternoon if she wanted to be fresh for the evening's festivities.

The sun had come out from behind the clouds as horse and rider cantered through the trees. Louise felt its welcome warmth on her face, enjoying the sensation of the wind in her hair. This evening was important to her, and she was happy because everything was going so well.

She decided that she would ride as far as the stream and then turn back. Guiding her horse towards a small rise ahead of her, she reined in suddenly as two figures came over the top. They were walking side by side, obviously deep in conversation, the woman's hair shining like a streak of silver in the autumn sunshine. All at once, the woman turned towards her companion, throwing herself at him in a burst of passion. He seemed to freeze for one moment, then his arms went round her.

The sight of Helen in Raphael's arms was too much for Louise. She could not bear to watch them kiss, so she tugged frantically at the reins, turning to ride away in a blind panic, the tears streaming down her cheeks. They were lovers! They had been meeting in secret because of the scandal it would cause if anyone guessed what was going on. It was too soon after Helen's husband's death for them to let their love be seen openly, so they stole away to hide from the world.

What a stupid fool she had been not to realise it before! She had believed that there was really a place for her here; she had taken pride in her position as châtelaine of Raphael's house, enjoying the small triumphs that came her way. Now she saw that she had been providing a cover for the true mistress of the house, and Helen must be laughing at her behind her back. They probably both laughed to think what an innocent little fool she was! Louise saw it all now.

She had been foolish to hope that Raphael might be learning to care for her: it had been hopeless from the very beginning. For a time, in France, she had caught his interest, probably because he was bored and could not be with the woman he loved—the woman he had loved since childhood. How could Louise hope to compete with an emotion so strong that it bound him to Helen in spite of all she had done?

The answer was that she could not. As her storm of grief gradually turned to anger at the way she had been used, Louise saw that there was only one hope for her. She must somehow escape from this intolerable position she had been tricked into. She would not stay here to be laughed at and duped by Helen.

If only André were alive, she thought desperately. It was no longer feasible to think of marriage with the Chevalier de Leconte. He would believe she had been the English lord's mistress, and would scorn her now. Her flight to England would have damaged her reputation, but it did not matter. She did not wish to marry. All men were false and cruel!

At this moment she did not care that her life might be in danger if she returned to France. She was humiliated and desperate, and it took all her courage to ride calmly back to the house. Yet thoughts of precipitate flight were far from her mind. She would not let either Helen or Raphael see that their despicable behaviour had hurt her. She would play her part as the hostess tonight—and only when the guests had all gone would she face Raphael with the truth.

CHAPTER TEN

LOUISE STOOD looking at her reflection in her hand-mirror. Her eyes glittered with cold pride, hiding the pain and anger inside her. She knew she looked her best, having taken great pains with her hair and gown. Her eyes twinkled with malicious delight as she looked at the neckline of her dress. After her ride, she had sent for her maid, and together they had worked on the ivory satin gown she was now wearing. Louise had deliberately slashed the décolletage to dip daringly over her breasts, almost exposing the rosy nipples. Even at the French Court such a gown would be worn only by the most daring of the ladies, but here in a quiet English manor house it was almost shameful.

Raphael would be furious with her when he saw her, she knew. That was why she had chosen to wait until the last minute before leaving her room, so that there would not be time for her to go back and change. Looking through her jewels, she selected a magnificent collar of huge rubies, fastening them round the slim arch of her throat and admiring the effect. Matching eardrops and bracelets completed the ensemble. Tonight, no one would be able to ignore the châtelaine of Carleton Manor!

There was a knock at the door, and Mrs Beacham asked if she could come in. Louise called out that she might.

'Excuse me, mademoiselle, but his lordship sent me to ask if you were ready. The guests are beginning to leave their rooms and gather downstairs.'

Louise hid her smile as she saw the housekeeper's surprised stare. Her own determination hardened as she sensed her inward disapproval, though there was no sign of it on her face. Tonight, the girl did not care what anyone thought of her—she was tired of being dutiful and responsible. She was sick of being used for other people's devices. If Raphael did not desire her himself, other men would, and she intended to enjoy herself.

'I shall go down now,' she said, picking up her fan as she swept regally from the room, her head high.

Just as she had hoped, the great hall was crowded with the guests she had greeted earlier in the day. Everyone had rested in their chambers before changing for the evening, and the scene below her was a glittering array of beautiful clothes and costly jewels, but not one of the women was dressed as magnificently as Louise. She and her maid had worked hard on the ivory gown, and it was typically French in its elegance and style.

Pausing at the head of the stairs, Louise waited until she felt everyone's eyes were turned in her direction. She heard someone gasp, and she could not help a little smile of triumph. Her entrance had caused a sensation, just as she had planned. Now, let them all think what they liked! She did not care if the ladies called her a French harlot; the gentlemen would have eyes only for her tonight, and if Raphael was shamed by her behaviour, that would be her revenge for what he and Helen had done to her.

As she walked slowly down, she knew that the whispers were circulating like wildfire through the huge chamber. She searched the sea of faces below her, finding Helen's first, and registering the shock and jealousy in those hard eyes. Then she saw Raphael making his way towards her determinedly, and her heart stopped beating for one terrible moment. There was no mistaking the fury in his face and the stiff set of his shoulders.

He met her at the foot of the stairs, and a shiver went through her as she saw his icy expression. He was looking at her as if he would like to murder her, and for a second Louise's courage failed her. She had expected him to be angry, indeed she had fully intended to provoke him, but never had she thought to arouse quite this fury. Her knees felt weak, and she wished she could turn and run back to the safety of her own room; then she remembered the scene she had witnessed in the park that morning, and her resolve stiffened. He had no right to look at her so accusingly after the way he had behaved!

Raphael's fingers closed cruelly over her arm, as if he meant to hurt her. Louise knew that he was fighting to control his temper, and she wondered if he would order her to go back to her room and put on another gown. If she had but known it, his first instinct was to do just that, and it was only the realisation of the scandal this would cause that saved her.

'You are late,' he muttered coldly. 'We both know why, and we shall discuss this matter later, make no mistake.'

He had spoken softly, so that only Louise could hear his words, but now he turned, facing the company as he said, 'Ladies and gentlemen, may I present Mademoiselle de Granvelle. Louise was forced to leave her home in France after the massacres you have all heard of. She speaks only a little English, but I know most of you will be able to communicate in her own language. She has kindly taken charge of my household, and I am sure she will try to make your stay here as comfortable as possible.'

A faint flush stained Louise's cheeks as she listened to his introduction. Was Raphael trying to protect her from her own folly? He obviously thought her outrageous gown would provoke an adverse reception, and his action made her feel humiliated. Her chin lifted a little higher and her eyes smoked with resentment. She did not need his help! She was not ashamed of what she had done, nor was she as ignorant of the language as he seemed to believe. Over the past weeks her English had improved rapidly, and she had intended to impress her

guests tonight with her ability. Now she smiled and
fluttered her eyelashes flirtatiously at the nearest gentleman.

'Good evening. I hope you found your room comfortable, my lord?' she asked in flawless English, made more
enchanting by her French accent.

'Perfectly comfortable, mademoiselle.'

The Earl of Harland stared at her like a man in a
trance. He took the hand she offered, lifting it to his lips
to kiss it lingeringly, his eyes never leaving her face for
an instant.

'Where did you come from?' he asked in a husky
voice, still holding her hand. 'Raphael said from France,
but surely it was Paradise?'

A delicious gurgle of laughter escaped her as she saw
the stunned look in his eyes. Here was her first conquest,
then, and he was the most prestigious of their guests.

'No, indeed, my lord,' she murmured throatily. 'I was
in Paris when the troubles started. Lord Carleton saved
my life, and brought me back to England to the safety of
his house.'

'Would that it had been me,' the Earl said fervently.
'Mademoiselle de Granville, I must tell you at once that
you are divine; the most beautiful woman I have ever
met. I offer you my heart, my name and my fortune, do
with them as you will. I am now, and for always, your
slave.'

A little flutter of apprehension ran through Louise as
she looked into his face. He was handsome, she supposed, with his grey eyes and light brown hair, but there
was something about his mouth that warned her of his
dissolute nature. Somehow she guessed that this was a
man who lived only for pleasure, and the signs of his
excesses were already beginning to show in his face,
though he could not be more than seven and twenty. Yet
he was exactly the kind of man who would best suit her
purpose this evening: she could flirt with him as much as
she liked without endangering his heart.

Gazing up at him with a wicked smile, she pretended
to believe his extravagant statement. 'You should be
careful, my lord! I might believe you, and take you at
your word. If I had a fancy to be a countess, do you not
think the title would suit me?'

'It was made for you,' he responded gallantly, his eyes
devouring her. 'Marriage would be a small price to pay
for the pleasure of owning you, mademoiselle.'

His eyes lingered on her exposed breasts, leaving her
in no doubt of what was in his mind. A tingle ran through
her as she saw the naked lust in his face, and she was a
little afraid of the passion she had aroused in him.

'Unfortunately, I am not for sale,' she said, giving him
a regretful smile to take the sting from her words.
'Excuse me, m'sieur, I must greet Lady Helen and Lord
Edward.' She moved away from him, conscious of the
scorching gaze that followed her wherever she went.

Musicians were playing in the gallery as the guests sat
down to eat the sumptuous feast prepared for them.
Course after course of rich foods were served, accompanied by only the choicest wines from the cellars. The
guests ate greedily, dipping their fingers in the succulent
sauces and wiping them on napkins of finest linen as they
attacked the next dish to be set before them.

Raphael had engaged a troupe of strolling players to
entertain the company while they feasted; they sang,
danced, tumbled and did feats of juggling that amazed
the watchers. Then, when the meal was ended at
long last, those with enough energy themselves began
to dance, or to indulge in more of their host's good
wine.

Seated in the place of honour beside the principal
guest, Louise was aware of Raphael's mounting fury.
She knew he had noticed the way the Earl's eyes lingered
on her exposed flesh and that he seized every chance to
touch her hand or arm. She gave her companion a
tantalising glance from time to time, never quite letting

him know what was in her mind. It pleased her that her behaviour was distressing Raphael. If he was humiliated by it, it was a just revenge for what he had done. She did not mind if everyone thought her a wanton; she would prefer them to think ill of her than to believe her a complacent fool who did not know what was going on behind her back.

Once her eyes met Raphael's across the table, and she shivered as they stabbed her with their accusation. She frowned and looked away. What right had he to pass judgment on her? He was no different from the man sitting beside her. Both of them were libertines who took a woman for their own pleasure.

Louise felt the Earl's leg pressed against hers beneath the table. She moved away, her eyes sparkling as she shook her head at him. He laughed, his hunting instincts aroused by the fascinating creature who seemed to encourage even as she repelled his attempts to capture her.

'Tell me,' he said, leaning nearer to whisper in her ear. 'Why has Raphael not made sure of you himself? He must be a fool to let a woman like you slip through his fingers—or are you already his mistress?'

'I am no man's mistress.' Louise sipped her wine calmly. 'I shall give myself to only one man, m'sieur.'

'You are a maiden?' The Earl looked at her in astonishment, his brows rising as she nodded. 'Then you have a prize I would give much to possess. It would indeed be worth my title.'

Her laughter made him stare, a slight indignation in his eyes. 'Oh, do not be offended, m'sieur,' Louise said, touching his hand. 'I am honoured that you should consider such a sacrifice, but I do not believe it would suit you to be married to me. You see, I would demand that my husband loved only me.'

He smiled ruefully. 'You ask a high price indeed, mademoiselle. Yet, for a woman like you, even this might not be too much to pay.'

It was Louise's turn to be surprised. 'Surely you are jesting, my lord?'

'You think me incapable of fidelity? Or perhaps you believe my fortune is not sufficient to keep you in such splendour as you have here?'

'Is any man ever entirely faithful?' Louise sighed deeply. 'I would marry the man I love if he had nothing! Like others of my kind, I ask only love. Even if it lasts but a short time, true love is the most precious thing a man can give to a woman.'

'Then your heart belongs to another.' The Earl shrugged his shoulders and laughed. 'That is a pity. Still, I am willing to bargain for what remains. Be my countess, mademoiselle, and take what pleasure you can from life. Give me a son, and I should not keep you a prisoner in my castle. Once we no longer enjoyed each other, I should not complain if you sought other lovers.'

'I believe you are serious.' Louise's eyes darkened as she looked at him. 'Forgive me, m'sieur, I cannot accept your offer, though I am honoured by it.'

'You refuse me because you are blinded by dreams of love. I shall not accept your answer now, Mademoiselle de Granvelle. You shall have some time to think over what I have said.' He smiled wickedly. 'There, see what a complacent husband I would make. I would never look at you as our friend is now. I think we should dance before he goes quite mad, don't you?'

Louise glanced towards Raphael and gasped. She got to her feet as the Earl held out his hand, knowing that it was her only escape. Raphael was on his way to claim her!

The musicians had been playing a slow, stately piece, but as Louise and her partner reached the floor it suddenly changed to the merry tune of a gaillarde.

'Ah, this is our good Bess's favourite dance,' the Earl said as he swung the girl off her feet. 'When you come to Court, you will see how merrily the Queen dances with her beloved Robert Dudley. I vow he is the only man she ever truly loved—had he never had a wife, England would have had a king before now.'

'Will she ever marry him, do you think?' Louise asked between springs.

'Nay, the scandal would be too great. Elizabeth will risk her throne for no man, no matter how much she loves him—or how prettily he dances.'

'Your words are treason, Harland!' Raphael's tones cut like the blade of a knife between them. 'I shall dance with my cousin now, before you corrupt her entirely.'

The Earl grinned, giving way good-naturedly. He bowed elegantly before Louise. 'Forget nothing I have said, fair lady.'

'What has he been saying to you?' Raphael asked, as the Earl walked away, leaving them together. 'He is a libertine and a gambler. You should not believe a word he says, Louise!'

She felt the pressure of his hand on her arm, and indignation flared in her breast. 'Oh, I know what kind of a man your friend is, Raphael,' she said scornfully, lifting her head provocatively. 'You are, I believe, very alike in many ways. The only difference between you is that you hide your vices and the Earl flaunts his openly.'

Raphael's face went white. 'What are you saying? I find your innuendoes insulting.'

'Really?' Louise smiled too brightly. 'Could it be rather that you are surprised that I am not the fool you thought me, my lord?'

'What?' Raphael's eyes narrowed dangerously, then his hand tightened on her arm. 'I must speak with you alone.'

'I have nothing to say to you,' she replied haughtily, but he ignored her, his fingers digging deep into her flesh as he propelled her through the thronged room.

Conscious of the curious eyes following them, Louise could do nothing but allow herself to be taken to a small antechamber at the side of the hall. She looked at Raphael sullenly as he thrust her inside and slid a heavy bolt into place, thus ensuring that she could not escape.

'I wish you will permit me to leave.'

'You will leave when I have finished with you, mademoiselle!'

'This is ridiculous,' Louise said, catching her breath as she saw the fury on his countenance. 'Just because I chose to wear a gown you do not approve . . .' Her words trailed away as he moved closer. 'You are not my father, m'sieur . . . You cannot tell me what I may do.'

'I am not your father—thank God!' Raphael muttered. 'It might be better if I were—at least you could not destroy me then!'

'You speak in riddles, m'sieur. I do not understand you.'

'Do you not?' Raphael sighed. 'Do you not indeed, Louise? Then it seems I have failed in my purpose. I thought . . .' He stopped and turned away, going to stand by the window, his back towards her as he gazed out into the night. 'I thought you were happy here, Louise. Pray, tell me, what have I done that offends you so?'

For a moment she thought there was pain in his voice, and her heart contracted; then she remembered the moment when his arms had closed round Helen and anger rippled through her.

'Do not pretend to be humble, m'sieur. I know you now for the cold-hearted rake you really are. I saw you with *her* this morning. I saw you embracing her. I know you have used me to give an air of respectability to your house while you carried on a secret affair with the wife of the man you killed. I know your secret, m'sieur—and I despise you for it!'

Raphael flinched as though she had struck him. He turned slowly to face her, and she gasped at his expression. 'You think I am Helen's lover . . . Is that what you are saying?'

A knot of sickness was forming in her stomach as

Louise gazed into the black hell of his eyes, and her knees shook as she formed the word with stiff lips.

'Yes.'

He was silent for what seemed an eternity, his eyes never leaving her face for an instant, and when he spoke, the sound of his voice turned her blood to water.

'So that is why you played the wanton tonight.' He looked at her in disgust and she shrank away from him, half expecting a blow. 'You believe that of me! You think I would use you—you!—to hide my shame from the world.'

'I saw you take her in your arms.'

'And then . . . What then, Louise?' he asked hoarsely. 'Did I thrust her to the ground and possess her in my lust before you?'

The colour drained from her cheeks and she felt weaker. Shaking her head, she backed away as he took two steps towards her, convinced now that he would seek to harm her in some way.

'I—I don't know . . .' she whispered, her hand flying to her throat. 'I rode away . . .'

'You rode away . . . condemning me as a lying, faithless womaniser in your heart—your icy heart that turns from me in disdain . . .' He paused, seemingly torn between disbelief and fury. 'Then there is no more to be said, is there? You condemned me without a hearing, and you took your revenge.' The coldness in his voice was more deadly than the sting of a scorpion. 'You wanted to twist the knife in my breast, did you not? Well, mademoiselle, I fear I must disappoint you. If you sought to make me jealous, you have failed. I wish you joy of your conquest, Louise. Indeed, I think you deserve each other.'

With that last thrust, he turned and slid back the bolt, leaving the room while she was still too numb to think clearly.

'Raphael . . .' she whispered through white lips. 'Oh, please, forgive me!'

Her words came too late: he had gone. For a moment, grief pierced her through the heart, and she cried out in her pain. If she had wronged him . . .

Movement returned to her limbs and she reached the door, knowing she must follow him. If her accusation were false, it would break her heart. She had never wanted to hurt him, only to make him see that she could not continue in his house while he betrayed her trust . . . But if he had not betrayed her. Oh God, what had she done?

Emerging into the crowded ballroom once more, her eyes were so blinded by tears that she did not see the woman until she stood deliberately in her path.

'He knows you for what you are now, you slut,' Helen hissed. 'Oh, you thought we were all fooled by that innocent look of yours, but I knew you for what you were the moment I saw you.'

Louise lifted her head, facing her enemy with pride. 'Pray let me pass, Lady Helen.'

'So that you can follow him and weep into his shoulder? I advise you not to waste your breath, mademoiselle. Your little tricks have failed. You thought you could make him jealous, didn't you?' Helen laughed harshly. 'All you have done is to destroy his dream of a perfect woman. Oh, yes, he thought you were above other women—now, he knows you are no better than the rest of us. He will come to me, and you will be sent packing to France, where you belong!'

Louise gasped at the hatred in Helen's eyes. 'I know you and he are lovers,' she said numbly. 'I know you have both been using me to keep your affair a secret.'

Helen's face showed suspicion, then she smiled. 'So you are not quite the fool we thought. Well, perhaps you have learned your lesson now. In future you will not give yourself so many airs. Remember I intend to be Raphael's wife, and nothing you can do will stop me.'

'You will destroy him,' Louise said. 'You have no shame!'

Helen's eyes went over her gown. 'At least I do not appear naked in company!' She broke off when Louise slapped her. 'You slut!' she shrilled as the music ended, causing everyone to look at them. 'How dare you?'

'Because I have the right,' Louise said quietly. She looked into Helen's eyes, expecting her to strike back, but surprisingly she flushed a dark red and walked quickly away.

The music had begun to play again, but no one was dancing. Louise raised her head, looking neither to right nor left as she walked calmly from the room. She would not run away, neither would she let anyone guess how much she was hurting inside. All her plans for this evening had been ruined. She knew that everyone would be laughing at her, but it didn't matter. Nothing mattered to her now.

She could not forget Raphael's look of disdain. He had given her a home and honoured her by making her his châtelaine, and she had destroyed his faith in her by behaving like a wanton in front of his guests. Her humiliation was complete, and it was her own fault. She should have confronted him and asked him for the truth, instead of trying to make him jealous. Helen had been right: this stupid masquerade tonight had been all for his benefit. She had told herself it was for revenge, but in her heart she had always known that it was meant to make him aware of her as a desirable woman. She had hoped that when he saw other men look at her with desire, he would want her again, as he had in France.

Now Louise saw that it was useless. Even if she had been wrong about what she thought she saw that morning, Helen was determined to be mistress here, and she herself could not find the strength to fight her any more. It was pointless to go on living here with a man who did not want her. She had thought she could cope with the pain, but she had been wrong. Louise knew that she had to leave this house quickly, before her own jealousy destroyed her. Already she had begun to change, doing things she would never have thought herself capable of. She would never have worn this gown tonight, she knew, and now she was shamed by it.

Louise forced herself to walk slowly up the stairs, knowing that she was still being watched, but once the lights and the music were left behind, she ran to her own room. Locking the door behind her, she began to rip at the fastenings of her gown, tearing it in her haste to get it off. She ripped the fine material across, throwing it to the floor in disgust. Then she flung herself face down on the bed and wept as if her heart would break.

Raphael hated her now. It was all finished. She must leave his house tonight, before he could guess how ashamed she was—before all pride was gone. She sat up, looking about her miserably as she tried to collect herself and make plans for her escape.

Suddenly a slight noise from her sitting-room made her start up in alarm. She put her feet to the cold floor, catching at a thin silk wrap to cover her nakedness.

'Who is it?' she whispered. 'Is someone there?'

She was trembling as she went into the adjoining chamber. Surely she had locked the door behind her? As she saw the man standing by the fireplace, the colour drained from her cheeks and she swayed unsteadily, her stomach contracting with nerves.

'How did you get in here?' she whispered.

For a long moment Raphael stared at her in silence, his eyes glittering strangely. She had never seen such a terrible coldness in him, and it terrified her. It was as if she were looking at a stranger: a man she did not know and could not recognise.

'Have you never wondered why I gave you these rooms, Louise?' he said at last, and the flat tone of his voice was somehow chilling. 'The painted panel conceals a door that leads into my chamber. I thought it might come in useful one day—and now it has.'

His face was deathly white in the flickering light of the

candle, etched with lines of strain about his nose and mouth. Louise's fascinated eyes clung to his tortured features as the silence deepened and stretched between them, and the beating of her heart was like the fluttering, torn wings of a wild bird in a trap.

Her tongue moved slowly over dry lips as the fear grew in her mind and she felt her throat closing. She tried to speak, and the words stuck to her lips, issuing at last as a hoarse whisper. 'Why have you come?'

'I have thought of you lying here alone so many nights . . .' he muttered, and his voice sounded choked, as if he found it difficult to put his thoughts into words. 'Imagined you lying in your bed, flushed in sleep . . .'

His eyes moved over her with a kind of feverishness, piercing the thin silk of her wrap which scarcely concealed the warm curves of her slender body, protecting her not at all from the probe of his gaze and giving a silver sheen to her flesh.

Suddenly his eyes narrowed to thin slits and his mouth twisted in a sneer, sending a spiral of fear through her. She flinched as he moved in closer to her, his fingers fastening about her wrist in a grip that made her wince.

'I have come . . .' he said with a dangerous softness that belied his words. 'I have come to take what is mine!'

Louise drew her breath in sharply as she heard the menace in Raphael's voice. She could read the intention in the hard glitter of his eyes—eyes that seemed to burn her as they moved slowly over her.

'No . . .' she whispered, backing away from him, her limbs beginning to tremble. 'Please do not do this, my lord. Do not shame me, I beg you!'

'You have no shame,' he muttered and his words were like the lash of a whip. 'You forget, Louise, I saw you flaunt yourself before them all this evening. I saw the way you looked at that—that libertine!'

'I was merely flirting with him,' she whispered. 'I wanted to punish you for what—what you did . . .' Her breath stopped in fear as she saw his rage. 'If—If what I thought was not so, I beg your pardon, my lord.'

'It is too late to beg, Louise.' He reached out and tore the thin wrap from her fingers, laughing harshly as she tried in vain to cover her nakedness with her arms. 'Do not sicken me with your false modesty!' he rasped. 'It will protect you from me no longer.'

'Please . . .' Louise began, but the words were lost beneath his ravaging mouth as it took possession of hers, bruising her with the punishing kiss.

Her naked breasts were pressed against the velvet of his doublet as he crushed her to him, forcing her head back to allow his invading tongue to explore her yielding mouth. Bending down suddenly to catch one arm behind her knees, he swept her up in his arms without taking his lips from hers and carried her back into the bedroom.

Laying her down, he left her at last to unfasten his doublet and smallclothes. Louise looked up at him, her heart pumping wildly. She had longed for him to come to her every night as she lay alone in the big bed, but she wanted him to take her with tenderness, not in anger.

'Please do not, Raphael,' she whispered. 'Take me if you will, but not in bitterness. I shall not resist you.'

A smile tortured his mouth as he looked down at her, seeing the way her nipples had hardened to rosy points and the smoulder of desire in her wonderful, smoky eyes. She wasn't even going to fight him. The little wanton had been laughing at his chivalry all this time —she wanted him to take her!

For a moment Raphael was tempted to walk away and show her the measure of his scorn, but her lips parted invitingly and she made an involuntary movement towards him, as though entreating him to hold her. A torrent of hot desire flooded through him, robbing him of all conscious thought so that his body's urging became paramount. He had held back his need of her for too long, and he could control himself no more. Jealousy and rage had driven him to the limits of his endurance, and now the barriers were swept before the tide of his passion.

He knelt beside her on the bed, gathering her body to him. As their flesh touched, he was torn by deep shudders that set him trembling from shoulder to thigh, and his anger melted in the heat of a passion long denied.

'Louise, my beautiful, wonderful girl,' he whispered, his lips pressed against the sweet arch of her throat. He inhaled the fresh, warm scent of her body, his senses spinning. 'What a fool I have been to wait so long! You were always mine . . . I should have told the world so from the start.'

She did not understand his fevered words, but her heart responded to the tenderness in his voice just as her body leaped beneath the touch of his hands. She lay unresisting as he stroked her quivering flesh, her legs parting willingly to allow him access to the warm secrets of her womanhood.

A tiny sigh escaped her as his fingers probed the silken flesh between her thighs; then his lips opened over hers as he moved to cover her with his body. The sudden pain of his entry made her stiffen in shock, and a single tear trickled from the corner of her eyes. Then the first wave of some strange new sensation swept through her, lifting her and carrying her away to a place she had never been—a wondrous place that was not quite Heaven and not quite Hell.

Her breath came faster as desire melted her body and she became one with her tormentor, her flesh seeming to mingle with his so that she was nothing more than a beat of his heart. She had no will, no mind of her own, only the fear that he would leave her. When the end came at last, it was as if she were torn asunder, tossed into the air like sea spray, to vanish for ever. It was like death and rebirth simultaneously.

Afterwards, Louise lay curled against his side like a kitten seeking warmth before its eyes had opened. She nestled against him, utterly spent, the salt taste of his sweat on her lips as she slipped into an exhausted sleep.

Raphael looked down at her, his face sombre in the flickering light of the dying fire. He knew now he had wronged her, and the bitterness of it twisted inside him. She was as innocent as she was warm and beautiful. He had taken something perfect and destroyed it. She would never forgive him for lying to her all this time, yet it was too late for regrets. It was time to tell her the truth.

He touched his lips to her forehead, a tenderness spreading through him that set him wondering at himself. She stirred but did not waken as he stroked her hair, and he smiled. Suddenly, the future held a golden promise. Easing himself from the bed, he dressed swiftly. Tomorrow he would tell her all the things he should have told her at the start.

Someone was making a noise. It reached through the misty webs that held her, forcing Louise to open her eyes. The throbbing pain in her head hit her with a blinding force as she tried to rise, and she lay still for a moment. She wanted only to stay where she was and die, but the knocking continued, and she pushed back the covers, stumbling out of bed with a groan. There was a terrible tightness in her chest that seemed to threaten her breathing. Reaching for a wrap to cover herself, she held it with nerveless fingers round her body. The room whirled crazily as she walked on bare feet to the door, feeling the cold strike into her even while her throat felt as if it were on fire. After what seemed a nightmare journey, she fumbled with the key, swaying dizzily on her feet as the heavy door swung open at last and she found herself looking into the anxious eyes of Mrs Beacham.

'God be praised, mistress,' she said. 'I was beginning to think I should never wake you.'

'I—I seem to be ill,' Louise croaked. 'What time is it?'

'Late afternoon . . .' The housekeeper frowned as she looked at her. 'You've caught an ague. I knew how it would be. You are not used to this climate, my lady. You should wrap yourself warmly.' She sniffed disapprovingly. 'And I see the fires have gone out.'

'Please do not scold me.' Louise's eyes filled with weak tears. She felt so ill, and it was all she could do to stand upright. 'I know it was wicked of me to wear that shameful gown last night. I—I should not have done it.'

'It was not wise,' Mrs Beacham agreed, but her face had softened as she looked at the girl. The child was naught but a babe after all, and there were things the housekeeper did not approve of in this house, but it was not for her to say. She shook her head, smiling slightly. 'Well, we all make mistakes, my lady. Now, come back to bed. I'll have the maids see to the fires and I shall make you a nice hot posset myself with something special to ease your chest. I've thought you were sickening for something these past two days, and it seems I was right.'

Louise felt too weak to argue. She allowed the housekeeper to fuss round her, only too glad to slip into bed and close her eyes as she moved about the room, tidying it and putting everything to rights.

'Now just you try to rest,' Mrs Beacham said, standing to look down at the girl's face and shake her head. There had been mischief here last night if she was not mistaken, but at least there was no evidence left to set the tongues of the servants wagging. 'I shall come back soon, and you must drink all your posset. It will do you more good than a visit from the physician, I promise you.'

Louise nodded weakly. She did not think she could bear to swallow an emetic or have hot plasters applied to her forehead. A visit from the physician was always a painful experience, and at this moment she felt she would almost rather die than endure those dreadful blood-sucking creatures on her body. Leeches always made her feel sick, and she already ached in every limb. She preferred to trust the housekeeper's knowledge of healing herbs. After all, it was only a chill, and she would be better in a few days. She shut out the shameful soreness between her thighs, trying to block the forbidden pictures that kept sending hot shivers all over her.

As Mrs Beacham left at last, Louise lay with her eyes closed, fighting the emotion that washed over her as the taunting memories flooded back. She had behaved like the wanton Raphael had called her, wearing that outrageous gown and flirting shamelessly with the Earl of Harland. She had meant to provoke Raphael, and her plan had succeeded only too well. It was her own fault that he had decided to use her like a whore. She had not even tried to fight him after her first, feeble attempt.

Tears stung her eyes as she remembered how easily she had given in. She ought to have defended her honour with all her strength, but his kisses had destroyed her resistance. She had wanted him to take her . . . wanted it so badly that she would have begged him to stay if he had tried to leave her. She knew her surrender had been complete, for she had been able to hold nothing back.

The realisation of her weakness where Raphael was concerned frightened her. What kind of a woman was she to give herself with such abandon to a man who did not love her? The truth was that he had made her his slave; she had not the will to fight him. His possession of her was total. He could take her whenever he wished and discard her when she no longer pleased him. And because she was so bound by her love for him, she would submit to it all.

The pain twisted inside Louise, destroying the pride she had always had in herself. What had she become? What might she become in the years ahead, when Raphael turned his face from her in disgust as he sought another's arms?

She turned her face to the pillow in sick despair. Her only chance was to leave his house before it was too late. Yet she was helpless, tied to her bed by the illness that had sapped her strength.

Sensing someone beside the bed, she opened her eyes, expecting to find that the housekeeper had returned with her posset. She gasped, shrinking beneath the covers as she saw that it was Raphael.

'Go away!' she whispered. 'I beg you, my lord, leave me in peace.'

He laid a cool hand on her fevered brow, frowning as he saw the look in her eyes. 'There is no reason to be afraid,' he said. 'You are ill, but it will soon pass. Forgive me, Louise. I have not used you well.'

'You used me like a whore,' she choked, turning her face to the pillow again so that he should not see the shame in her eyes. 'You dishonoured me, and I hate you for it.'

'There is no dishonour in a union such as ours. The blessing of the church is a mere formality, Louise. A true union is that of a man and woman who belong to each other . . .'

'I do not want to belong to you,' she lied wretchedly.

A nerve jumped in his throat, and he clenched his hands to stop himself reaching for her. He had hoped to explain everything to her this morning, but how could he, now that she was so ill? What he had to say would cause her pain, and he must wait until she was well. Last night she had given herself to him more completely than any woman he had ever known. He could not believe she would turn from him now.

'Louise, listen to me! I know I have deceived you, and I accept that you are hurt by this. When you are better, we shall talk, and you will see that I had no choice. You will see that this is best for you. You have been content here . . .'

'Leave me,' she moaned, covering her face with her hands. 'You are cruel to taunt me when I am ill.'

Raphael struggled to control his emotions. He wanted to make her look at him, to force her to accept the inevitable, but it was impossible at present. He took a turn about the room, his thoughts sombre as frustration engulfed him. She was being unreasonable, and he had no time to plead his case. He went to stand by the bed once more, looking down at her flushed face and tumbled locks, his senses stirred by memories of the previous evening. He could not let her go now, even if she hated him.

'I must go to London,' he said at last. 'The Queen has summoned me, and I cannot disobey her again. I would not leave when you are sick if it was not important, Louise. Please tell me that you will try to understand why I lied to you. I realise it must seem that I tricked you into coming to England with me, but I had no choice. I hope, in time, you may be able to forgive me?'

'No, never,' Louise muttered, suddenly finding the courage to face him. He was admitting he had deceived her with Helen! 'What you have done has destroyed my life. I wish I had never met you!'

'This is foolishness.' Raphael stared at her in mounting resentment. 'I have done nothing that was not my right. There is a moment in every maiden's life when she must become a woman.'

Anger swept away the shame, and Louise sat up in bed, her aching limbs forgotten. 'I have given you no rights over me, m'sieur.'

'You little fool!' Temper snapped in the black eyes, and he sat beside her on the bed, taking hold of her shoulders. 'You are mine, Louise, and have been from the first night I saw you! I was patient with you because of your innocence, and the grief you had suffered—but I will have no more of this nonsense. You belong to me, and I shall never let you go! So accept what is done and be ready to welcome me to your bed when I return. If you do not, I shall take what is mine, whether you wish it or not.'

Louise could feel the cruel grip of his fingers through her wrap, and she was powerless to prevent the tear sliding down her cheek as she whispered, 'You are hurting me, Raphael. My—My head aches . . .'

The fury died out of him and he looked at her helplessly, unable to come to terms with her rejection. 'Forgive me,' he said stiffly. 'I meant not to hurt you. I shall leave you to rest.'

'Thank you.' She sank back against the pillows, a little moan escaping her lips as the feverish shudders gripped her body. 'Please send Mrs Beacham to me.'

'I am here, my lady.'

The housekeeper frowned as she moved towards the bed, her eyes darting accusation at the man who still hesitated there. 'Forgive me, my lord. I did not know you were here until I heard your voice. I have a hot posset for Mademoiselle de Granvelle. With your permission, I will have the maids make up the fires before she freezes to death.'

Raphael's nostrils flared as he saw the stubborn look on her face. He knew that she must have been in the adjoining room long enough to have overheard what was said between them, and it was clear she had put her own interpretation on his words. There was a challenge in her eyes, though her manner was that of an obedient servant. Damn her! She knew he could not refuse her reasonable request. Yet they both understood that she was protecting her mistress from him, forcing him to leave. He felt angry and frustrated, yet he knew there was no more to be said for the moment.

'Then I shall place Mademoiselle de Granvelle in your care while I am away. Be warned that I shall hold you personally responsible for any harm that may come to her.'

'She will come to no hurt at my hands, my lord.'

He appeared to be taken aback at her unspoken message; then he smiled oddly. 'Then I can go in peace.' He strode from the room, as she stared after him in bewilderment.

As soon as the door had closed behind him, Louise clutched the housekeeper's arm. 'You must help me,' she whispered hoarsely. 'I have to leave this house before he returns!'

Mrs Beacham saw the fear on the girl's face. If she had not overheard her master's words, she would never have believed him capable of such cruelty; but there was no doubting the evidence of her own eyes and ears. She became grimly determined; it might mean the loss of her position, but she was brave, and she had a little money to see her through her old age. She could not stand by and see this poor girl destroyed: it would be a sin, and she could not bear it on her conscience.

'Rest now, my dear mistress. His lordship will be gone for at least two weeks. I shall help you to leave as soon as you are well enough to travel.'

CHAPTER ELEVEN

LOUISE STOOD at the window, gazing out towards the park. The trees were beginning to look bare as autumn turned to winter and the mists curled across the damp ground. It would not be so cold in France, the girl thought, trying to cheer herself. Once she was there, she would learn to live with her pain. Perhaps she would even be able to discover what had happened to André, though she feared he must be dead, for there had been no word from him.

She had been ill for five days, but Mrs Beacham's cures had eased her aches and she was almost well enough to travel. The housekeeper had been very kind to her, sending word to her brother's son in the next county and arranging for him to escort Louise to France. Her own maid had agreed to accompany them, and in a day or two she would be leaving Raphael's home. It was a bitter wrench for her to go, but she knew she could not stay. If she did, her own jealousy would destroy her. Much as she loved Raphael, she would not be used and cast aside when Helen became his wife.

Louise felt sad as her gaze travelled slowly round the room she had come to think of as her own. She could have been so happy here, if only . . .

The door opened and Mrs Beacham came in. 'Forgive me for disturbing you, mademoiselle, but there is a gentleman below who wishes to speak with you.'

'A gentleman? Not—Not the Earl of Harland?' Louise blushed as she recalled how shamelessly she had flirted with Raphael's friend. He had responded gallantly, but she did not believe he really wished to marry her. Besides, she had made up her mind that she would never marry. She would live quietly on her estates in

France and find some impoverished matron to be her companion.

The housekeeper sounded uncertain. 'No. He says he is your brother, but . . .'

'André? *Here?*' Louise turned faint as the room spun, holding on to the edge of the table to steady herself. 'Can it really be him?' Her heart was pounding. 'Where is this man?'

'Downstairs in the hall.'

Louise waited no longer. Her feet flew along the gallery to the head of the stairs. A man was standing in the hall with his back turned to her. As she called his name, he turned, and then she was hurtling down the stairs and into his arms.

'André!' she sobbed, flinging herself at him in an excess of joy. 'André, you are alive!'

André seemed rather startled by her greeting, but he held her briefly before pushing her away from him.

'I had not thought to find you so pleased to see me.'

The coldness in his voice dimmed her pleasure. She drew back, looking at his face in bewilderment. She had forgotten that her brother disliked any show of affection from her.

'It is just that I am so glad to see you,' she said. 'I thought you were dead.'

'Perhaps it might have been better for you if I were,' he sneered. 'Or have you lost all sense of shame?'

'I—I don't know what you mean!'

'Are you married, Louise?'

She dropped her eyes before his cold stare. 'No.'

'That is what I heard from a man who was a guest in this house a few days ago. We met in a Portsmouth inn and shared a glass of wine together. He was struck by my name, and he told me about a young woman he had met with a similar title.' André glared at her. 'The Earl of Harland has hopes of making you his mistress, Louise.'

'He has no reason to hope, André! He—He asked me to marry him, but I refused.'

'Because you are Lord Carleton's mistress.' André
gripped her wirst. 'The Earl is a patient man, Louise. He
will take you when your lover has done with you.'

'I—I am not a harlot! You are unfair to accuse me so!'

'Then why did you run away with him?'

'He rescued me after you left me alone in the street
that night, and he took me home.'

'Why did you not stay and wait for me?'

'My life was in danger.' She saw a startled look in his
eyes and pleaded with him. 'Oh, you must believe me,
André! Lord Carleton was warned that the Cardinal de
Lorraine was plotting to kill us both.'

His grip tightened on her wrist. 'Do you swear to me
that this is the truth?'

'I swear it, André.' She winced. 'You are hurting me! I
would not have left France if I had known you were still
alive. What happened to you after we lost each other?'

'I searched for you, of course. I spent days trying to
find you, searching among the dead and injured; then
someone told me you had left Paris with the Englishman. When I finally reached La Rochelle, they told
me you and he had been there, but had disappeared
suddenly.'

Louise frowned. 'Did you not get Raphael's letter to
the steward?'

'There was no letter.' André stared at her. 'Why did
you not marry the Chevalier de Leconte?'

No letter? How could that be? Had Raphael lied to
her?

'I have never even met him. I did not know how to
contact him—nor did I wish to.'

André's eyes narrowed and she sensed a strange
urgency in him. 'You are not lying to me, Louise?'

'Why should I lie?'

Louise avoided his searching gaze. She had not told
him the whole truth, but some things would have to
remain her secret for ever. She raised her head at last,
puzzled by the odd look of triumph on his face.

'Your servant said her master was in London, is that true?'

'Yes. Why?'

'I had hoped to pay my respects to him—but perhaps we shall see him in London.'

'We?' Louise stared at him. 'Are—Are we going to London?'

'I have business there, and you shall come with me. Now that I have found you, you cannot stay here in this house.'

It was strange, Louise thought, she had prayed constantly for André to be alive, and yet now that he had come to fetch her, she felt almost reluctant to go with him.

She raised her eyes to meet his. 'No, I cannot stay here . . .'

Raphael paced restlessly about the ante-room, his patience stretched almost to snapping-point. This was the tenth day he had attended Court, waiting to be summoned to an interview with the Queen. Each day he had been left alone for several hours, and then told to come again the next morning. It was her Majesty's way of showing her displeasure, and while accepting Elizabeth's right to punish him, Raphael felt the frustration mounting within. Only the realisation that a second offence could lead to his arrest and imprisonment in the Tower kept him from returning home.

He stared moodily out of the window at the river. A thick fog was spreading across the surface of the water, and the trees along its banks had lost their leaves. Winter was upon them, and every day that passed increased the danger of the roads becoming blocked by snow. If that happened, it might be weeks before he could get back to Louise.

'Damn!' he muttered, striking his fist against the wall in impotent rage. 'How much longer must I wait in this accursed place?'

'It seems that, like us, you have little love for Whitehall, Lord Carleton—since you are impatient to leave it. Perhaps you would prefer a sojourn in the Tower?'

Hearing the coldness in the Queen's voice, Raphael hastily turned to face her, dropping to one knee. 'Your pardon, your Majesty, I did not hear you enter.'

'Methinks your mind was elsewhere, sir.' Elizabeth looked at him coldly.

'I will not deny I have anxious thoughts concerning someone who was ill when I left home, but my frustration came from impatience to see you, ma'am. I had earned your displeasure when we last met, and it has troubled me. Your Majesty must know that I have always been your loyal subject.'

'You call it loyal to disobey our orders, sirrah?' The clear, intelligent eyes began to twinkle. 'You deserve some punishment for your presumption. Yet we shall listen to your excuses, for the love we bear you. We are not so fickle as those who profess to love us.'

Raphael drew a sigh of relief. The Queen was not really angry, or he would even now be cooling his heels in a dungeon. He reached into his doublet and brought out a small packet.

'I had this portrait of the Duke of Alençon commissioned for your Majesty,' Raphael said. 'It was not ready when I left Paris, but my cousin, Jean Montpellier, brought it to me when he arrived in London three days ago.'

The Queen accepted the package graciously but did not open it immediately. 'You seem to have a surfeit of French cousins. We have heard tales of a young Huguenot girl you rescued from the massacre. We would hear of this—and your reasons for visiting France in disobedience of our orders.'

'I went in response to a letter from my uncle's housekeeper. He had died of violent stomach pains, and she believed he had been poisoned.'

'And was this Jean Montpellier's father?'

'No, ma'am, my uncle died without issue. As the eldest male relative, I am his heir. It was my duty to investigate the stories of murder.'

'Yes, that is clearly so.' Elizabeth frowned. 'I met your mother once when I was a child—was she not Marie de Leconte before she married?'

'That is so, ma'am.'

The Queen nodded. 'Come, sir, rise and walk with me. I would hear your opinion of these terrible happenings in France. My people demand justice for the Huguenots; they would have me send help to La Rochelle to aid the defiance of the royal army, but my ministers plead caution. If I give the French cause for anger, they may try to assist the Queen of Scots. They tell me there are plots to place Mary on my throne —there are those who say she has more right to rule than I.' Elizabeth's eyes glittered. 'I believe you had a private audience with Catherine de' Medici. What think you of her?'

'She is cleverer than some would have you believe, ma'am. She works in secret like a serpent, striking suddenly when the moment is right.'

'Was it she who plotted the slaughter of the Huguenots? Her ambassadors say it was in response to a plot against the royal family.'

'I believe she miscalculated the feelings of the people. I am certain it was her intention to rid herself of Coligny, but the rest was done in haste, and I believe she was shocked by the extent of the massacre.'

'A prince's life is sometimes hard.' Elizabeth sighed. 'What will history say of me, I wonder?'

'That you were the best king England ever had.'

Laughter lit the clear eyes. 'You flatter me, sir. Yet your words are sweet. You have given me a gift, and I have one for you. There are some documents that I think will interest you—they concern Mademoiselle de Granvelle.'

'Documents?'

'They were sent to me by Catherine de' Medici. It seems that she wishes you well, and she thought you should have them.' Elizabeth quirked her brow. 'Be patient a little longer, sir. In a few days you shall return to your home, and next time you come to Court, I shall expect to see your wife—do you understand me now?'

A gleam of amusement lit his eyes. 'I pray your Majesty enjoys a long and healthy life. England was never served by a wiser prince. I believe there is not another ruler in Christendom can defeat us while you reign, ma'am.'

'You have a honeyed tongue, sir. We have missed you at Court, and can spare you no longer. Now, tell me how you came to rescue this charming girl.'

'But, André, I would prefer to go home,' Louise said, looking at her brother across the table where they had just eaten. 'Could you not send a servant with me and continue your mission alone?'

He touched a kerchief to his lips fastidiously. 'No, Louise, I want you to accompany me. It will not be necessary for you to attend the Court, but you may amuse yourself in London by gathering a new wardrobe. Besides, it would be dangerous for you to travel alone. It was difficult enough to avoid the French fleet on the voyage here; when my mission is over, we may have to travel first to Navarre.'

Louise looked down. She did not want to risk seeing Raphael in London, but she could not explain her reasons to André.

He was watching her face, a tiny smile playing about his thin lips. 'My mission is important, Louise. If I can persuade the English Queen to help us, substantial gains may yet be made for our people, despite the blow that was struck against us in Paris. We owe it to Coligny and our father to do what we can.'

'Yes.' Louise shuddered. 'Is it true that they dragged the Admiral's body through the streets?'

A muscle twitched in his cheek. 'Yes; they were not content with his murder, they had to humiliate his corpse, too. You should not ask about these things, Louise; it is not fitting for a lady to speak of such unpleasantness.'

'I—I pray that Father did not suffer before he died.'

'He died for his beliefs.' André frowned. 'Father wanted you to marry the Chevalier de Leconte, Louise. Do you still wish to wed him?'

Louise looked at him in surprise. 'You know I have not met the Chevalier, André.'

'Then perhaps you would prefer to remain as you are for a while?'

'Are you giving me a free choice?' Louise could scarcely believe it when he nodded. 'Then—Then I should prefer not to marry at all. I would rather stay at home and act as your hostess until you take a wife.'

'Good. I did not approve Father's choice of a husband for you, but I could do nothing to prevent it. I hope you will allow me to guide you in future, Louise. You need not fear that I shall force you to marry against your will. Indeed, I should be sorry to lose your company too soon.'

Louise blinked, feeling touched by his concern. It was unexpected and brought a rush of emotion flooding through her. Perhaps she had misjudged her brother all these years, she thought regretfully. It must have been only his stern manner that had made her think he resented her in some way. She smiled mistily at him across the table.

'I am grateful for your kindness, André. I shall try to be worthy of your trust in me.'

'I am your brother,' André said, clasping her hand briefly. 'Remember always that I want only the best for you. Now, if you will excuse me, I must make preparations for our journey.'

Louise had never known André to be so kind to her. She was sure he knew she was hiding something from him, and yet he had not pressed her for the truth. Why? Sighing, she turned her thoughts to the journey ahead. Since André insisted she should go with him, she could only hope that Raphael would be on his way home before they arrived.

'Gone? How can she be gone?' Raphael glared at his cousin. 'She was too ill to leave her bed when I set out.'

Jean looked at him anxiously. 'You asked me to visit your home to enquire after her health. When I got there, your housekeeper told me her brother came for her . . .'

'My God!' Raphael exclaimed, his face ashen. 'I did not believe he would dare to follow us to England. I have suspected for some time that he killed our uncle, but until now I had no proof. It is hard to believe a man could be so evil, Jean.'

Jean nodded. 'When you first told me he had tried to abduct his own sister, I thought you were mad—but now you have the last pieces of the puzzle. What will you do?'

'I must find her and get her away from that madman before he harms her.'

'But can you be sure he does mean to harm her?' Jean asked, unwilling to believe it, even now.

'Among the documents sent by Catherine de' Medici was proof that he poisoned our uncle. She has ordered that he be arrested as soon as he returns to France. I am sure now that he killed the Chevalier to prevent Louise's marriage—and he will kill again rather than lose what he believes is his. But he may wait until he has first disposed of me. I believe his henchman was searching for those documents, not the jewels, the night I captured him at the inn.'

Jean stared at him. 'Then she is safe until he can get to you?'

'I pray it may be so, but there is little time to be lost. I shall see her Majesty today, and then I must begin the search for her.'

'We shall both search for her, Raphael. Louise told Mrs Beacham that they were coming to London, so perhaps he means to confront you?'

'Who knows what goes on in the mind of a man like that?' Raphael's face was grim.

Louise gazed out of the window in frustration. Snow was falling on the rooftops and the branches of the trees. As yet it had not settled on the ground, melting beneath the tramping of feet and the rattling carriage-wheels, but if it did so by morning, it would make her trip to the silk merchants unpleasant. André had promised to take her there when he returned, and she wanted to see the sights of London. Bored with being alone, she decided she would not wait for him to finish his business. There was no reason why she should not go out in a litter, with the stout porter to walk by her side.

She would need money, Louise realised. André could not object if she helped herself from the chest in his room, since he had said she could spend what she pleased to amuse herself. Their father had always been a prudent man, but André seemed to be spending money liberally now that he was in possession of the estate. They had travelled to London in great style, and the house he had hired was very grand.

Upstairs in her brother's chamber, she found the small iron-bound chest with little difficulty and pulled it out from under the bed. It was locked, but Louise knew that he always kept the key hidden in the binding of his Bible. Opening it, she found some documents lying on top, and beneath them the jewels she had brought out of Paris in her bodice. André had asked for them, and she had returned them to his safe-keeping. Among them was the gold locket and chain the Chevalier de Leconte had given her as a betrothal gift. Picking it up, Louise impulsively put it round her neck. It did not belong to

André, and she intended to return it to the Chevalier when she went home.

Taking a few gold coins from the pile beneath the rest of her family's jewels, Louise began to return the documents to the chest when a bold signature caught her eye. When she looked more closely, she realised that it was her marriage contract, and curiosity made her examine it. As she did so, a little shock went through her. She had seen that handwriting before—and yet it could not be! She looked at the signature again, her eyes wide with disbelief as she read:

'*Signed this day by Raphael, Chevalier de Leconte.*'

It had been witnessed by André, and in her father's neat hand was his own signature at the bottom.

Raphael was the Chevalier de Leconte? No, it could not be true! The room seemed to spin as Louise stared at the document in her hand. It was impossible, and yet in a strange way it explained so many things that had puzzled her. But why had Raphael never told her the truth—why had he told her she must not marry the Chevalier unless it would make her happy?

The only explanation that occurred to her brought a flush to her cheeks and a quick thrust of pain to her heart. Could she have misjudged him all this time? She had told him that she did not want to marry the Chevalier; could he have been waiting for her to trust him before telling her the truth?

All kinds of doubts and suspicions were whirling in her head. André must know the full identity of the Chevalier, since he had witnessed the contract. Why had he not mentioned it to her?

Running down the stairs, Louise called for her maid, wanting to leave the house before her brother returned. Her interest in visiting the silk merchants had evaporated with her discovery, but she needed to get away to think by herself. There was some mystery here, and now she was remembering so many things that suddenly made sense.

After spending an hour at the silk merchant's, Louise purchased a length of blue velvet and some lace, asking for the goods to be delivered as soon as possible. She was frowning as she stepped into the street. There was little pleasure in buying new gowns when she was so confused. She knew she must ask André for the truth as soon as he returned. Why had he deliberately deceived her when he came to Carleton Manor?

Pausing outside the shop, Louise looked about her at the colourful signs of the merchants of Cheapside, listening to the cries of the street-costers and the rumble of heavy wagons on cobbled stones. The streets of London were narrow: in some places the overhanging second storeys seemed almost to touch. Women hung from upper windows, calling to their neighbours as they flung the slops into the gutters, and laughing if a passer-by cursed when his fine smallclothes were stained by the filth. Yet there were grand houses, too, with gardens that reached right down to the river, and the new palaces of the wealthy along the Strand. The spires of churches could be seen all over the city, and their stained-glass windows were the finest to be found anywhere in the world. Across the river in Southwark were both the Bear and Bull houses, where the baiting of dumb animals provided fine sport for the citizens of London.

Shivering as the cold wind bit into her flesh, Louise sighed. She was very much afraid she had made a terrible mistake, and she did not know what she ought to do about it. Signalling to the men bearing her litter, she climbed inside. She must discover the truth from André as soon as he returned to the house.

Across the street, a man observed her being born away, doubt creasing his brow. He had thought for a moment . . . and yet he could not be sure. Jean watched as the litter was carried down the street and round the corner. He could hardly run after her and demand that she come with him, even if it was Louise. Short of abducting her by force, he could not prevent her from returning to her brother. Even if he told her of Raphael's suspicions, she might not believe him. Yet he knew that Raphael would have done something.

'I am not my cousin,' Jean sighed. He shrugged his shoulders, about to walk away. Then he grinned: he might not be as forceful as his cousin, but he understood the ways of women. He crossed the road, and went into the shop he had seen the woman leaving.

Louise sat looking at the beautiful locket Raphael had given her as a betrothal gift. What a blind, wilful fool she had been to throw away her chance of happiness. The truth had been there for her to see, if only she had looked for it. Why else should he have risked his life for her? Why else should he have brought her to his house as an honoured guest unless it was because he cared for her? Now that it was too late, she had begun to understand the kind of man he was. Beneath the passion and the arrogance was something precious she had barely glimpsed as yet.

A pang overcame her at the thought that it was too late to ask for his forgiveness. She had said such dreadful things to him . . . He would never forgive her. Realising at last how advanced the evening was, she washed away the tear-stains. It was time she went downstairs to face André. He had lied to her, and she was determined to have the truth from him. He must have known that Raphael was the Chevalier de Leconte; why had he not told her on the morning the contract was signed?

Leaving her bedchamber, Louise walked slowly along the gallery. She was not looking forward to the confrontation with her brother, knowing how violent he could be when he was angry. But she must ask him why he had hidden the truth from her. Somehow she felt it might be important, though she did not know why. Hearing the sound of raised voices from below, she paused at the head of the stairs, her heart racing as she recognised Raphael's deep tones.

'I intend to speak to Louise before I leave,' he was saying. 'She is my wife by law, though the church has not yet blessed our union. The marriage contract was signed by her father, and a copy of it is in my possession—as is his Will. You cannot deny me the right to see her.'

'So you had them all the time!' André replied angrily. 'It will do you no good, m'sieur. You will not see my sister. She chooses of her own free will not to marry you.'

'Then let her tell me so herself. I am warning you, m'sieur! I shall not leave this house without her.'

'She has given me her decision. Leave now while you can, Chevalier, or I shall have my servants throw you into the street.'

'No, André! I will speak to him.'

Both men turned to look at her as she stood on the stairway. She saw surprise in André's face, then anger, and something akin to hatred.

'Go back to your room, Louise!' he snarled. 'Leave this to me.'

She shook her head, confidence spreading through her as she read the expression in Raphael's eyes with a new insight. She had thought he must hate her, but now she knew she had been wrong. He had come here tonight to claim her as his own. He still wanted her!

'Louise, I want you to leave this house tonight,' Raphael said quietly, moving towards the foot of the stairs. 'Please trust me. Ask no questions, just come with me now.'

The entreaty in his voice puzzled Louise, but she knew the time had come to choose. She must go with him now, or lose him for ever. Smiling, she descended the last stairs, offering him her hand as she looked into his eyes.

'I am ready,' she said. 'I was wrong to leave you. I love you, Raphael, and if you want me, I shall be honoured to be your wife.'

Fire leapt in the dark eyes as he looked at her. 'It was my fault,' he said his smile sending little shivers of delight through her body. 'Whatever has happened is in the past. Forgive me, Louise.'

'How very touching. Unfortunately, you have just signed his death-warrant, my dear sister.'

André's chilling tones made Louise suddenly aware of the danger. She gave a cry of alarm as she saw how close he was to the man she loved, and the significance of the sword he had drawn. Her cry warned Raphael, but he turned too late. Before he could defend himself, André drove the blade deep into his back. He groaned once, falling to the ground as his hand clutched the wound. Blood was pumping through his fingers in a crimson tide as he lay unmoving on the floor, his eyes closed.

Louise's screams echoed wildly in the lofty hall as she stared at her brother in disbelief, unable to move from the spot. 'You—You murderer!' she breathed. 'You killed him!'

'You killed him yourself, Louise,' André said, a horrible smile twisting his mouth. 'If you had kept your promise to me, I might have let him live. I cannot let you marry anyone—so I shall have to kill you, too.'

'No . . .' Louise whispered, her face white as she stared into his eyes and saw the light of madness there. Her brother had lost his reason! 'I see it all now. It was you, was it not, André? You planned to abduct me . . . You murdered Pierre de Guise!'

'He was a weak fool,' André boasted, laughing in a strange high voice. 'He walked into my trap because he was blinded by your beauty. Do not weep for him, Louise. He was less than nothing, and it gave me great pleasure to kill him. The other one has caused me far more trouble. I would have had you long ago if he had not interfered—and everyone would have believed you had run away with that pretty boy. It was all so easy—even Marie helped me because she was jealous of you. I gave her gold and she persuaded de Guise to rescue you in the forest—the poor fool even thought it was his own idea!'

'You—You are evil,' Louise said as the sickness rose in her throat. She made a move towards Raphael, but André pushed her back with the tip of his blade. 'Why? I do not understand—why have you done all these terrible things? Why do you hate me? You are my brother.'

'Your half-brother,' André said, his face contorting with hatred. 'When I was young, I was fond of you, but when you grew up I saw that it was you who stood in my way. Father told me before you were to have married Étienne that you would inherit everything because you were his child and I was a bastard. There was to be nothing for me—except one small estate in Languedoc that had been my mother's dowry. You were to have it all—just as you had all his love . . .'

'No . . .' Louise shook her head. 'It was you he loved, André. I was always the one he punished, don't you remember?'

'He punished you because it mattered to him that you should be beyond reproach. I was my mother's shame, and he never let me forget it, even though he loved her. He married her, knowing she carried me inside her womb, and he promised her he would bring me up as his own son—but he never loved me. I was not of his flesh.'

She heard the anguish in his voice and suddenly she understood what had made him the way he was, twisting his mind. If she had suffered from her strict upbringing, how much worse had it been for André, knowing the truth? And the cruellest blow was that he had not discovered it until just before she was due to marry Étienne. She realised why he had changed towards her, and she pitied him for the pain he had suffered, even now when she knew the extent of his wickedness.

Tears slipped silently down her face as she looked at him. 'Why did you not tell me?' she asked. 'You were my brother—I would never have agreed that you should be disinherited. I would have shared it all with you.'

'No.' André's voice had dropped to a harsh whisper. 'I

wanted him to think you had run away with a de Guise. I
wanted him to believe you as worthless as the bitch who
gave us life . . . Then he would have turned to me. He
would have loved me as his son.'

She tried to move nearer Raphael again, but he thrust
his sword into the padded stomacher of her gown. 'Get
back, Louise!' he warned. 'I told you. I shall kill you,
too.'

'You can have the estate, André. Only let me tend my
betrothed husband, I beg you.'

'The estate is rightfully mine,' he said, not listening to
her. 'I bear his name. He had no right to let me believe I
was his son all those years, if it was not true. I was
so proud of all that he stood for. I wanted to please
him.'

'I'm sorry, André,' Louise said, her tears spilling
over. 'Take the money—take everything! Just leave us
alone.'

'You should be sorry,' he said, his face twisting with
anger and hatred. 'You stole everything that should
have been mine—and now you are going to pay for it. I
want to see you suffer before I kill you!'

Louise gasped as she saw the menace in his face,
backing away from him in terror. 'No, André,' she
whispered. 'Please do not do this . . .'

The madness lit his eyes with an unnatural glow, and
saliva trickled from the corner of his mouth as he gave a
foolish giggle. 'You should thank me, dear sister. I am
sending you to join your lover.'

There was a sound of banging doors and of booted
feet. André halted in surprise, his arm poised to strike at
her.

'Touch her and you die, m'sieur!'

Jean's ringing tones caused André to swing round with
a curse. He stared at the newcomer, seeing the sword in
his hand and a score of armed men crowding into the hall
behind him.

'Who are you?' he demanded harshly.

'I am Jean Montpellier, and I have come to arrest you for murder in the name of her Majesty Queen Elizabeth of England.'

André's eyes swivelled desperately as he saw he was outnumbered, seeking a way of escape and finding none. Turning suddenly to face Louise once more, he drew back his sword, its blade already stained with Raphael's blood, preparing to plunge it into her. 'Then let her die!' he cried, his eyes burning with the insanity that had him in its grip.

Louise stood as if rooted to the ground as he raised his arm to thrust into her. She could not move or cry out as she watched the blade descend. She was held by a strange fatality, hardly caring at this moment whether she lived or died. Then a look of surprise came into André's face and he jerked backwards, the sword falling from his grasp. In that second, Louise saw that Raphael had somehow managed to get to his knees, and his hand was round her brother's ankle. From deep inside him, he found the strength to pull André off-balance, causing him to topple from the stair.

She screamed as she saw that Raphael was trapped beneath her brother's body. They were both trying to reach the sword, but the wounded man's strength had been used up by the effort he had made, and the girl saw that he could never hope to reach it in time.

She swooped on the sword, holding it with both hands as she prepared to drive it into André's back, knowing that she must save Raphael somehow. Then strong hands were about her waist, lifting her clear as a dozen men surrounded the writhing figures on the floor. As they dragged André away, he suddenly began to scream, twisting wildly and frothing at the mouth as he fought like a mad beast. He was still screaming at her, vowing to be revenged on her, as they dragged him from the room.

Louise turned her face away in horror, hiding it for a moment against Jean's shoulder as the shudders went through her. 'He is insane!' she whispered. 'My brother

is insane . . .' The sword fell unheeded to the ground as
she wept.

'It is over now,' Jean said, his big hands stroking her
hair as he held her. 'They have him fast—you are safe at
last.'

Louise pulled away from him, going to where Raphael
slumped exhausted on the floor. She saw the dark
crimson patch of blood on his doublet, and caught her
breath.

'Help me, Jean!' she cried desperately. 'He is badly
wounded.'

Raphael opened his eyes and smiled at her. 'I am not
dead yet,' he said, and fainted.

It was just before dawn that Louise stirred. She had been
sitting beside Raphael's bed, her head resting against his
arm, and it was the touch of his fingers moving in her hair
that brought her to full consciousness.

'Raphael?' She bent over him, moving the candle
closer to peer at his face. 'Are you in pain? Can I help
you?'

'Thirsty . . . Water . . .' he croaked.

There was fresh water in a ewer beside the bed. Louise
poured some into a cup, slipping her arm behind his
head to lift him as he gulped a few sips.

He murmured as she lowered him gently to the pillow,
catching her hand as she would have moved away.
'Don't leave me.'

She stroked the dark hair from his forehead, smiling at
him lovingly. 'I shall never leave you again, my lord.'

'That feels good,' he said. 'You are kinder to me than I
was to you when you were ill.'

'You were not unkind to me. I did not understand. If I
had known the truth, I would not have said such terrible
things to you. I—I thought you meant to keep me as
your mistress, and then discard me when I no longer
pleased you.'

'Did you really believe I would use you so ill?' He

sounded weary, and she caught his hand, holding it to her cheek.

'Forgive me, my lord! I loved you, but I did not trust you.'

'Can there be love without trust?'

'Do not doubt me!' Louise pleaded. 'Forgive me for hurting you.'

His searching fingers found her hand and held it. 'You must not distress yourself. If anyone was to blame, it was I . . . I had allowed my own bitterness to cloud my mind . . .' His words trailed away as his eyes closed. 'Forgive me, I feel strange. This weakness is foreign to me.'

'You have lost much blood. You must rest now.'

'Lie here by my side, Louise, so that I know you are near.'

'Yes, Raphael, I shall stay with you always.'

He closed his eyes with a sigh of content as she nestled against him, his hand reaching for hers.

Tears trickled down her face. He was very weak, and she was so afraid that he would die. Because he was normally such a strong man, his weakness terrified her, and her lips moved soundlessly in prayer. If he died, she would not want to live.

Later in the morning, Raphael was burning with a fever, but he clung to life with a tenacity that amazed the physician Louise had summoned.

She listened to his advice respectfully, but Jean had already bound his cousin's wound and she would not let the doctor torture her beloved with his hot plasters. When he produced a case containing leeches, she dashed them to the floor in a fury.

'He has already lost too much blood,' she snapped. 'If you can do nothing for him, please go away.'

'If you refuse my advice, you must care for him yourself, mademoiselle,' he replied, offended.

After he had gone, Louise bent over her patient, bathing his forehead with cool water and watching him anxiously. She had already sent a servant to fetch Mrs Beacham, and for the present she could do nothing but watch over Raphael, and pray.

She glanced at Jean as he came into the room. 'I have sent that quack away. If Raphael can but hold on until Mrs Beacham comes, she will know what to do.'

'Is she a witch that you have so much faith in her?'

Laughter showed in her face. 'No, just a sensible woman who has some knowledge of healing herbs.'

'I like to see you smile,' Jean said. 'I fear you have had little reason of late—and now I must tell you something that may add to your troubles.'

She felt a prickle of fear at the nape of her neck. 'What is it, Jean?'

'André has escaped. They were taking him to the Tower by boat. He was sitting quietly, apparently sunk in a daze; then, all at once, he hit the guard beside him and dived into the water. They searched for him for an hour, but he had disappeared. The guards said he must have drowned, but I shall take no chances. He would stop at nothing to be revenged on you.'

'I know.' Louise shivered. 'It is not for myself that I fear. You must put a guard over Raphael's room always, Jean.'

'You know I shall do everything in my power to protect you both. It may be that we are anxious for nothing. André could have drowned as they say.'

She shook her head. 'No, I am sure he got away from them, but they dare not admit it for fear of the Queen's anger. There is a deep river on our estate in France and André used to swim there; he can stay beneath the surface for a long time. He saved me from drowning once, when I fell in . . .' She caught back a sob. 'I know you will not understand, but I am glad he has not been shut away in that gloomy place.'

'I can understand why you feel that way, yet for myself I would feel happier if he were a prisoner. It was I who went to the Queen when Raphael came here. He hoped to persuade André to let you go without a fight, because he did not want to cause you to suffer more than necessary. I came to arrest him because he is insane, Louise. While he is free, you will never be safe.'

Louise sighed. 'I know you are right, but I pity him.'

'You are a woman of compassion,' Jean said. 'Raphael is fortunate to have found you.'

She glanced towards the bed, catching her breath. 'Raphael may be dying.'

'He will live for you.' Jean smiled at her. 'Rest now, Louise. I shall watch him for you.'

A protest rose to her lips, but she realised that Jean was right. She must rest, or she too, would be ill. 'You will call me at once, if—if . . .'

'If the fever breaks, I shall send for you,' he promised.

For several days the fever continued to hold Raphael in its grip. Louise and Jean took it in turns to sit by him, while armed guards patrolled the house at all times. Sometimes Raphael had moments when he seemed to know them; he would ask for water and talk lucidly for a while, then slip back into the fever.

Mrs Beacham arrived three days after Louise had sent for her, having come as quickly as the roads would allow. Fortunately, the snow had vanished overnight and there was now a heavy frost, turning the earth to iron and decorating the cobwebs with fronds of crystal white. She took in the situation at a glance, showing no surprise at finding Louise with her master. She dressed his wound with ointment, pouring a little of her fever mixture down his throat, despite his attempts to stop her.

'Master Raphael always was a bad patient,' she said to Louise. 'You have already done all that was possible. His wound is healing slowly. If the fever breaks, we shall save him.'

'Will it break soon?'

'That is entirely in God's hands, my lady.'

For three more days they could only wait and pray.

Then, as Louise sat beside him one night, a change came over him. He ceased to toss so restlessly, his breathing becoming less laboured. She bent over him, laying her hand on his brow. His skin was much cooler, and he seemed to have passed into a natural sleep. The fever had gone, and she knew he would live. A wonderful sense of peace filled her and she went down on her knees to offer up her thanks. Her prayers had been answered! God had been merciful.

When Mrs Beacham came to take her place, Louise was able to seek her bed with an easy mind. In the morning when she entered his room, Raphael was sitting up, propped against the pillows.

'You are better, my lord,' she said, smiling at him.

'I am, now that you are here,' he replied with a grimace. 'Your woman has been forcing me to swallow one of her wretched brews. Tell her I want wine and a proper meal.'

'She is *your* housekeeper, my lord! Besides, her possets will do you good.'

'A kiss from you would do more than twenty of her foul cures.' Raphael held out his hand with a hint of his old arrogance. 'Come here, wench. I woke, and you were gone. I thought you had left me.'

'I told you I would never leave you.'

'You told me you loved me—or was that part of the fever?'

'I do love you. I have always loved you.'

'Then why did you say you hated me when I tried to tell you you were mine?'

'Because—Because I wanted to hear you say you loved me. You swore that you would marry only if your wife possessed a fortune. You said you did not believe in love.'

'I have not yet said otherwise, so why have you spoken now?'

'Because I no longer need to hear the words. I know what is in your heart, even if you do not.'

'Indeed?' His brows went up, mocking her. 'And what of Helen? Do you still believe I was making love to her the morning you saw us together?'

'No. If you wanted her, you would have proclaimed it to the world. I know that now.'

'Do you?' The black eyes glittered, and his fingers curled possessively around hers. 'So you demand no explanations from me?'

'No. I shall listen if you wish to tell me, but I ask nothing.'

'Am I dead?'

She stared at him. 'I do not understand you, my lord.'

'Such meekness frightens me, Louise. I think you must be an angel, for the troublesome wench I brought out of France would never have been so patient.'

'I see you *are* better.' Louise smiled. 'Why did you take her in your arms, then? It looked to me as if you intended to kiss her.'

'Like this?' Raphael drew her towards him, his lips moving caressingly over hers. 'Why have you spoilt me for all other women, Louise?'

'Have I?' She looked at him shyly. 'Do you truly love me?'

'What is love? If it means that I cannot rest when you are not by my side, then I must love you.' He raised his brow as she frowned. 'You know it, Louise. You said it was so.'

'You are wicked to tease me thus!'

'What would you have me do? I am too weak to show you how I long for you. Will you drive me to madness with your sighs, woman?'

Louise flinched. 'Do not talk of madness, I beg you.'

The laughter died out of his eyes. 'Forgive me, I had forgotten for the moment.'

She swallowed hard. 'I can never forget that my brother tried to kill you.'

'It is over, Louise. It does not matter.'

'No . . .' She looked at him, her face stricken. 'André

escaped when they were taking him to the Tower. Jean was right: we shall never be safe while my brother is free. He is insane . . . my own brother is a murderer.'

'Your half-brother, Louise; you had different fathers.'

'But the same mother.' Louise looked at him fearfully. 'She was carrying André in her womb before she married my father. You said I was a wanton, and it was true. I am the child of a harlot, and I carry her blood in my veins.'

'No!' He heard the anguish in her voice, and gripped her hand. 'I was angry and jealous when I said those things. I know you were innocent when I took you, Louise.'

'Yet I drove you to that act with my wanton ways. Can you forgive for what I did that night? Will you ever really trust me?'

'Yes . . .'

The word came a little too slowly, and her face clouded. Even now he was touched by bitterness. She had confessed her love, surrendering her last defences, but still he withheld a part of himself. The hurt was too deeply embedded in him. He wanted her as he had from the beginning, but he could not bring himself to make the final commitment to her.

CHAPTER TWELVE

WITHIN A WEEK Raphael insisted on leaving his bed, though he was not yet strong enough to think of travelling, nor would he be for many weeks to come. He had been lucky that André's blade had scraped along his hip-bone and missed vital organs, but the loss of blood had sapped his strength.

Jean stayed on with them in London, keeping a constant guard about the house, but as the days and then weeks passed, everyone began to relax. There had been no sign of André in all this time, and it seemed that he had either returned to France or died in the waters of the Thames that dark night.

In February of the new year, Catherine de' Medici sent her two sons, the Dukes of Anjou and Alençon, to besiege the stronghold of La Rochelle, but as Raphael had foretold, the stubborn burghers would not give in and its defences could not be breached.

When the winds of winter began to give way to the gentler climes of early spring, Queen Elizabeth sent her personal physicians to inquire after Raphael's health. It was reported that his condition improved daily, and so it was decided that preparations for his wedding to Mademoiselle de Granvelle should go ahead.

They were married on a bright April morning at a grand ceremony attended by the whole Court. Louise wore a lavish gown of pale yellow silk, with wide skirts and a tight bodice, the stomacher thickly encrusted with pearls and gold thread. Her hair was swept up in shining coils, intertwined with a fine gold ribbon that held a large, pear-shaped pearl at the centre of her forehead.

Her serene beauty drew all eyes: even Queen Elizabeth smiled graciously on the lovely young woman who stood so proudly at her husband's side. Although the couple were to leave at once for their country estate, her Majesty expressed a wish to see them at Court in the autumn, hinting at an important new position for one of her favourite courtiers.

After the ceremony, a huge banquet was held at Whitehall, where the bride was fêted as her due. Course after course of succulent meats were brought to table: swans and geese, plump pigeons, and carp baked in a pastry case. Following the meal, a band of strolling players entertained them with music and a play.

Raphael turned to watch Louise, seeing the sparkle of laughter in her clear eyes. 'Are you happy, my love?' he whispered.

She smiled and blushed. What woman could fail to be happy on such a day? Gifts of all description had been heaped on her: silks and laces, precious spices from the east, a silver spoon and knife for her own use at table, perfumes and a velvet cloak lined with fur so that she would be warm on the coldest English day. So many gifts from all Raphael's friends that he was forced to buy a wagon to have them taken back to Carleton Manor.

Jean had given her a pair of embroidered gloves, a golden pomander filled with special herbs to ward off the plague, and a miniature of her husband that he had specially commissioned. She had thanked him with a kiss, while Raphael watched and smiled, though there was a spark of jealousy in his eyes.

They left London early the next morning. Jean travelled with them as far as Greenwich, where he was to board a ship for France. He had waited only to witness the wedding, and was impatient to be at home for the spring.

'You will visit us one day, I hope?' he said, as he kissed Louise. 'Be happy, my dear cousin, and think of me sometimes.'

'I shall never forget how much I owe you,' she replied, hugging him impulsively. In the months he had spent with them she had come to know the goodness of his heart, and she would miss him.

She watched the men take leave of one another, smothering a sigh. It would seem strange without Jean; and though Raphael had now completely recovered, there was an anxiety in her mind that would not be banished. Her husband had dismissed the guards, refusing to live his life in the shadow of fear, and keeping only a few of his most trusted followers about him. It was his wish, and Louise never mentioned her own fears, but they lingered in her mind. She still believed that André was alive, but she prayed that he had gone home to France.

She was pensive and silent as they continued their journey, and Raphael glanced at her in concern.

'What troubles you, Louise? Are you sad to see my cousin go?'

'I shall miss him,' she admitted, smiling as she saw that he was a trifle jealous. 'Peace, my lord! Jean has been a good friend to us. I love him as—as I would a dear brother.'

'Only as a brother?' Mockery glinted in the black eyes, and she shook her head at him.

'You have me, my lord, can you not rest easy now?'

'I do not wish to rest, my lady. I am sick of too much ease. I wish only to hold you in my arms—and then I shall know that you are mine.'

'For that you must wait a little longer.' Louise laughed as she saw the fire in his eyes, remembering the kisses which still stung her lips from the previous night.

It was so good to be at home again. The housekeeper had gone on ahead, so that everything was ready for their homecoming. Raphael had given strict instructions, and there were no guests that evening. They dined alone in Louise's apartments, drinking wine from the same cup, and watching each other's faces in the flickering candlelight. Then Raphael put down his goblet, and came round the table to draw her to her feet and into his arms. He kissed her gently, looking down into her eyes that had suddenly become smoky with desire.

'So you are truly mine at last, Louise?'

'Yes, my lord.'

'Then we must have no secrets between us.' He smiled as her eyes questioned him, tracing the white arch of her throat with his finger. 'I have known other women in my bed, Louise—and, for a time, Helen was one of them, but she was never more than that. I never promised to wed her, and I was not her first lover.'

'Yet—Yet she hurt you terribly. I saw it in your face the first night you brought me here.'

'It was Richard's death that hurt me.' Raphael's face tightened with remembered pain. 'Helen always wanted to be mistress here. When I would not marry her, she used Richard to taunt me. She threatened to wed him, and when I laughed at her, she carried out her threat. He was always her slave. I told her it would be the end of everything that had been between us, but she would not believe me. She pleaded with me to take her to my bed, and I was angry that she thought I would lie with my cousin's wife—and so we quarrelled.'

Raphael stopped abruptly and Louise turned anxious eyes on him. 'Please go on, my lord.'

'She went to Richard and told him that I had raped her.' Louise gasped, and her husband smiled grimly. 'Even Richard did not believe that, but he thought we were still lovers, and he was jealous. He accused me, and we came to blows. I thought that would settle it, but he followed me to London and forced a duel. Although I tried to avoid killing him, it was useless.'

'And so you killed your own cousin, and it hurt you deeply?'

'Yes.' Raphael's voice was harsh. 'I think he wanted to die, Louise. I had refused Helen's pleas, but there were many who had not. It seems that she must always find some new lover to taunt . . .'

'So you came to France feeling embittered and angry at the world?'

'Yes. The Queen banished me to my estates, but I had my reasons for disobeying her.'

'The murder of your uncle?' Louise whispered, hanging her head in shame.

'Did Jean tell you that?'

'Yes. He did not wish to, but I had to know the truth.'

'Then I must tell it all.' Raphael tipped her face towards him, brushing her lips gently with his until the shame had gone from her eyes. 'I suspected André at the start, but I did not know why until much later. It was only when I was in possession of your father's Will that I understood your brother had desperately tried to stop you marrying anyone.'

Louise wrinkled her brow, not quite understanding, even then. 'You came to Paris in search of revenge?'

'Yes, at first. I knew André had visited my uncle, but I was not sure if your father knew of the visit. He did not. He had never met the Chevalier de Leconte. He thought it was I who had written to him asking if he would consider giving you in marriage.'

'But it was really your uncle?' Louise shook her head. 'I still don't see why a man who had never met me should want to marry me? It wasn't for my inheritance, because Jean said he had large estates.'

'I can only assume it was because he loved your mother when she was a girl. I know that from something my own mother told me, Louise. She made me promise that one day I would visit your home—and if I liked you, marry the child of her dearest friend. Eventually I forgot the promise.' Raphael's arms tightened around her as she moved restlessly. 'Do not look at me like that, Louise. Listen until I have finished, please?' She nodded and he smiled, stroking her cheek tenderly. 'The Lecontes and your mother's family were neighbours, and for many years it was taken for granted that their houses would be joined in marriage. Then the two men quarrelled and the young people were forbidden to meet. Perhaps my uncle thought he could recapture his youth by marrying you . . . I do not know. I can only be certain that André visited him without your father's knowledge—and that he put poison in the wine they drank together. The Chevalier died some hours later in terrible pain.'

The colour drained from her face. 'Do you think your uncle . . . Could he have been André's father?'

'We shall never know, since your mother confessed her secret only to a nun who was present at the birth. When I left Paris after the royal wedding, I went to see if she would tell me the truth, but she took the secret with her to the grave. I pray with all my heart that it was not so.'

She crossed herself, shivering. 'And you went on with the marriage negotiations in the hope of discovering the truth?'

Raphael caught her chin as she hung her head, making her look up at him. 'I never intended to hurt you. I meant to withdraw at the last minute. I would have brought André to justice by any means I could.'

'By your sword if need be?' Her eyes flashed accusation at him.

'Yes, that was my intention at the beginning.'

'So why did you sign the contract?'

'It was after that night at the Louvre gardens. I knew then that I wanted you more than I had ever wanted any woman.' He smiled wryly. 'We were already entangled in a web, Louise. I was reluctant to tell you the truth —you distrusted me enough as it was. I thought you would hate me if you knew I had lied to you.'

'And that mattered to you?'

'You know it did! I wanted to marry you only if it would bring you happiness.'

Louise sighed. While Raphael was ill, Jean had told her all he knew of the affair. She was aware that her husband had not taken his opportunity to seek revenge for his uncle's murder, and she understood that it was for her sake he had spared André. That forbearance had almost cost him his life. It was all very sad. Through no fault of their own, they had been caught up by Fate and made to pay for the sins of others.

Raphael looked down at her, and a strange, almost humble, expression came over his face. 'Can you forgive me?' he asked.

'There is nothing to forgive,' she said, smiling up at him with love. 'The past is gone. I am your wife now. Forget what happened . . . Forget it, and tell me the future is ours.'

He took her face gently between his hands, kissing her with a tenderness that gradually deepened to passion. Then, catching her up in his arms, he gazed down at her with a hint of his old mockery in the dark eyes, his look sending shivers of delight coursing the length of her body.

'Words are easily spent and mean little,' he said huskily. 'I would rather show you what the future holds for you, my lovely wife.'

He carried her through to the bedroom, setting her on her feet as he began to unfasten her clothing, slipping down the soft silken robe to kiss one satin shoulder. Her flesh took on the glow of the firelight, turning to a soft gold as she trembled beneath the touch of his gentle hands that knew every part of her as they stroked and caressed her, bringing her to the crest of a wave. She was carried on a sunlit sea, drowning in the warm waters of love as his kisses swept her onward.

'You are so beautiful, my darling,' he whispered. 'So warm and giving. I have never known with any other woman the pleasures you give me.'

She melted into his flesh, dissolving in the river of his passion. Waves of sensation washed over her again and again as she tossed wildly beneath him, torn apart by the almost unbearable ecstasy of the climax, which shook

her as the earth moved out of orbit and she was flung into
eternity.

'Raphael, I love you . . . I love you . . .' she whim-
pered, her face buried in the warm dampness of his
shoulder as he held her.

He held her soft, yielding body closer, whispering
words of such sweetness that tears slipped from her eyes
and ran down her cheeks. His hands caressed her still,
stroking her back with firm, arousing fingers that soon
had her quivering as she pressed herself against him and
felt his passion leap to throbbing urgency once more.

It was a night that she would remember all her life,
when he seemed unable to quench his burning desire for
her, coming to her again and again until they both
drifted into a sleep of total exhaustion.

The siege of La Rochelle went on interminably, lan-
guishing through the long winter months of 1572 and the
spring of the following year. The Protestant Bayard, La
Noue, had pleaded with the stubborn burghers to give
up their struggle and come to terms with the royal party,
but the wounds inflicted on the Huguenots on that
terrible night in 1572 were deep and needed time to heal.
In April of 1573 a score of English ships under the
command of the Comte de Montgomery set out to bring
succour to the beleaguered city, but they were driven
back by the French fleet. Hearing of their shameful
defeat, Queen Elizabeth raged at the disgrace their
commander had brought on the English flag, refusing
permission for Montgomery to land on her soil. Yet,
despite their increasing isolation, the brave citizens
held on. Then, in June, Catherine de' Medici was
forced to make peace with the city, granting terms
that were to have far-reaching effects both in political
and religious affairs. The long struggle was over at
last.

It was summer now and it seemed a lifetime ago that
Louise had fled from the terror in Paris. Her country was

beginning to lick its wounds, and the threat of war was ended for now, at least. Life had begun to settle into a harmonious pattern. She was the undoubted mistress of Carleton Manor at last, secure in her husband's affection and content—content save for the tiny doubts that still haunted her at times.

Helen and her brother sometimes came to visit, but not as often as they had. Louise knew she had no cause for jealousy, and she found she could accept her husband's friends for what they were. Helen's reputation had suffered because of the scandal at Court; to have shunned her completely would have been unnecessarily cruel. It was for this reason that Raphael had continued to receive her, and it was not in Louise's nature to be less generous than her husband.

Raphael was a good master. His estate prospered under his careful stewardship, and life was sweet. He and Louise rode together every day, often watching the hawks fly from his wrist or simply delighting in each other's company. Sometimes they would ride into a near-by town and wander through the market, attended only by their faithful Thomas Craven. Once, at a fair, Raphael joined the wrestlers in the square, and to her great delight he beat all comers. At other times he would show her his collection of beautiful illustrated manuscripts, and a volume of Chaucer's tales printed by Master Caxton himself. When the weather was wet, Raphael would read, while Louise played for him; and in the evenings they supped with the constant stream of friends who came and went as they pleased.

Louise wondered at herself that she should ask for more, yet even as she lay content and satiated in her husband's arms at night, a need in her went unsatisfied. She knew he loved her, but she felt a barrier between them. It was scarcely discernible, but it saddened her. In her heart she carried the secret hope that the last barriers would fall when he held his son in his arms.

She could not yet be certain that she carried her

husband's seed in her womb, but with every day that passed, her hopes grew stronger.

One sunny morning in July, Louise shyly confided her hopes to Mrs Beacham, asking her advice.

'Ay, you've good cause to hope, my lady,' the house-keeper said with a smile. 'I've suspected as much for some time—but it was not my place to say.'

A thrill of excitement ran through Louise and she impulsively hugged the older woman, her face lighting up. 'Then it is safe to tell my husband? I would not want to disappoint him.'

'I think you are as safe as any woman can be, my lady. Childbearing is never certain until the babe is in your arms.'

Louise laughed, hardly listening to her. She was carrying Raphael's child! Surely now their happiness was complete?

'My lord is with his hawks,' she cried, her eyes glowing. 'I must find him and tell him my news!'

The housekeeper watched as Louise hurried from the room. Knowing how often a babe miscarried or was born dead, she had not the heart to spoil her mistress's pleasure by making her doubt her ability to carry a babe full term. Although the girl was a mite narrow in the hips for childbearing, she was strong and healthy and had every chance of bearing a living child.

Unaware of her servant's thoughts, Louise was already running from the house. It seemed to her that the sun was somehow warmer and the birds had never sung more sweetly. She was conscious of her happiness, hugging it to her as she contemplated Raphael's surprise and pleasure at her news. It would mean so much to him to have a child to inherit his estate, she was sure, and perhaps he would really love her, now that she could give him such a precious gift.

A brief enquiry at the stables told her that her hus-band was in the woods as she had expected. He had a young hawk he was training to fly after the lure, and

Louise knew exactly where she would find him. Deciding to walk rather than ride, she strolled at leisure through the trees, delighting in the beauty of her surroundings. It was cooler here, but pleasant and very peaceful.

Perhaps because she was so wrapped up in her own little world, Louise did not at first notice the odd rustling sounds in the undergrowth. It was not until she had almost reached the tiny clearing, where she knew Raphael would be with his hawks, that she heard a sharp noise like the snapping of a twig beneath someone's foot.

Halting abruptly, she looked over her shoulder. Suddenly she felt cold, despite the warmth of the sun. 'Is anyone there?' she called, looking around anxiously.

For a moment there was silence, and she thought she must have imagined the noises; then, as she prepared to go on, she heard a muffled groan and more rustling sounds. Instinct told her to run as fast as she could to find Raphael, but something made her stay where she was as the ragged figure stumbled through the trees towards her.

She held her breath in horror as the filthy creature came steadily nearer. The man's clothes were hanging in tatters about his emaciated frame, and his hair clung in matted tangles about his face—a white, haunted face with hollow eyes. Panic caught at her throat as he advanced, shuffling slowly as if it was almost too much effort to put one foot before the other. She screamed, feeling terrified as he held out his hand as though to touch her, the fingers crooked like claws; then the fear stilled in her and she looked into his face, seeing him clearly for the first time.

'André . . .' she whispered, pity driving all other thoughts from her head. 'Oh, my poor, poor brother —what has happened to you?'

'Water . . .' André muttered through cracked lips. 'Louise . . . Help me . . .'

As Louise moved towards him unthinkingly, he suddenly collapsed, sinking into a heap at her feet, his body twitching as if he were in a convulsion. The girl knelt beside him, wondering how he had come to be here and in such a condition. Had he been wandering in a state of near madness all this time, living rough in the woods and afraid to approach anyone in case he was captured once more and taken to the Tower? She knew it must be so, and a deep compassion filled her. She gently rolled him over so that he lay on his back, shaking violently.

'Help me!' he croaked, his eyes staring wildly as he clutched at her with skeletal hands.

'Yes, I must find someone,' Louise said, trying to rise.

His hands grasped at her, fastening round her wrist with surprising strength. 'Water . . .' he muttered. 'Water . . .'

She tried to free herself, but he would not release her, however hard she struggled. 'Please let me go, André,' she begged. 'I have to fetch help.'

'No!'

Suddenly his eyes lit with a strange glow. Giving a strangled cry, he lunged at her, knocking her backwards to the ground, his hands encircling her throat.

Louise fought wildly, gasping for breath as she felt André's cruel fingers pressing deeply into her flesh, choking her. She tried to tear his hands away, but he was strong despite his emaciated appearance, and there was a fanatical gleam in his sunken eyes. She knew that, even in his madness, his one desire was to kill her.

'Please, André . . .' She tried to form the words but no sound came out. She was choking, her vision clouding as the terrible hands closed tighter on her throat, and she realised she was dying. Then the blackness closed in on her and she knew no more.

From somewhere far away a man's voice was calling to her, pleading with her to do something. Sometimes he sounded angry, sometimes he seemed to be crying as he begged her to come back to him. Louise tried to open her eyes and tell him he must not weep for her, but she was too weary.

She was in a strange, grey place where there was neither light nor darkness, but only shadows. Something evil lurked in these shadows, waiting for her. It hovered close to her, hiding its face behind a veil of mist, and its skinny claws reached out for her, raking at her flesh. She cried out as she felt the pain tearing at her, screaming and writhing in terror until the strong hands quietened and the gentle voice soothed her.

The evil one was coming for her again, pushing her towards a black, bottomless pit. She screamed over and over again. Now there were two figures in the mist, who were fighting, rolling over and over on the ground as she lay suspended over that wide, dark chasm. Then one of the figures lay still and the other came towards her, reaching out for her.

Louise sat upright in bed, screaming wildly and shaking her head from side to side in a frenzy. 'No! No, André, don't . . . don't. . . .'

Suddenly strong arms held her, comforting her as the shudders convulsed her body. 'I'm here, my darling,' the gentle voice whispered close to her ear. 'I'm with you, Louise. André has gone: he can never hurt you again. You are safe now.'

'Safe?' Her lips moved but her eyes remained closed; then the shudders ceased and she lay quietly.

'Don't go away again, my love,' the voice pleaded close to her ear. 'Stay with me. I need you! Stay with me, Louise, I beg you.'

She wanted to stay with him, but the shadows were closing in on her again, dragging her down into that grey world where there was no pain. Then the hands were on her shoulders, the fingers no longer gentle as they dug into her flesh.

'No, I will not let you go,' the voice said, suddenly

becoming harsh. 'You shall not leave me, Louise. You shall not!'

Now the hands were shaking her as if she were a rag doll. The pain was all around her and she cried out, wanting it to stop.

'You must stop it, my lord,' another voice said. 'Can you not see you are hurting her?'

'Leave me be, woman. She's slipping away again. I cannot let her go. I cannot!'

Louise felt the sharp stinging slap across her face and jerked violently, spasms running through her body. Then she opened her eyes, staring into the face of the man who held her. Tears began to slide silently down her cheeks.

'Why did you hit me?' she whispered.

'Louise,' he said in a strangled voice. 'You have come back to me at last!' Then he gathered her up in his arms as she began to sob, holding her pressed against him. 'Yes, cry, my darling. You will be better soon.'

'God be praised.' Mrs Beacham's voice reached Louise. 'I thought we had lost her.'

The housekeeper crossed herself, whispering a prayer of thanks. Then she went quietly from the room, leaving them alone.

'Why are you crying, my lord?' Louise stared at Raphael in wonder, touching his wet cheeks. 'Have I been ill?'

He stroked her hair, smiling at her. 'You had a fever, my love, but you are better now.'

Her brow wrinkled. 'Something happened to me, but I cannot remember . . .' She looked up at him. 'I was coming to you . . .' A sudden shiver went through her as the memories began to crowd into her mind. 'It—It was André . . .'

'Hush, Louise. He will never hurt you again.'

'Is—Is he dead?'

'Yes. He is at peace at last, Louise. You should not grieve for him. He could not have lived much longer.'

Louise sank back against the pillows. 'How he must have suffered these past months. He looked so pitiful.'

Tears of weakness came to her eyes, and she lay quietly as Raphael held her hand in his.

'Have I been ill long?' she asked. 'What was the matter with me? I cannot remember . . .'

Raphael hesitated, fearing to tell her why she had been so ill lest it prove too much for her. On the morning she was attacked, he had heard her screams and rushed to help her; the struggle with André had been swiftly over, but he had feared it was too late. Louise lay limp in his arms as he carried her into the house, and in his agony he had thought her dead. It was Mrs Beacham who discovered that she was still breathing.

For several days Louise had lain in the bed like a broken doll, knowing nothing as the fever raged. The physicians had not understood why she would not wake up, and they held out no hope for her recovery. Only her faithful servant's nursing had brought her through the fever, and even she had been able to do nothing about Louise's refusal to come back to them. Now, Raphael was afraid to speak in case she slipped away once more.

Sensing his reluctance to answer her, a sudden fear clutched at Louise's heart. 'My child,' she whispered, her eyes dark with distress. 'Have I lost my babe?'

She read the answer in his eyes and turned her face to the pillow, a feeling of hopelessness spreading through her.

'There will be other children, Louise.'

He did not understand, she thought, the misery washing over her. 'I—I wanted my child,' she whispered. 'I wanted to give you a son so that you would love me.'

'What?' Raphael's eyes narrowed as she hid her face from him. He lifted her from the bed, gathering her against him, feeling the frailty of her body. 'Please, Louise, listen to me.'

'I failed you,' she whispered. 'I have lost our child.'

Raphael held her away from him, looking into her face. 'I, too, want our child, Louise, but there will be others.' He shook her gently as she turned her face aside. 'Listen to me! You are more important to me than any child could ever be.'

'But . . .'

He stopped her protest with his lips, kissing her with such tenderness that she was silenced. 'I love you, Louise. I love you more than I ever thought possible. When I believed you were dead, I wanted to die too. I couldn't face the empty years without you. I need you. Your warmth and your sweetness is something I never expected to find in any woman.'

'Oh, Raphael . . .' Louise laid her head against his shoulder, letting her body relax. 'How long have I wanted to hear you say those words!'

He held her close again, brushing his lips over her hair. 'The bitterness inside me has all gone, Louise. When I realised how empty my life would be without you, I understood at last why my mother needed to take lovers. She could not bear to marry again because no one could ever take my father's place—just as no other woman could take your place, my love. But she needed something—some warmth and human contact—to help her through the lonely years.'

Louise looked up at him, her eyes shining as she realised what his words meant. 'And you have forgiven her, my lord?'

'Yes, my darling. You have given me so much more than you can ever know. I am at peace now—now that you have come back to me.'

'I told you I would never leave you, my lord.'

'Yes, I know you did.' Raphael kissed her brow as her eyelids fluttered. 'You must sleep. I shall stay with you until you wake again.'

Her eyes felt heavy and she wanted to sleep, but she forced herself to hold on a little longer, gripping his hand as he drew away from her.

'Raphael . . .'

'Yes, my love?'

'We shall have other children?'

'Many women miscarry in the early months, Louise. Mrs Beacham says it is often so, but you are young and strong. When you are well again, God will give us another child.' He smiled and touched her cheek. 'I promise you it will be so, my dearest love.'

Louise smiled and sighed contentedly. The ache inside her eased as she saw the look of love in her husband's eyes. Raphael was right, she thought, as the healing arms of sleep reached out to enfold her. God was good, and one day she would give her beloved husband the gift of a son. . . .

Merry Christmas one and all.

CHANCES ARE
Barbara Delinsky

THE GIFT OF HAPPINESS
Amanda Carpenter

ONE ON ONE
Jenna Lee Joyce

HAWK'S PREY
Carole Mortimer

AN IMPRACTICAL PASSION
Vicki Lewis Thompson

TWO WEEKS TO REMEMBER
Betty Neels

A WEEK FROM FRIDAY
Georgia Bockoven

YESTERDAY'S MIRROR
Sophie Weston

More choice for the Christmas stocking. Two special reading pack from Mills & Boon. Adding more than a touch of romance to the festive season.

AVAILABLE: OCTOBER, 1986   PACK PRICE: £4.80   Mills & Boon

MASQUERADE

YOU'RE INVITED TO ACCEPT

2 MASQUERADE ROMANCES
AND A DIAMOND ZIRCONIA NECKLACE
FREE!

Acceptance card

| NO STAMP NEEDED | Post to: Reader Service, FREEPOST, P.O. Box 236, Croydon, Surrey. CR9 9EL |

YES! Please send me 2 free Masquerade Romances and my free diamond zirconia necklace – and reserve a Reader Service Subscription for me. If I decide to subscribe I shall receive 4 new Masquerade Romances every other month as soon as they come off the presses for £6.00 together with a FREE newsletter including information on top authors and special offers, exclusively for Reader Service subscribers. There are no postage and packing charges, and I understand I may cancel or suspend my subscription at any time. If I decide not to subscribe I shall write to you within 10 days. Even If I decide not to subscribe the 2 free novels and the necklace are mine to keep forever.

I am over 18 years of age   EP22M

NAME _____

(CAPITALS PLEASE)

ADDRESS _____

_____

_____ POSTCODE _____